CHRISTINE ROBERTS

SECOND TO NONE

THE HEATHEN BROTHERHOOD

Copyright © 2021 by Christine Roberts.

All rights reserved. This book or any portion thereof may not be reproduced or used in any manner whatsoever without the express written permission of the publisher except for the use of brief quotations in a book review.

This is a work of fiction. The names, characters, incidents, and places are products of the author's imagination, and are not to be construed as real except where noted and authorized. Any resemblance to persons, living or dead, or actual events is entirely coincidental. Any trademarks, service marks, product names, or names featured are assumed to be the property of their respective owners and are used only for reference. There is no implied endorsement if any of these terms are used.

Publishing Services provided by Paper Raven Books
Printed in the United States of America
First Printing, 2021

Paperback ISBN= 978-1-7366543-2-3
Hardback ISBN= 978-1-7366543-3-0

DEDICATION

"Don't marry the one man you can live with, wait and find the one you can't live without." These are the words my grandmother shared with me when I was in college. These are the words that encouraged me to wait for love. These are the words that led me to the most wonderful man, the happiest life — one I have shared with my soul mate for more than 20 years. This book is for you Gigi. For not only encouraging me to wait for all of life's best things, but for being the best thing yourself.

CHAPTER ONE

The small gray light that passed for the Oklahoma winter sun wasn't enough to ward off the bite of the wind. Ian pulled his jacket collar up closer around his neck and strode toward the arrivals gate of the city's only airport. During the last year, he learned quickly that everyone at the Leaning H Ranch had a job to do. Some days, it was a good job, like riding your horse across a meadow looking after the cattle. Some days, it was mucking out horse stalls in the barn. And some days, it was picking up your sister's new nanny from the airport. If he had the choice, he would have much rather been mucking stalls.

It was hard to believe his baby sister, Molly, was having babies of her own. The birth of her third son earlier that week had not gone as smoothly as the first two. Her doctors were concerned about her uncontrolled high blood pressure. The truth was, it had everyone concerned. Especially Molly's husband, Wyatt, and, of course, Ian. They expected to keep her at least a week in the hospital while they tried to get it under control. That would mean someone would have to take care of her two older boys and the new baby.

Wyatt's entire family—his mom, four brothers and their wives, and a passel of kids—all lived scattered around the ranch. And they were perfectly capable of helping out. But Molly insisted her family wouldn't be a burden to her sisters-in-law, who were admittedly already stretched thin caring for their own broods of rowdy youngsters. Having only grown up with his baby sister, Ian was unfamiliar with the dynamics of large families. And he'd never known a family with so many children. They seemed to be everywhere. It took him the first six months he was living on the ranch to learn who was who. He still got the names wrong from time to time. There were nineteen of them, after all.

When Molly insisted she could not get better without knowing her boys were properly cared for, Wyatt surrendered almost instantly to her request for a nanny. The truth was, he would have given her anything she asked for in the first days after the baby was born. He was just thankful to have his wife and child alive after a nail-biting birth.

Molly had poured over resumes sent by an agency in Oklahoma City. After a couple of phone interviews, she selected a woman named Charlotte Poole. She was young, only twenty-five, be she'd graduated top of her class at some fancy British nanny academy. She spoke with an accent that had Molly imagining Mary Poppins when they spoke on the phone. When Molly made up her mind about something, she was never easily swayed. So when she decided that Charlotte Poole would join the Hampton family at their cattle ranch in Oklahoma, Wyatt wrote a check. Two days later, Ian found himself freezing to death at the arrivals gate at the airport, waiting to ferry the nanny out to meet the family. He was really wishing he was mucking out horse stalls now. But he would, of course, honor any wish Molly made of him. He didn't like the idea of a stranger taking care of his nephews. Those boys and Molly were the only family he had. At least, they were the only family that would have him.

Until his retirement last year, his army special forces team had been his family. His team leader and best friend, John Galloway, was more like a brother than a boss. They were all brothers, born of battle, bullets, and blood—the Heathen Brotherhood. Ian found himself thinking of them often. He wondered what they were doing, where in the world they were, and which one of more than a dozen bad guys they had in their crosshairs. Some days, he really missed that old life.

John was known to the team as the Preacher. Ian had given him that nickname in bootcamp. He deserved it with all his idealistic talk of Jesus, chivalry, and tempered anger—sort of ironic because he'd been the one to rise in rank to lead their band of foul-mouthed, bad-ass soldiers.

A newly married couple posing for pictures in front of their honeymoon flight reminded him of the last time he'd seen John—his wedding day nearly a year ago. Ian shook his head, thinking about how his wife, Andie, so quickly won his heart. Preacher decided to leave the teams and work from behind a desk. In fact, they were expecting their own baby in just a few days.

Just as the thought buzzed through his mind, his phone vibrated in his pocket. He smiled when he saw John's name and picture on his caller ID.

"You sorry piece of shit," Ian answered, mock disdain in his voice. "You don't call me for months, and then here I am wondering about how the hell you are, and you call. What's going on, man?"

"Ha!" John answered back with a laugh. "I'm sending you a picture. Don't hang up."

Ian heard his phone chime notifying him of an incoming text message. He tapped the screen to reveal a picture of John lying in a hospital bed next to his red-headed wife. The two embraced a newborn baby in their arms. Obvious signs of fatigue, tears, and exhilaration masked their faces.

Ian smiled and returned the phone to his ear. "Congratulations, man. When did this happen?"

"This morning," John said. His voice sounded more euphoric than Ian had ever heard it in their fifteen years of serving together. "I have a daughter. Can you believe that? A girl!"

"Well, you know what they say about special forces soldiers having daughters?" Ian's voice gave a chuckle. "Guess you blew the balls off that one."

John laughed heartily. "She's so perfect. I swear, you never saw such tiny fingers and toes in your life. She's beautiful, Ian. Thank God she looks like Andie. She even has her read hair."

"What did you name her?"

"Allyson," John said. "After Richard and Judy."

Richard and Judy Allyson had taken John in during his late teens. It was Richard who had helped John get into the teams, having served himself years ago. Ian could hear the slight tremor in John's voice remembering his late father. Ian liked Richard Allyson instantly.

"That's perfect, man. Richard would have loved it. I bet Judy is over the moon. How's Andie doing?"

"She's OK. Just exhausted," John's voice choked a bit. "Ian, man, I never knew how strong women were. Watching her go through that." John's voice trailed away.

"I know." Ian cut in. "I was there when Molly had Robert. Makes you rethink that whole 'weaker sex' descriptor, doesn't it?"

"Hell yes. My wife is a fucking rock star! Hey, how is Molly?"

"Better, thanks. The doctors hope she'll get to go home soon. They've just got to get her blood pressure under control a bit better."

"Tell her we wish her the best. I can't imagine Andie having to stay in the hospital and the baby discharged home. It would kill her."

"Yeah, to say Molly's less than pleased would be an understatement. She's convinced Wyatt to hire a nanny for the boys to help out, for God's sake. I'm at the airport to pick her up now."

"A nanny? That's so un-cowboy like of you," John teased. "Can't you just tie them to a horse or something?"

The two laughed at the joke. "Tell me about it," Ian said. He glanced up at the board that listed the arriving flights. Flight 421 had just arrived.

"Good luck with that," John said, still laughing. Ian heard the sound of a newborn cry in the background. "I gotta go. Daddy duty."

Ian could hear the joy in his friend's voice. A pang of jealousy rang through his own heart. "Congrats, man. Tell Andie for me, OK?"

"Roger that. Out here."

Ian hung up the phone and smirked at the idea of his team leader holding his own new baby girl. John left the operator lifestyle a little reluctantly but had found something far more worthwhile with Andie. It had been seeing them together that had gotten Ian to thinking seriously about his own life. There had been too much war, too much death. He was ready for life, for some peace, not just with the people around him, but in his heart. He wouldn't even mind a couple of kids of his own someday.

Ian slipped his phone back into his pocket and retrieved the small sign he penned before leaving the house. He'd written the name CHARLOTTE POOLE in tight military capitals across it. He held it up while a stream of passengers filed through the gateway.

A tall, thin, fair-complected, blonde woman approached him. She was balanced with a large black leather tote bag on one shoulder and a large black purse on the other. Her hair was pulled back off of an alabaster face. There wasn't a drop of makeup on it. She had shining chocolate brown eyes that Ian thought looked like they'd been happy once. But now they just looked tired and, perhaps, a bit lost. Her thin, rose-tinted lips were pinched into a tight line under a long thin nose. But her face looked soft somehow. She was undoubtedly one of the most beautiful women Ian had ever seen.

He swallowed, feeling his mouth a bit dry. It was impossible not to notice the odd contrast in her sunlight yellow hair and dark espresso eyes. She had an exotic look about her that reminded him of the women he'd seen in the Middle East. But her features and complexion were clearly European. She wore a plain black shift, black pumps, and a gray and white striped scarf that was tied loosely around her neck. A black coat was folded neatly over one arm. She was absent the carpetbag and umbrella, but she certainly looked the part of a no-nonsense nanny to Ian.

"Dr. Hampton, I presume," she said. Her tone was stiff and cold, but her accented voice was so sexy—a combination of Scottish with a hint of the Queen's English. The alto lilt was like music. Ian licked his lips. What would that voice sound like saying his name, he wondered.

She stood with her shoulders back and her spine ramrod straight. She nodded slightly to the sign Ian held in his fingers. "Thank you for meeting me. I hope my arrival was not inconvenient. I am Charlotte Poole. I will need to collect my luggage, and then we may be off."

Ian found himself staring. "Um," he stammered, trying to reclaim his thoughts. His eyes and his imagination wandered a bit farther down her figure from her voice and mouth.

"Actually, I'm not Doctor—" he began. But Charlotte had already turned on her heel, clicking toward a sign that indicated the carousels for baggage claim. Ian trailed behind, trying to finish his sentence.

Molly had cheerfully described her as happy and "practically perfect in every way." He'd even heard their laughter on the short calls they'd had during the interview process. Molly bragged about her wonderful sense of humor. Ian stared at Charlotte tapping ahead of him. Surely, this icy woman wasn't the same Charlotte Poole Molly described?

"I'm not . . . um, Dr. Hampton—Wyatt, that is," he said, finally.

Charlotte stopped and pulled two identical black suitcases from the conveyer belt and dropped them at Ian's feet.

"Ian McGuire, ma'am," Ian said. He extended his hand in greeting. "Wyatt and Molly asked me to meet you."

Charlotte looked down at Ian's open hand. She didn't reach to shake it. Instead, she just sniffed and nodded her head toward the suitcases. "Delighted to meet you, Mr. McGuire. Shall we, then?"

Ian looked down at the suitcases, then looked back up at Charlotte, but her heels were already snapping furiously toward the exit signs that led to the parking deck. He snatched up the suitcases and stalked after her. Charlotte Poole might be gorgeous, and Molly might be impressed with this woman, but he certainly wasn't. There was no way he was going to like her at all.

Ian maneuvered his pickup down the interstate toward the turn off that would take them to the Hampton's cattle ranch, the Leaning H. To Ian, it was five thousand acres of the most beautiful land God ever created. He loved the wide, open sky and the large expanse of land that met the horizon in both startling sunrises and glorious sunsets every day. It was green—a sharp contrast to the orange sand that covered Middle Eastern deserts. And it was flat, unlike the unforgiving mountains of Afghanistan. Those landscapes painted a backdrop he'd only ever associated with struggle and pain. And he'd seen enough of that to last him a lifetime. For him, it was nearly eight square miles of perfection.

He remembered the day he'd arrived there nearly a year and a half ago. Molly and Wyatt had come to pick him up at the airport. His sister had almost instantly dissolved to tears seeing the damage the IED explosion had done to his body. He was still using the cane then. Ian rubbed his thigh. Damn thing still hurt when he pushed too hard or rode too much.

He'd been offered Wyatt's old room upstairs in the main house where Wyatt's mother lived. She fed him, talked to him, and, as his body healed, gave him work to do for her around the ranch. It had felt so good to use his body for something other than kicking in doors and neutralizing targets. He liked that his hands were used for building fences and growing gardens and not destroying terrorist cells. His brother-in-law, Wyatt, was a veterinarian by trade. Occasionally, he'd asked Ian to help deliver calves or lend a hand with a horse. Life, not death, sprang forth from the ranch like new grass in spring. He'd been able to heal not only his body but also his heart and his mind. When the army offered him a chance to leave after his injuries healed, he took it.

For nearly a solid hour of their ride, the woman in the passenger seat didn't make a sound. She hardly moved. She just sat, hands folded neatly in her lap, staring out of the window, seemingly transfixed by either the landscape or her thoughts. Occasionally she let her gaze drift through the front windshield. But only for a minute or two before she was turning away and looking back out over the Oklahoma countryside again.

"Is this your first time in Oklahoma?" Ian asked casually. The truck turned onto a gravel road that led to the main part of the ranch.

"Of course," she replied flatly. Charlotte didn't even turn her head to look at him while she answered.

"I think you're going to love it here," Ian started again. "It's just beautiful. And the Hamptons are very nice people. I know Molly and Wyatt are grateful to have your help."

Charlotte replied with a soft hum that sounded like she doubted Ian's statement would prove true.

"The boys are great," Ian started. At the start of this statement, Charlotte turned her cold eyes and held him with a frosty stare.

"Mr. McGuire," she said, cutting him off. "Forgive me for interrupting what I am certain would no doubt be a series of quaint anecdotes. I appreciate that you wish to entertain me with your version of polite conversation on this interminably long journey to our destination, which, as it appears, is located in the middle of nowhere. But I can assure you that it is not necessary. I am quite content to be left alone with my thoughts. Thank you." When she concluded her speech, she once again turned her head to stare out of the window.

Ian ground his teeth together in outrage. His only reply was a discontented hiss. Rude bitch. He was just trying to be nice. There was no spoonful of sugar in this woman at all, of that he was sure. And he didn't like the idea of a woman like her taking care of Robert, James, and Logan.

Robert, who had just turned five, was a fighter. He'd never stand to be treated rudely by anyone. James, however, was younger than his brother by two years and hadn't quite developed Robert's tough demeanor—yet. But he was a quick study and mimicked everything his big brother did. Logan, who was just days home from the hospital, would need constant attention and affection. Ian didn't want his first weeks to be under this woman's unfeeling hand. While he drove, Ian planned out exactly how he was going to tell his sister that this woman was not what the family needed. Charlotte Poole had to go.

All Charlotte wanted was quiet. And she was thankful the ranch hand they'd sent to drive her thought so too. At least until he decided that forty-nine minutes was as long as he could go without speaking. She knew he wanted to charm her with his version of the good-old-boy southern grace for which men in this part of the country were known. She didn't have tolerance for charm or grace. She just continued to stare out of the dirty truck window. It was the only place where she could somewhat avoid the stench of barn animal and manure that seemed to be clinging to everything and everyone in the truck. What sort of bumpkin backwater had the agency sent her to?

Her conversations with the mistress had been pleasant. Mrs. Hampton seemed to be a kind and well-educated woman. She had been so certain she'd like it here. Until she was met at the airport by the field hand with his dusty jeans and overly familiar demeanor. He'd actually wanted her to shake hands with him. As if she couldn't see what sort of dirt and animal feces that potentially covered them. No, thank you.

She swallowed and tried to force down the lump of tears threatening to rise up again from her throat to her eyes. She'd thought the nine-hour flight would have allowed her to cry all the tears she had. But clearly, there were more. She thought of her sister and her father. She was here for them. For them, she would endure cowhands that smelled of manure, dirty pickup trucks, and changing nappies for other people's children. For them, she reminded herself. She was doing this for them.

CHAPTER TWO

The truck finally came to a stop in front of a large, butter yellow, wood-sided, two-story farmhouse. A wide porch striped with stark white spindles wrapped around every inch that could be seen from the gravel drive. More like a narrow dirt road, the drive wound around the house in an S configuration providing access to the main road through the ranch and a large parking area for a myriad of trucks and SUVs. To Charlotte, the whole scene looked more like a movie set than a farmhouse on a ranch in the middle of nowhere.

Ian pulled in beside an old Ford pickup with faded dark green paint and large patches of orange rust spattered across the sides and wheel wells. Waving to them from the front steps of the porch was a woman who appeared rather tall and very trim. She had silver hair cut in a modern pixie style and was dressed in jeans, square-toed cowboy boots, a bright red sweater, and a blue quilted jacket. But what stood out most was her sweet smile that shone up from her rosy cheeks to her bright clear eyes.

"That's Midge Hampton," Ian started. He turned and gave Charlotte a hard stare—fire and ice in equal measure. "She's the Hampton matriarch, Wyatt's mother, and one of my dearest friends. You will be nice to her."

Ian frowned at her and gritted his back teeth together. Evidence of his displeasure with her was revealed in the tightening muscle that twitched at his jaw. Charlotte rolled her eyes at him. Honestly, what did he think she was going to do?

"You *will* be nice to her, or I'll see to it that you're on the next bird back to the Frigid Bitch Academy you came from. I don't give a damn what Wyatt and Molly say. Are we clear?"

Charlotte's mouth dropped into a rounded O. The nerve of this man. "I beg your pardon," she said, offended by Ian's overt insult.

He didn't answer. But before she could say more, and she certainly had more to say to this low-born cretin, he popped open the door of the truck and started unloading her suitcases from the back

Charlotte pushed her door open. She let out a deep breath, adjusted her practiced smile, and strode up the steps to meet Midge.

"Welcome to the Leaning H," Midge said warmly. She wrapped her long, thin arms around Charlotte, bringing her in for a tight hug. Her gesture was unexpected, but, Charlotte could admit, she'd needed it.

"I'm Midge Hampton, Wyatt's momma. Come on in. We're so glad you're here."

Charlotte stepped inside to a warm, cozy space. The scent of freshly brewed coffee, cinnamon, and lemon-scented furniture polish quickly replaced the smell of dust and cow from her nostrils. She shed out of her coat and glanced around. From the front entrance, she could see a large modern kitchen to her left. It was immaculately clean and outfitted with shiny stainless steel appliances and gleaming light granite countertops. A huge island was encircled by no less than eight mismatched barstools that all looked well used but in good shape. The kitchen space had a wide opening to one side that appeared to access a large dining room. Taking a half-step closer, she could see it was anchored by a long wooden farmhouse table flanked with sturdy benches. It could easily sit at least twenty.

Her gaze was directed to the opposite side of the entry where Ian hung her coat in a tidy closet just behind the front door. There was a small study to the right of the entry with a large desk and well-worn red leather chair. A yellow-orange glow deeper in the room hinted at an unseen fireplace inside. In front of her, a wide staircase, lined with a dark gray brocade runner, climbed to a small landing and then twisted to lead farther up to the second floor. The entire house was as charming on the inside as it was on the outside. Charlotte felt her body relax slightly. This assignment was starting to feel a little less overwhelming.

Charlotte was unwrapping her scarf from her neck when two small boys slammed through a rear screen door and ran through the house to clutch at Midge's legs. A burst of noise and screams following their rush.

"Nan! Nan!" they shouted. "He's going to get us. You have to save us!"

Midge laughed at the two boys. Their faces were flushed pink from the cold and play. Ian bent down and scooped up the smaller of the two boys.

"Who's after you, Luke?" The cotton-headed child stared back at Ian with wide eyes. "Brandon is."

The older boy grabbed Midge's leg tighter, burying his face in the soft denim of her jeans. "He said we have to do school work and then get a bath. He's gonna torture us, Nan. We hafta hide."

"Well," Ian said. "If it's a hiding place you're after, you can't do better than Nan's barn. He'll never find you in there." Ian set the boy he'd called Luke back down on his feet again.

"C'mon, Will, let's hide in the barn," he said. He grabbed the older boy's mitten-clad hand, and the two shot through the front door as fast as they had come in the back.

Two seconds later, the back door slapped again. This time, a tall man with a ruddy complexion and bright brown eyes came striding through. He looked to Charlotte to be about the same age as her younger sister, twenty or so. He removed a gray stained cowboy hat from his head and walked quietly up to Midge, who was still laughing at the two boys who had just launched out of her front door.

"Hey Nan, Ian," the young man said politely. His voice was a low, soft baritone. He gave Midge a kiss on the cheek and shook Ian's hand. "Momma and Aunt Lacy sent me to get hold of those two delinquents. I know they ran through here. Any idea where they're hiding this time?"

Midge's face spread into a sweet smile. "Ian sent them to the barn." She turned a hand, palm up, toward

Charlotte. "Brandon, I want you to meet a new guest at the ranch. This is Charlotte Poole. She's going to be helping Wyatt and Molly out with the boys for the next few weeks until Molly gets better. Charlotte, this is my oldest grandson, Brandon."

Brandon extended his hand. It was calloused and stained from work and just as filthy looking as Ian's had been. She didn't feel obligated to touch a stranger, so she gave a polite nod but refused to take it. She quickly moved her hand instead to finger a small string of pearls that hung at her neck and offered him a weak smile.

"Nanny Charlotte," she said. It was clear she needed to set some boundaries between their social stations. Directing the family as to what she wished to be called was a good start.

Brandon quirked his brow and cast Ian a quizzical look. Ian only gave a little shrug. "Well, best of luck to you with that rowdy brood," Brandon said. "You're gonna need it, Nanny Charlotte. Thanks, Nan. Momma said she'd send a casserole over to Uncle Wyatt's tonight if you can take one tomorrow."

"Oh, that won't be necessary," Charlotte broke in. "Tomorrow, I mean. I'm happy to prepare supper for the family." Light housework and some cooking had been part of the contract she'd signed with the Hamptons. She didn't have much experience preparing meals, but how hard could it be?

Midge cocked her head to one side with an expression Charlotte couldn't quite discern. Her face quickly shifted into another tender smile. "Well, of course. Tell your mom that'll be fine, Brandon. But Nanny Charlotte will be cooking for them from now on."

Brandon smiled at Nan. Charlotte couldn't help but feel as if their expressions were sharing the punchline of some sort of private joke. There was definitely something mischievous hiding behind the glance they shared. What in the world had she gotten herself into?

"It was nice to meet you, ma'am," Brandon said to Charlotte and then turned toward Midge and Ian. "I'll see you later, Nan. Oh, and Ian, Dad said he could use your help with some of the west fences tomorrow morning if you're free."

"I'll be there first thing," Ian said. He gave the young man another hardy handshake. And with that, Brandon strode purposefully out the front door toward what Charlotte suspected was the direction of the barn.

"Well, you've met Brandon, Luke, and William. He insists on being called Will these days. You'll meet the rest as time goes on," Midge said. She started up the staircase, clearly wanting Ian and Charlotte to follow her.

"The rest?" Charlotte asked, following Midge up the steps to the second-floor landing.

"Uh-huh. All of my kids, except Lizzy, live on the ranch. And my grandkids are quite a flock. There are eighteen of them, very soon to be nineteen." She turned and stared at Charlotte. She was just two steps below Midge on the stairs but somehow felt as if the woman towered over her in more ways than one. She seemed to possess an inner peace that was beyond description. It elevated her somehow to a stratum of serenity and self-control Charlotte had only ever dreamed of achieving.

She always thought of herself like a duck on a pond. Above the surface, there was placid quiet and calm. Below the water, however, there was a frenzy of chaos and movement necessary to sustain the illusion. Midge, however, was different. Under the surface, she would be just as calm as she appeared on the exterior. It was a state Charlotte envied.

"Nineteen?" Charlotte repeated. Midge replied with a hearty laugh.

"Yes, ma'am. And yes, we've heard all the jokes. We definitely know how it happens, and yes, there is more to do out here on a ranch. We just like big families. And I wouldn't trade a single one of those noisy young'uns for the world."

Midge stopped at the top of the stairs and turned sharply to a door on the right. She opened it and stepped inside. Charlotte moved to follow. Before she could enter, however, Ian pushed past, dropping her suitcases down before sliding out again and pounding down the stairs. She was forced to employ more unseen frantic actions under the surface to sustain a calm demeanor—although she doubted she was very successful. The man was a bull. He lacked any social grace and was too large to fit into any circumstance delicately. No, delicate was never a word one would use to describe him.

"This is my special guest room. The kids know not to come in here. And it will be your room. I hope you'll find everything you need. If you don't, just ask Ian or me. We'll be happy to get whatever you need to feel comfortable.

"Ian's room is across the hall. The bathroom, I'm sorry to say, you two will have to share." She pointed to a partially opened door at the end of the long corridor. "But don't worry. No one cleans a bathroom like our Ian. I'm sure you'll find it all right. The coffee pot is always on, and the kitchen is always open. I don't cook a whole lot these days, but you're welcome to whatever is in the fridge or pantry."

Midge walked in a tight circle around the room, taking it all in and giving it one final inspection before turning around and facing Charlotte again. She paused a moment and offered her a tender, understanding gaze. Charlotte got the overwhelming sensation at that moment she was being evaluated somehow by this woman. And she couldn't explain why, but she desperately hoped she wouldn't be found lacking. Although they had just met, Charlotte got a distinct impression that Midge Hampton was a woman you wanted to be your friend.

"We are so very glad you're here, Charlotte. I want you to be happy while you're with us." She laid a warm hand on Charlotte's shoulder. Her touch was light, but she could feel the strength of her fingers as she gave a soft pat. "Now, we'll let you get settled in. Ian will take you over to see the boys in the morning."

Midge turned to leave. "Excuse me," Charlotte said. "At the risk of sounding unappreciative of these beautiful accommodations, I thought I would be staying with Dr. Hampton and his family."

Midge gave her another easy smile. "That house is already overflowing. And trust me, my dear, you're going to want someplace quiet to escape to at the end of the day. Wyatt knows you're here. He'll come by on his way home from the hospital this afternoon and fill you in on everything you need to know. Don't worry. We'll take good care of you."

Charlotte let out a soft breath. She was the one hired to take care of the Hampton boys, and here she was, being assured she would be taken care of. This job was going to be all right, she thought. Then she noticed the closed door across the hall and the beast who slept on the other side of it. As long as she avoided him.

"Thank you," she said simply. Midge turned and closed the door behind her, leaving Charlotte to look around the space that would be her new home. Home. The word burned in her heart, leaving a singed hole where the once-familiar sounds and smells had filled her. Home was where the people she loved were. And it was so far away. With just that single thought, her tears came again.

Downstairs, Ian poured a cup of coffee into his favorite mug. "You didn't tell me she was staying here," Ian said.

"Is that a problem?" Midge asked. She poured her own cup of coffee and sat down on one of the barstools around the island.

"No, ma'am. Of course not. This is your house. It's just . . ." Ian didn't quite know how to finish. "She's not what I expected. I don't think she's going to fit in here. You saw her. She didn't even shake Brandon's hand."

"Ian," Midge said softly. She set her cup down and drummed her fingers lightly along the thick handle, her manicured nails making a soft tinkling sound as they clicked on the ceramic rim. "Have you forgotten how long it took for you to adjust to life out here? You came to us a bit broken and lost too." She paused and considered the doubtful expression Ian cast at her. "Oh, sure, she doesn't have the bruises and broken bones you did when you came to us. But I can see that poor girl is hurting just as much as you were when you arrived. Charlotte is in a strange country, with strangers—and a lot of them. She'll need a chance to find her . . . what did you call it . . . battle rhythm? Give her a little grace while she figures things out. The poor girl is probably scared to death."

"If just being here scares her, Midge, she doesn't stand a chance with Molly's boys," Ian said. He let out a humored snort into his coffee mug. Those boys were little heathens-in-training. His nephews were going to eat her alive.

"Then we need to pray harder for Nanny Charlotte," Midge said. "Just like we did for you." Midge stood and gave Ian's shoulder a light tap. "I'm going to the study if you need me."

Ian stood with his coffee cup on the front porch looking out over the wide expanse of gray Oklahoma winter sky. The weather forecast wasn't calling for snow, but he could smell it in the air. And he could feel it in the wound in his leg. It always ached before any weather moved in. The sounds of cattle lowing and children laughing tickled the back of his ears. He thought again about John and opened his messages to see the picture of his best friend and his new family.

Without warning, the flashes of memory came. Unbidden. Unwanted. Bursts of white light. The sound of the explosion. The memory of the IED bombing in Afghanistan flared through his mind. His eyes squeezed shut. He tried to breathe, to just breathe. His nostrils flared at the memory of the acrid smoke and the smell of blood and burning flesh. Ian shuddered and forced his mind to pack away the images. That life was over. It was over.

His eyes opened slowly to see streaks of soft pink light trying to push through the low gray clouds. The colored sky announced the end of another day. Another day, and he was no closer to finding what he had come here to find.

He'd left the army to find peace and purpose. But the truth was, he'd only found out how lonely it could feel living on a ranch with so many other people. Looking back at his phone, he flipped through pictures to see his teammates again: John, Jake Morgan, Bill Greer, Mark Freedoms, and Nate Fairsmore. The faces of so many brothers lost over the years drifted through his memory. He had wanted a new life, a fresh start. But what that looked like, he had no idea.

Ian's thoughts were interrupted by the sound of a large white SUV crunching its way up the drive. It slid to an easy stop, and Wyatt popped out of the driver's seat. Tall with a broad-shouldered frame, he wore the strength of a man who worked hard every day. His dark brown hair was hidden, as it usually was, under a well-worn cowboy hat.

After he'd freed them from their car seats, two small boys assailed Ian, tackling him in a giant hug. Wyatt gently swung an infant carrier on one hand, a large blue bag with a brown dear head embroidered on one side draped over his shoulder.

"Hey there, Ian. Our new nanny make it over the pond OK?"

"She's upstairs." Ian took the carrier from Wyatt and ushered the boys into the cozy living room at the back of the house. Midge had started a fire in the oversized stone fireplace. Wyatt threw an extra log onto the small flicker. Poking at it with a long andiron, he stoked it to a roaring blaze that quickly warmed the room.

Ian looked down at his newest nephew sleeping peacefully in a cocoon of cloud-soft blankets and carefully extracted him from the straps that held him securely in place.

"How's Molly?" he asked. He unbuckled the infant and cradled his tiny pink body in his oversized arms.

"Good. She seems to be responding better to this new medication. She was awake for nearly our whole visit today. She still cries when we leave, though. It kills me every time. I'll feel so much better when she's at home where she belongs."

"She will too," Ian said. Logan stirred in his arms, cracked open one eye, and stretched his mouth into a wide yawn before closing it and drifting back to sleep again.

"How are you doing, little man?" Ian whispered. "You behaving yourself and giving your older bothers hell?" Logan let his eyes open a slit and looked as if he wanted to focus on Ian's face. He grimaced as if he was going to smile, then sneezed. As if the sneeze was his reply, Ian responded, "That's good. You keep up the good work."

"Hey, you two better be helping your poor old man take care of your little brother," Ian called out to the boys, mock severity in his tone. Robert and James knew their Uncle Ian would never be cruel to them. So they just smiled and nodded.

"Only I don't help with the poop," Robert said. The smaller version of him in the form of the middle brother, bobbing his own head in agreement. Ian laughed.

"Well, guess who else had her babies?" Ian quizzed. He lowered his voice to a faint whisper, which physically drew the boys closer to hear the secret he was about to impart. "That crazy old barn cat of Nan's. I bet there are kittens in the hayloft if you go look."

The two older boys wasted no time flapping through the back door to head out to the barn, each bearing an excited look on his face.

"He just ate," Wyatt said. He gestured with his chin to indicate the sleeping infant in Ian's arms. "So he should be good for another," Wyatt checked his watch, "hour, at least. I'd like to meet the nanny. What did you think of her?"

Ian felt himself scowling. "Maybe you should make up your own mind about her," Ian said. He settled the baby comfortably in his arms.

"That bad, huh?" Wyatt leaned back in a chair and crossed an ankle over one knee. "Molly seemed to like her, though."

"She's just . . ." Ian searched for the right word. "A bit cold to me. To hear Molly talk, I had this picture of this warm-natured person with a nurturing personality, you know. Someone who'd get on the floor and build blanket forts with the boys. This woman is ice, man."

"Molly didn't get that impression from her at all," Wyatt said. His brow knit together with a look of concern. "She said she had a kind face. A pretty face, if I recall her words correctly."

"Oh, don't get me wrong, she's beautiful," Ian said. His mind thought back to the lithe body that swished through the airport in her sleek black shift. He remembered the sway of her hips when she walked and the way her breasts bobbled when she yanked her luggage from the carousel. He felt his body respond, and he squirmed uncomfortably in his seat. What the hell? He didn't even like her. Geez, had it been that long since he'd gotten laid that the Ice Princess was turning him on? Well, she was beautiful.

Wyatt grinned. "I see. So no playtime in blanket forts for the boys, but maybe for Uncle Ian?"

Ian cut him a look of daggers. "Hell no. I want someone who's nice and warm-hearted. I'd probably get frostbite putting myself anywhere near that woman." Without wanting to, he found his mind conjuring images of what it would be like to put himself *very* near that woman. His body responded further, pressing lightly against the zipper of his jeans. He willed himself to put away these ridiculous ideas. More for his body's own benefit than for Wyatt, he said, "She's definitely not my type. And I'd think twice before letting her stay on. You know that the women on the ranch said they'd help you with the boys. And I can pitch in too. The boys need family, Wyatt."

Ian thought a moment about each of the Hampton brothers and their wives that lived scattered across the family land. Even before he could retract his statement, Wyatt spoke the logic he knew had forced them into bringing Charlotte Poole to the Leaning H in the first place.

"Susan and Kip have six kids, Ian. And Kip works cattle every day and is trying to build himself a barn before spring. Mattie and Ginny have three of the loudest little girls God ever put on this planet, and she's going to have another one in less than a month. She's got no energy for two boys and a newborn."

"What about Lacy?" Ian suggested and then instantly regretted it when Wyatt cast him a glare. If there was a single Hampton wife on the ranch who could match Charlotte icicle for icicle, it was Timothy's wife. Ian thought better of his idea. "Never mind."

"I know Momma would probably want to help, but she can't keep up with those boys for the long days I work." Wyatt let out a breath. "No, Molly was right to bring in some help. Besides, it'll only be for a couple of weeks until Molly is back home. How much damage could she do?"

Ian cast him a skeptical look.

Wyatt rose to his feet and went upstairs to tap on Charlotte's door. When he returned, she was behind him, her hands folding gently at her waist, wearing the same black dress and heels she'd had on from the airport. But Ian noticed her face seemed pinker, her eyes reddened. Had she been crying?

Robert and James burst through the screen door, each carrying a mewing newborn kitten in their hands. "Look, there's five of them," Robert said. He thrust his sample toward his father for inspection. "Can we keep one?"

Wyatt nodded. "When they're ready to leave their momma, you can pick one out to guard our barn at home and keep the mice out of Mommy's garden," he promised. He turned to face Charlotte. "I'd like you boys to meet Miss Charlotte. She's going to be helping me take care of you two while Mommy gets better."

Robert made a face and stuck out his tongue.

Ian reached up and gave him a light thump on the back of his head. "Manners, young man." Inwardly, however, he grinned. She wouldn't stand a chance.

Robert looked temporarily abashed before quickly wrinkling his nose again and adding, "Why can't we just stay with Aunt Susan?" He crossed his arms, carefully tucking the kitten into the crook of one. His actions were meant to demonstrate his obvious disapproval of the family's new addition.

Little brother James copied his nose wrinkling and arm-crossing movements in a show of solidarity. But, he had a bit more trouble negotiating the kitten and gave up to resume stroking the cat's head.

"I don't need a nanny. I'm not a baby," Robert said.

Wyatt smiled at his oldest son and gave his shoulder a gentle squeeze. "We're doing this because it will make Mommy feel better. And we want Mommy to feel better, don't we?" Robert gave a hearty shake of his head. After examining what his reaction should be based on his big brother's, James followed suit.

"Good, then you're going to be good for Miss Charlotte, right?" Robert shook his head, this time meaning it. James beamed in agreement.

Ian snickered. "Take those two fleabags back to their momma," he said. The two boys walked slowly through the back door, once again letting it smack against the frame as they trudged much more slowly this time to return the kittens to the barn.

Ian suddenly felt Charlotte's eyes on him. He was cuddled in an oversized recliner, gently rocking his sweet nephew. If his time with Robert and James had taught him anything about babies, it was that they didn't keep for long. He'd enjoy every chance he had to hold and rock the infant. In the blink of an eye, he knew Logan would be wiggling out of his arms to run on his own. Still, he supposed he should allow him to meet his new nanny.

"You've met Ian, I understand," Wyatt said, gesturing for Charlotte to sit across from the recliner on the sofa. He took a seat in a larger chair next to the recliner. "And this tiny little man is our newest, Logan."

Ian stood up and reluctantly handed the baby to Charlotte. She laid him on her narrow lap, leaned over, and breathed in the sweet newborn smell of him. She gently stroked his head and then let him clutch her index finger tight in his miniature fist. Her face broke into a wide smile. Her smile, this one more genuine than the others she'd forced that day, changed her entire face. Ian could see her icy facade melting with what was obviously an instant affection for the baby. And with that smile, she morphed from beautiful to simply stunning.

"I remember the day my sister was born," Charlotte said in a soft voice. She gazed into Logan's face. "I remember the way she smelled, the softness of her skin and hair, and the way she held my finger just as Logan is now. One simply cannot be near a baby and be unpleasant."

Ian let his heart ease a little. Perhaps Midge had been right. Maybe she did just need a little time. He hoped.

"Hello there, little man," she addressed Logan directly. "Aren't you just perfect, then? Yes, you are. You are," she cooed in a softer accent. "Is your wife nursing?" Charlotte asked Wyatt. Her eyes didn't leave Logan's face, but a more businesslike expression washed over them.

"No. The medications they have her taking make that impossible. There's formula at the house."

"Well, that will mean longer periods between feedings," she said matter-of-factly. "And more time for us to get to know one another, eh little man?" Charlotte finally managed to take her gaze away from the baby when the back door smacked open again and Robert and James, now accompanied by two little girls of about the same age, pushed into the living room. The girls crowded instantly around the baby.

"We're getting a baby at our house too," one of them said. Her long blond hair was in desperate need of a good brushing. A dirty dress hem peeked out beneath a bright pink puffer coat. Her legs clad in fleece leggings adorned with ducks, and her feet clad in bright green mud-caked rainboots. "Only ours is going to be a girl baby and not a boy baby."

"We already have a baby at our house," replied the other girl. Her soft brown hair gleamed with streaks of red and gold. Her entire body clad in some variation of pink sequined garments—to include her shoes, which were, of course, put on the wrong feet. "And when Aunt Lizzy comes, we'll have three babies. You'll just have one, Abigail," she shot back.

"Ladies, please lower your voices. You'll wake the baby. And kindly step back. You may touch him only after you have sufficiently cleaned the mud from your hands." Charlotte captured the older of the two girls' wrist between two fingers and slid it carefully away from the baby's head, just a mere inch below her touch.

The girls frowned at her. "Who are you?"

"I'm Nanny Charlotte. I'm going to help Doctor, that is, your Uncle Wyatt, with the baby while Aunt Molly is recovering."

"We don't have a nanny at our house," the older girl said. "We have a Caroline. She's my big sister, and she's super bossy."

Wyatt laughed and cut in, scooping up the smaller girl in his arms. "Charlotte, this little bottle of vinegar is Abigail. She belongs to my brother Matthew and his wife Ginny," he said, bouncing the girl in his arms. "And that little bottle of vinegar is Elise, one of my oldest brother Kip's kids."

Abigail crossed her arms and poked out a plump pink lip in protest. "I am not a bottle of vinegar, Uncle Wyatt!" Her loud declaration caused Logan to wriggle in Charlotte's arms.

"Mind your volume, dear miss," whispered Charlotte. Abigail instantly lowered her voice. Ian was nearly impressed at the gentle authority Charlotte seemed to have with the children. OK, so maybe she'd manage not to screw things up in the next couple of weeks, Ian prayed.

Behind the two girls, Wyatt's older boys stood proudly.

"Bobby says we're not supposed to like you," James said. His tiny voice tried desperately to sound older than his three years.

"Is that so?" Charlotte asked. "And why is that?"

James cocked his head and looked back to his older brother. He clearly hadn't thought to ask him for any sort of reason for the order.

Robert squirmed under the now six pairs of eyes examining him and waiting for an answer.

"I never said that," he lied. "I said you didn't have to like her if you didn't want to." He crossed his arms over his chest. This time, James did not mimic his movements.

All the protestations seemed to have seeped through the air and between Logan's blanket. The infant gave a discontented squiggle and began to fuss in Charlotte's arms. Ian leaped to his feet and immediately took his nephew from her.

"I think our little man may need a clean nappy," she said, handing him the infant.

"I'll do it," Ian said. He was determined not to give her a second longer with his nephews than he had to. He snatched the bag from the floor and went upstairs to change the baby. Before rounding the corner to the stairs, he looked over his shoulder and gave Robert a reassuring wink. If Robert had already made up his mind not to like Nanny Charlotte, Ian would enjoy watching her try to change his mind. The next two weeks might be a disaster, but it was going to be damned entertaining to watch.

"I expect you boys to obey Miss Charlotte. Am I understood?" Wyatt said in his most commanding fatherly tone. The boys stood a bit straighter, Charlotte noted, and responded with an enthusiastic "Yes sir," before turning and running with the girls back outside, letting the screen door flap behind them again.

Wyatt resumed his seat on the chair. "Charlotte, I need to be honest with you. My boys are a real handful. Robert, my oldest, is testing authority right now. Honestly, I don't know how Molly does it with them. She makes it look easy, but I've come to learn in the last week or so, it's not. Don't hesitate to reach out to Ian or to me if you need a hand with them."

"Ian?" Charlotte looked confused. "The ranch hand?"

Wyatt gave her a hearty laugh. "Ranch hand? Well, he does work here at the ranch. But Ian is Molly's brother. And the boys respect and obey him. So don't hesitate to employ a little male muscle if you need it."

Charlotte flushed with embarrassment. There was no way she would ever give Ian McGuire the satisfaction of coming to her rescue to do this job. How difficult could three little boys be, anyway?

"I'm certain I can manage things, Dr. Hampton," she said, giving him a reassuring smile.

"Please, call me Wyatt. We're all kin here, and we want you to feel a part of the family while you're with us."

"I usually prefer to maintain a more professional distance, but I suppose I can make an exception, Wyatt."

"Good. We start early here. I'm usually gone by five. The older boys get up around seven. I'm helping cover for the vet in town this week, so occasionally, I have runs to farms in the area. I like to visit Molly in the afternoons, around two or so. That way, we can have a nice visit without wearing her out and get back here in time for the boys to have dinner and get to bed by eight. Logan eats every two to three hours or so." Wyatt cracked a smile. "He's the easy one."

Charlotte smiled and stood as Ian returned with a contentedly clean infant. Behind him, a man nearly as wide at the shoulders as he was tall came in through the front door behind a curvaceous redhead with a wide, warm smile. The man had to be one of Wyatt's brothers.

Second to None

The two men were both massive and looked as if they could be twins, although the one that just entered looked considerably older. The woman, carrying a foil-draped casserole dish, had long thick auburn hair sprinkled with a few gray strands. Rather than make her look older, it defined her as a leader of the family and made her appear wise and trustworthy. Charlotte instantly liked her. Her eyes smiled as warmly as her mouth.

"Hey there, little brother. We were on our way to drop off dinner when we saw your truck. Looks like we're in time to see the new baby." The man strode over to Ian and scooped up the infant. Charlotte clutched the beads about her neck. He hadn't washed his hands.

"Kip, Susan, is that you?" Midge appeared from around the banister of the stairs in time to greet a young teenaged girl carrying a baby on one hip, a toddler loping along after her.

"Caroline, here, let me take Margaret from you." Midge relieved the teen of her squiggling burden. She gave her a squeeze and a kiss on her chubby pink cheek. The red-haired woman, who had disappeared from the crowd into the kitchen, reappeared and hugged Midge, Wyatt, and then Ian in turn. She then took the baby from the man she came in with. Charlotte's cheeks flushed again. Did no one care about infecting this infant?

The room was suddenly filled with more children who came by way of the perpetually slapping screen door. And with them came the noise. Chatter and greetings seemed to increase exponentially into a hum that rang in her ears. Charlotte clasped her hands tighter. This noise would disturb the baby. She looked over at Wyatt, who was chatting contentedly with his brother and sister-in-law and then scooping up the toddler that came in with the teenager called Caroline. Her eyes roved around the room and rested on Ian, who was standing alone in a corner. He was watching her.

Ian's long legs strode to her side. He leaned in and spoke into her ear—the sound pressing goose flesh onto one arm.

"The tall one is Kip, the oldest. His wife, the redhead there, that's Susan. Great lady. You met their oldest, Brandon, and their son Will earlier today. The rest of their brood is Caroline," Ian pointed to the thin teenager, "Elise and Max," Ian said, waving a finger in the direction of one of the little girls who had come in earlier and a slow-moving toddler, "and baby Margaret. I've taken to calling her Maggie because it irritates Susan so much." Ian pointed out each member of the clan as he mentioned them.

"How many brothers are there again?" Charlotte asked, swallowing. Her anxiety tightened the air around her. There were so many people. So many strangers. So much noise. The air grew hot, and she tugged at her neckline.

"Wyatt is the youngest brother of four. After Kip comes Matthew, Mattie. He's married to Ginny. They have three girls. And all of their names start with the letter A. Don't ask me what that's about. Timothy is the next. He's married to Lacy." At the mention of her name, Ian let out an exasperated sigh. "She's a bit high maintenance, but nice."

"I see. And . . . and that's all of them?" Charlotte stammered.

Ian shook his head. "The baby of the family is Lizzy, the only girl. She lives in town with her husband and their twin girls, Ruby and Pearl. Everyone calls her fella Blue. And to be honest, I don't even know if that's his real name."

Charlotte felt her face scrunch with worry. How could she keep an eye out for strangers who didn't belong when there were so many new faces and new names to keep track of?

"There are so many of them." She dabbed at her upper lip, now moist with sprinkles of perspiration.

"Don't worry. They're all nice people. They'll help you out." Ian looked down into Charlotte's face. "You OK? You look a bit pale."

"Just a little jetlag. Perhaps a breath of air, I think," she said, fanning her long slender fingers in front of her face.

"Come with me," Ian said. He placed a hand at her waist and led her outside the flapping screen door onto the back porch. Charlotte took in a long breath.

The biting winter air stung her flesh. It instantly froze the moisture on her face, but she was thankful for it. She closed her eyes and took in deep breaths of air, willing her heart to slow and her fears to quiet. She was safe here. She was safe, she repeated to herself over and over. Slowly, she opened her eyes to see Ian's staring back at her.

Closer now, she could see soft lines around his dark blue eyes. She had thought them brown before, but they were a deep shade of navy. Dark brows hooded them and gave him an air of mystery. He had a tiny bump on his nose where it looked to have been broken once—maybe twice. Her eyes traced a razor-thin scar that slid down one cheek and over his jawbone. Following it, she could see the dark stubble of a day's missed shave shadowing his chin. Full, tanned lips opened slightly, revealing a mouth of straight white teeth. A shiver ran down Charlotte's spine as she stared at his mouth. *A mouth that had been made for kisses.* She'd read that in one of her favorite Violet Dunn romances and hadn't understood what the writer meant until now. A soft pink tongue peeked out and brushed over his bottom lip. His mouth was moving. Was he speaking to her?

Charlotte shook her head and heard his voice ask again.

"Better?" His hand softly rubbed a shivering shoulder.

"Yes, thank you, Mr. McGuire," she said, breathing in deeply again. Her head felt dizzy. The ranch hand was rude, reeked of unwashed cattle, and annoyed her to exhaustion. But Lord, if he wasn't one of the most beautiful men she'd ever seen. Beautiful wasn't a word often used to describe men. They preferred to be thought of as handsome or rugged. But Ian was simply beautiful. He had well-angled features and a work-honed body. The muscles that rounded his plaid flannel shirt evidenced the hard work he did every day. Under them, Charlotte had no doubt he was sculpted as well as any of the great Renaissance statues in Florence—marble hard, smooth, and begging for fingers to reach out and touch.

"It gets pretty crazy when they all come together. It took me a while to get used to the noise and the constant movement too," he offered. He leaned his forearms over the railing of the porch.

"Of course," Charlotte smiled. She took in one final breath, smelling snow in the air.

"Dr. Hampton informed me you are Mrs. Hampton's brother. I apologize for confusing you with a hired hand. I had no idea you were a member of the family."

Ian turned his head and stared at her as if a horn were suddenly sprouting from the middle of her forehead. What was that look for? Didn't he know she was apologizing to him?

"I mean, you weren't exactly what I was expecting when I arrived. And I'm sure my reaction was a bit less congenial than it should have been. I meant no disrespect."

Ian continued to stare at her with the same puzzled expression. He stood up straighter now and tucked the ends of his fingers into the front pockets of his jeans. "I wasn't what *you* expected?"

"I'm sorry. I thought you were just a ranch hand. You understand."

"No, I'm afraid I don't." Ian's gaze morphed quickly into one of anger.

"I didn't mean to insult a member of the family; that's all I'm saying," Charlotte said. She suddenly began to feel quite warm again despite the frigid air that clung around her.

"But you have no problem insulting a hired hand, is that it? Forgive me for saying so, Nanny Charlotte, but you are quite possibly the biggest snob I've ever met. I can't believe my sister thinks you would be good for my nephews."

"I beg your pardon," Charlotte said, her eyes wide.

"This is a working ranch, Miss Poole. We all work very hard around here, family or hired help," Ian growled. "That alone deserves respect, wouldn't you agree?"

"Well, of course. You misunderstand, I . . ."

Ian dismissed her with a grunt. "No, I think I understand you perfectly. But just so *you* understand, until you got here, all those people you just met have taken care of my sister and her family. They've changed diapers, done laundry, cooked meals, and cared for her without thinking about how much they already have to do for their own families. I won't allow you to insult any of them. Do you understand?"

"I do." Charlotte looked up, straightening her spine and squaring her shoulders. "You have my apologies, Mr. McGuire."

"I love my sister and her family more than anyone in this world. They are all I've got." Ian let out a frustrated groan. "And for their sakes, I'll put this behind me and move on." Ian turned on his heel and took a single step toward the door. He turned and looked back at her, his gaze hard and steely. It sent a shudder through Charlotte's body.

He extended his hand toward her. This time, Charlotte took it in hers, sealing their truce. She was surprised by how soft and warm it was. Her skin tingled when he gave it a tender squeeze, demonstrating both strength and tenderness of body and of character.

"You can call me Ian," he said, releasing her grip. "You've had a long day; maybe you'd like to go back upstairs for a while?"

Charlotte nodded and, with Ian's hand guiding the small of her back, was danced through the living room and kitchen of the house as he introduced her to each of the Hamptons. The family, already gathered together, decided to linger and enjoy Susan's casserole. So, Brandon and Caroline pulled plates, forks, and cups down from the cabinets to serve food.

"Charlotte, hun, aren't you hungry?" Midge said, calling to Charlotte. She had already climbed to the landing headed to her room as Ian suggested. "Stay and eat something. There's always plenty."

"Thank you, Mrs. Hampton. But I think fatigue has won out over hunger. I have an early start to the day tomorrow and would just like to retire if that is agreeable."

Ian stopped at the bottom of the stairs. He raised his brows and then departed with a cheerful, "I'll eat."

Charlotte closed the door on the strangers, the noise, and everything unfamiliar. She felt like a fish out of water here among these people. They were a family. She was the outsider. Hired to help out and then be sent on her way. And, without even realizing it, she had probably alienated the only person who could have been a friend to her while she was here. She'd felt bad about getting things off to such a bad start with Ian. What was it about that man that so convicted her to remorse?

She missed her own family. More than anything, she wanted to go home to them. But that was impossible now. Without even undressing, she laid down on her bed and let her misery overtake her. And as it had each night since she'd left home, her tears eventually dripped into dreams.

CHAPTER THREE

Charlotte's eyes flew open at the sound of a fist pounding on her door. If that thumping continued, the door would come down, she thought.

"Rise and shine, Charlotte. I'm leaving in ten minutes if you want a ride over to Wyatt's." Charlotte cracked open an eye at the sound of Ian's voice booming through the door. He had the sort of voice that rumbled from deep in this throat. No matter what he said, it sounded like he was a drill sergeant barking a command to a line of disobedient troops. Charlotte was certain, if he wanted, he could use that voice to shake the very bones in a person's body.

Her eyes were swollen and burned from another long night of crying. Her jetlagged stomach lurched, the time feeling more the middle of the night than the first part of the morning. She sat up and looked around the dark room. There was no light. She checked her watch:

4:40 a.m. She wanted to cry and bury herself back under the soft blankets of her bed. But instead, she forced herself to put on clean clothes and made a quick trip through the bathroom. She somehow managed to be downstairs in time for Ian to hand her a cup of coffee and hold open the door to leave. The biting winter air was colder than Charlotte expected. The coat she'd brought from home would be woefully inadequate for the knife-like winds.

"Is that what you're wearing?" Ian asked while she pulled her weary body into the front seat of his truck. She shivered and wrapped her hands around the hot coffee. Her fingers burned with cold.

"Is there a problem with my attire, Mr. McGuire?" Charlotte asked coldly. She looked over her dark gray wool trousers, pink and gray cashmere sweater, and shiny polished black leather loafers. It was what she would have expected any nanny she'd ever had to have worn.

"These boys live on a working cattle ranch. You're aware of that, right?" His lips curled into a knowing grin.

"I am aware," Charlotte said with a condescending glare. She sipped the coffee. It was strong, bitter, and black. She hated coffee but forced down the swallow. She hoped the heat would help warm her cold body. Oh, what she wouldn't give for a cup of properly brewed tea.

She'd see to getting some on her first day off, she vowed to herself. Surely, even bumpkin backwater had a tea shoppe.

"OK then," Ian said. He cocked his head and let an amused smile lift one corner of his mouth. He shifted the truck into drive, and they bounced down the gravel road that connected Midge's farmhouse to the back acreage of the ranch. Wyatt and Molly's home turned out to be a beam and stone two-story. It rose up before Charlotte's eyes as they crested a small rise about two miles down the long gravel path. It looked like a quaint cottage from her childhood. Visions of the cabin where her father and mother took her and Maisie skiing on school holidays flitted through her mind. Warm yellow light flooded through the downstairs windows. The bright round moon reflected on a large pond hidden behind the house where Ian stopped the truck.

"This is so beautiful," Charlotte found herself saying out loud. "Like something from a fairy story."

"Yeah, Wyatt picked a good spot on the ranch." Ian took a long sip of his coffee.

"Do all of the brothers live on the ranch?" Charlotte asked. She pulled her gaze away from the house and collected the large tote bag she'd brought with her.

"Yeah, they each were deeded a small piece to put their house. There's a spot for Lizzy and Blue too, but they want to live in town. He's an engineer and wants nothing to do with cattle ranching."

"I see. Well, thank you for delivering me this morning," Charlotte said. Without realizing it, she found herself smiling at Ian, thinking of the beautiful house and the coziness of having one's family so close by.

"Good luck," he said. Then added under his breath, "You're going to need it."

Charlotte cast him a sardonic stare, rolled her eyes, and slid from the truck. She picked her way through a litter of toys on an expansive back porch into a large kitchen overlooking the pond.

Inside, the house was quiet and warm. Wyatt was sitting in a kitchen chair at a small table, Logan cradled peacefully in his arms, a bottle at his mouth. He was smiling down at his son in a way that made Charlotte's heart ache with a pang of jealousy. What she wouldn't give to walk in on a scene like this in her own kitchen one day. Piped dreams of whipping cream, she scolded herself. There would be no such thing.

Charlotte cleared her throat to announce her presence. "Good morning, Dr. Hampton," Charlotte said in a soft whisper.

"Good morning, Charlotte. And please, again, call me Wyatt."

Charlotte gave a slight nod. "Would you like for me to finish up? You said you needed to be on your way early this morning."

"Oh, he's done. He's just chewing the nipple and having a nice talk with his dad, huh?" Wyatt gave the baby a kiss on the top of his head and laid the bottle down on the table. "But I do need to get going. I'll be back around two. I want the boys cleaned up so we can get to the hospital to see Molly and then back here in time for dinner. Can you manage to get something started? There's a pot roast thawing in the fridge."

Charlotte nodded. "Consider it done. I have matters well in hand."

Wyatt handed over the sleepy infant and slipped out into the blackness, his truck rumbling away from the quiet house.

Charlotte took a deep breath and looked around. The kitchen was a generous size, with a long farmhouse table tucked beside a wide window. The living room was comfortably furnished, with even more toys scattered about the floor. The home was clean, but one would think more than just two little boys lived there with the amount of clutter that lay strewn about. Charlotte laid the baby down in his bassinet by the fireplace that blazed just off the kitchen in a small hearth room. She flopped down in a chair beside him with a sigh. If this was going to be her new life, at least for now, she was going to have to make the best of it.

The winter sun made a show of itself that day, silencing the icy wind and raising temperatures. The weather felt perfect. Ian stretched his back and sore leg as he dismounted his horse and walked it to the main barn.

"Turned out to be a beautiful day, didn't it, girl?" he said. He brushed her coat and then set about to fill her feed trough and water bowl. As he laid the hose down beside the spigot outside the door, he saw a tiny pair of cowboy boots stuck ankle-deep into a soggy mud hole left by running water. Ian shook his head. There were so many kids on that ranch there was no telling who'd let their wards wreak this havoc. Pulling the boots out, his eye caught a glimpse of a pair of tiny jeans, then a trail of clothing leading back into the barn that included a t-shirt, flannel button-down, and a pair of Captain America underpants. Ian followed the trail to a low growling sound, followed by hysterical laughter. The source of it, he soon discovered, was his nephew Robert.

He was completely naked and caked from head to toe in drying mud and horse manure. At some point, when the mud and manure concoction was wet, he'd rolled himself, it seemed by the looks of him, in the loose hay on the barn floor. Shoots of straw poked out from his head, arms, knees, and elbows. He was a sight. Ian couldn't resist a smile.

The laughter came from Will, who was also naked, caked with the same mud-manure and straw mixture as his cousin and rolling on his back, clutching his stomach in a fit of hysterical laughter.

"What on earth are you two boys doing?" Ian said. He was desperate to hide the amused smirk spreading across his face. But he failed miserably.

"I'm the hay monster," Robert said. He held up his hands in a claw-like grip and gave a loud, low growl, showing a mouth full of angry teeth. The sound produced more fits of laughter from Will.

"I see," Ian said. "Where's Miss Charlotte?" Ian looked around for the nanny. There was no sign of any adult around. That wasn't uncommon. When they were old enough, children were allowed to roam the ranch together in groups. Robert just shrugged.

"And where's James?" Ian said. He looked around again. The nearby chicken house erupted in a flurry of flying feathers and angry squawks. Ian suspected that's where the little brother had gotten to. He started striding in that direction when he heard the boy let out a pained scream.

Ian broke into a run. When he skidded to a stop in front of Midge's chicken coop, he saw James with his leg caught in a low voltage electric fence used to keep the chickens from getting out into the yard. The shock wouldn't have caused any serious damage, but it was certainly enough to scare his three-year-old nephew to death. Ian grabbed the wire with his gloved hand and wrenched the boy through, pulling him tight into his arms. Tears streaked through his mud-spattered face as he sobbed and buried his eyes into his uncle's shoulder.

"You OK, James?" Ian said. He quickly examined him for any injuries.

"My leg hurts," James said through tears. Ian wasted no time in pulling the child's jeans down to reveal a bright pink line striped across his thigh. He'd have a little mark for a few days, but he'd live with no real harm done. And he'd learned a valuable lesson about electric fences. At least he hoped he had.

"You'll be all right," Ian said, redressing James. He once again looked around again for Charlotte. Where was that woman?

"And you're gonna leave Nan's chickens alone from now on, aren't you?" Ian patted the little boy's back and soothed him the best he could. "Let's get you home and cleaned up. Daddy's taking you to see Mommy in a bit. You'll like that, won't you?"

The boy raised his arms for Ian to hold him. After ordering Will to put on his pants and get himself inside to Nan's bathtub, he carried Robert and James back to Wyatt and Molly's house. James sat in his lap, pretending to steer them the whole way home.

From the driveway, Ian could hear Logan wailing inside the house. White smoke was billowing through two open kitchen windows and the open back door. Ian found himself running for the second time that afternoon, this time toward his sister's house. His heart hammered in his chest. He burst through a curtain of smoke to find Charlotte pulling a large pan from the oven.

A black charcoal-colored lump was smoking on top of it. The smoke detector was screeching, causing the baby to scream from his Moses basket on top of the kitchen table. Ian snatched two kitchen towels, wrenched the pan from Charlotte, and flung the burning meat, pan and all, into the pond beyond the back porch. A column of steam hissed from the cold water as it sunk to the bottom.

When he stomped back inside, he stabbed at the smoke detector with a long wooden spoon to silence it. Scooping up the baby in his arms to soothe him next, he glared at Charlotte, who stood still, choking on the smoke.

Robert's hay monster alter ego appeared in the doorway, pushing a startled scream from a gasping Charlotte.

"Robert, what on earth . . ." She couldn't finish her sentence. Ian had already picked the boy up like a sack of onions in one arm and cradled the infant in the other. He was headed toward the upstairs bathroom. His jaw clenched in rage.

"C'mon James, bath time."

Charlotte trailed after, holding a still-sobbing James in her arms. She appeared in the bathroom doorway several moments behind Ian. "James said he's hurt."

"He's fine," Ian ground out. "He got tangled in Midge's electric fence."

"An electric fence?" Charlotte screeched. Horror edged her voice.

"I said he's fine. Just leave them both here with me. I'll get them cleaned up. You get Logan settled and get that mess cleaned up downstairs before Wyatt gets home."

Charlotte stood in shock as Ian turned on the water and quickly had both boys in the bathtub.

"Now!" he barked. Charlotte went into Logan's room, scooped him up from his crib, where Ian had left him, and soothed him in the rocker.

Wyatt came in nearly an hour later to find the kitchen clean, his children bathed and ready to go to visit their mother at the hospital, and a weary-looking nanny standing beside his brother-in-law.

"Ian?" Wyatt looked a bit surprised to see him standing there. "Were you wanting to go with us? Molly would love to see you."

Ian shook his head. "Not today, Wyatt. Kiss my baby sister for me, and tell her to get better quickly. Her boys are missing their momma." He cast Charlotte an accusing glare as he said the last few words with pointed condemnation.

He'd not spoken a word to her outside of giving her the command to clean up her mess and tend to Logan. He couldn't. He was too angry. While the ranch was free for the children to roam, there were dangers. His mind could create a thousand scenarios that could have either or both of the boys badly hurt. And she'd been hired to look after them. Where had she been?

"I'll do it. You didn't need to come fetch Charlotte, though," Wyatt replied. "I was going to carry her back to Momma's house." He pulled a piece of straw from Robert's head. He looked at it oddly before tossing it to the floor.

"Don't worry, I'll take her," Ian said. He cast a menacing stare at the nanny. He wouldn't need the whole two miles in the truck alone with her to be sure she knew how miserably she'd failed today.

After getting the three boys buckled into their car seats and waving goodbye to Wyatt, Ian turned and stabbed a long finger into Charlotte's face.

"What the hell happened today?" Ian shouted, fury burning his face a deep scarlet. "Do you even know where I found the boys? All the way at Midge's place by the barn, that's where. How the hell did they get there? Robert was . . . well, you saw what he looked like. And James got tangled in the electric fence by the chicken house. An electric fence! If I hadn't been right there . . . if anything had happened to those boys . . ." Ian raked his hand through his raven hair. "I swear, woman, I would have wasted no time in mounting your heart on a spike. Where the fuck were you?"

Charlotte forced her shoulders back and straightened her spine. "Mr. McGuire," she began in a weary but firm-sounding tone, "I would kindly ask that you refrain from using such vulgar language. I will admit things got a bit out of hand today . . ."

"A bit out of hand?" He began to speak in clipped tones as if Charlotte was some sort of slow-learning child. "James was electrocuted. I found Robert naked and covered in mud and horse shit. Both of them miles from home. Miles! The baby was screaming, and you were apparently trying to set fire to my sister's house with a pot roast. I think a bit of vulgar language isn't out of line at all."

"I think I'd like to go back to my room now if you please," Charlotte said, turning to head for the truck. Ian grabbed her arm and spun her around to face him, his eyes just inches from her face. Fury burned behind the navy orbs like flames, ready to lick her soul into hell. Her spine shuddered, and she swallowed, trying to remember to breathe.

"You are in way over your head here, woman," he barked.

Charlotte wrenched her arm from his grip, rubbing the place his fist had pressed into her arm. It throbbed from his tight grip. "If you are not intent to deliver me, Mr. McGuire, then I shall walk."

Charlotte hiked her tote bag over her shoulder and started toward the gravel path that would take her back to Midge's house. Ian growled but said nothing. He slid behind the wheel of his truck and skidded down the road ahead, spewing a cloud of dust over her.

Charlotte watched his truck disappear over a low hill. When he was well out of sight, she let herself collapse. She flopped down on the top step of the front porch, buried her face in her hands, and cried. The day had been a disaster. She had failed. Ian was right. He was no doubt phoning his sister and brother-in-law right now to tattle on her miserable experience of the day.

Charlotte swallowed hard, and her shoulders slumped under the heavy weight of Ian's convictions. The day had spiraled out of control before she knew what happened. The older two boys constantly ate, which meant she could barely get the kitchen cleaned up after one snack before she was making another. Feeding the baby was done in between trying to unclog the toilet, which James had filled with toy cars for a car wash, and stripping Robert's bed after he'd spilled chocolate milk all over the sheets. By the time she'd tossed the meat into the oven and sent Robert and James out to play, she had just enough time to remake Robert's bed. Looking around, there were more toys scattered on the floor than before she'd arrived. How did one woman do this all day, every day?

She was embarrassed to think she'd lost track of Robert and James. She'd told them to go outside to play to have ten minutes of peace to try to tidy up but had lost track of the amount of time after Logan started crying. No matter what she did, he couldn't be made happy again. And then the smoke alarm started screeching out a warning that dinner was burned. What a miserable day! Her feet hurt, her back ached, she'd not eaten all day, and her ears rang from the constant noise. But she'd be damned if Ian McGuire saw her defeated. She was down, definitely, but she wasn't out. Not yet. Failure was not an option.

But if Doctor and Mrs. Hampton found out what happened today, she'd be sacked for sure. If it hadn't been for his . . .

Charlotte looked up at the lengthening shadows and wiped the tears from her cheeks. If Ian had wanted Wyatt and Molly to know what a miserable nanny she was, why did he help bathe the boys and clean up the kitchen? Why had he helped her? It couldn't be possible that this hardened boar of a man had a soft place anywhere on his body. Apparently, however, he had one for his sister and her family. Charlotte let out a long, tired breath.

"Tomorrow's got to be better," she said quietly to herself. "If there is a tomorrow."

With that, she hiked the bag back onto her shoulder and started the long walk back to Midge's farmhouse.

Skidding the truck into the drive at Midge's, Ian slammed the door of his truck and then pounded through the back screen door, letting it slam with such a hard bang that Midge nearly spilled the water she was measuring for dinner.

"Ian, what the devil has gotten into you?" Midge said when he stomped into the kitchen. "You look like you're on the verge of murder."

"I am!" he spat.

"What happened? Was it Kip? Did the two of you argue again?" Midge stood with her hand on her hip.

"No!" Ian went to the sink and filled a glass of water, drained it, and then filled it again before he spoke. "That woman," he started. "That woman that my sister hired is an utter disaster. You should see the state of the house. And there'll be no supper when they get home; she burned that. She nearly set the damn house on fire! I should probably tell Wyatt I found Robert and James all the way up here in your barn. Alone. Robert was butt naked, covered in cow crap and mud. James got tangled up in the chicken fence. Poor kid nearly scared himself to death. And Logan was screaming his lungs out when I ran into a house filled with smoke from a burning pot roast." Ian took a breath and glanced at Midge.

She was covering her mouth with her coffee cup.

"I mean, this isn't exactly rocket science." When Ian stopped to take a breath from his rant, he discovered Midge was covering her mouth to hide a fit of laughter. She was laughing!

"You're laughing?" Ian barked. "What if something would have happened to those boys?"

"Ian, Robert and James are smart enough to follow a path up here and back to their house. I know they're little, but they are safe on the ranch. There are so many people around. I saw them playing in the barn."

Midge picked up a knife and set to scraping long orange carrots over the sink. Ian flopped down onto a barstool. "I didn't know Robert had gotten naked, though," she continued. "But Will told me when I hosed him down in my shower. And I was already at the back door to get James out of my chickens when you pulled him from the fence. I've been telling that boy to leave those poor birds alone. Now maybe he'll listen to me."

"She's not cut out for this, Midge. That was negligence, and you know it."

"I remember my first days of motherhood weren't any better, and no one accused me of neglecting my kids. Charlotte just lacks experience, that's all. She'll learn. No one got hurt, Ian." Midge wiped her hands on a clean kitchen towel, then turned, and laid a hand on his back. The heat of his anger radiated through his shirt, and his heart pounded in his chest underneath.

"But they could have—" Ian cut in.

"But they didn't," Midge said softly. "I'll have a word with Wyatt tonight. I suppose I'll be taking him some supper anyway. How about we help her out? Having her here means a lot to Molly. And you want her heart at ease about her boys, don't you?"

"That's an emotional ambush, Midge. You know I can't refuse Molly anything. I suppose we can help the nanny," he said grudgingly. "I'm going to take a shower. I need to cool off." He started up the stairs.

"Ian," Midge stopped him. "Where is Charlotte?"

Ian shrugged. "Well, if she's as smart as my nephews, she's following the path leading from Molly's to here," he said wryly. "I'll help with dinner when I get down."

It took Charlotte nearly an hour to carry herself back to Midge's house by foot. Her body ached. Her shoes were not cut out for the terrain, as she felt every sharp piece of gravel cutting into her heels. And she was tired. More tired than she'd ever been in her life.

The sky darkened quickly. She barely made it back to the farmhouse before the last sliver of sun slipped away for the night. She found Midge and Ian in the kitchen laughing. Ian was cutting vegetables, and Midge was stirring something in a pot. The aroma filled the entire house and set Charlotte's mouth to watering. She'd prepared a dozen snacks, two different lunches, and eight bottles of formula but hadn't had a single bite herself all day.

"Hello there, Charlotte," Midge said casually as she entered. "Did you have a good day?"

Charlotte gave a weak smile and nodded. "It was busy," she said. She was unsure how much Ian may have said about what happened. If she had to guess, he'd told her every horrid detail as soon as he got through the door. Still, she couldn't be mad at him. He had helped her. Although, she still hadn't figured out why.

"Well, that's good," Midge said absently. She returned her attention back to the pot. "Dinner is ready if you're hungry."

Charlotte shook her head. "I'd like to have a bath. May I eat in my room later?"

Midge stopped stirring and stared hard at Charlotte in the doorway. She had no doubt she looked as exhausted as she felt. Midge would be able to clearly see the bedraggled misery of defeat surrounding her. She glanced toward Ian, which proved to be a huge mistake. As if she couldn't feel any worse, his judgmental stare bore into her, making her feel even more embarrassed. After the scolding he'd given her an hour ago, she would have thought that to be impossible. Yet, here she was, more deeply humiliated than she'd ever been.

"Of course," Midge answered.

Charlotte slipped upstairs and into the shower, letting the water wash more of her tears down the drain. For the sake of her family, she had to make this work. She had to. Failure was not an option.

Feeling only mildly refreshed from her shower, Charlotte stood in her robe in front of the full-length mirror of her bedroom, brushing out her wet hair. Someone knocked softly at her door.

Ian's voice came from the other side. "Midge asked me to bring a tray up to you."

Charlotte opened the door and took the proffered tray. "I hope you like chicken and dumplings," he said.

Charlotte stared at the gravy-coated pile of pale yellow food on the plate and gave a slight grin. "We shall see then," she said, laying the tray on the bed and picking up her hairbrush again.

"You need to eat," Ian said gruffly. "You didn't eat yesterday, and I'm betting you didn't eat today either. The first rule of war is to feed the troops."

"War?" Charlotte mocked. Why did that word seem to fit her new job more than "nanny" or "caregiver"? She'd felt she'd battled the boys. She had fought her own weariness and a constant state of overwhelm all day. Ian was right. It was a battle. And it was one she was losing. "I very much doubt you should call it war, Mr. McGuire," she lied.

"All evidence to the contrary," Ian shot back. He folded his arms across his chest and leaned onto the door jamb. "It certainly looked like you were losing the battle today, Miss Poole."

Charlotte cast her eyes down and played with the bristles on her hairbrush, shame coloring her cheeks like a bright flame. He was right. Her first day was an unholy failure from start to finish.

"My first day with special forces, I was tasked with helping our supply sergeant load pallets for an upcoming deployment. I failed at every step. She'd made me load and unload those damn pallets over and over until I got it right. By the time I was done, I could barely stand up. It was well after 2100 when I finally finished. I wanted to head back to my bunk or at least get some food, but my team leader sent me to the range to catch up on all the training I'd missed that day because I was a screwup that couldn't load bags and boxes in the right order. I felt humiliated. Turns out the whole thing was a test. There was no deployment. They just wanted to see how I handled failure. Turns out, that's where I'd actually failed."

Charlotte twisted the hairbrush in her hands, picking at the bristles. She turned to face herself in the mirror again, unable to meet Ian's eyes. Her usual rosy glow had turned sallow. Deep hollows were making shadows on her cheeks, and there were purple smudges smeared under each eye. She felt his gaze on hers, judgment still looming behind his eyes.

He had no right to try to understand. He would never be able to fully comprehend what she was living through and how badly today's disaster stung.

She scraped the brush through her hair, making it sound as if she was pulling the hair out rather than smoothing it. She could see Ian staring at her in the reflection. Her head jerked in protest against the brush as she struggled to get it through a mass of tangles.

"You're going to pull it out. Here," Ian commanded. He walked to stand close behind her and took the brush from her hand. "You have to start at these knots from the bottom."

Charlotte rolled her eyes. As if she didn't know that. But she reluctantly handed him the brush anyway.

He worked in small gentle strokes with the brush, starting at the ends of her damp hair and gradually pressed toward her scalp. He worked patiently until her silken hair slid easily through his fingers. It was still damp but shone like gold. Ian let it slide slowly through his fingers just once before handing her the brush.

"There," he said at last and handed over the brush.

"Thank you," Charlotte said softly. She was quickly losing hold of her equilibrium.

"It's no big deal. Molly used to have really long hair in high school. I'd have to help her get the back sometimes. I don't mind."

He turned to leave and got nearly to the doorway when Charlotte suddenly found her voice again and stopped him.

"Ian?"

He turned and met her gaze.

"I wanted to thank you for what you did for me today. At Wyatt and Molly's. With the boys." Her voice was small and quiet.

Ian nodded, receiving her appreciation. "You're welcome."

This man was confusing her. He kept juggling her emotions back and forth between his anger and disappointment and gestures of kindness. She was getting dizzy.

"Why? Why did you help me?" Charlotte asked, looking up into his dark blue eyes. "You've certainly made no secret of the fact you think me ill-suited for this work. So why did you help me? You could have let Dr. Hampton come in and see what a disaster the day had been. But you didn't."

Ian shrugged. "I guess I love Molly and the boys more than I dislike you."

Charlotte squared her shoulders and clutched her opening bathrobe tight around her neck.

"Then I am in debt to your sense of honor and loyalty. And I offer my assurances that my performance will improve," she said.

"We'll see about that." Ian turned on his heel and left, clicking the door closed behind him.

CHAPTER FOUR

"I'm sorry about the boys' behavior yesterday," Wyatt said when Charlotte arrived at his house the following morning, promptly at 5:00 a.m. Ian had dropped her off again after a silent drive down the long gravel path that connected the two houses. "They know they're not supposed to walk up to Momma's without a grown-up."

Charlotte nodded. She opened her mouth, ready to offer her apologies and pledges that it would never happen again. But Wyatt stopped her with a raised hand before she could speak.

"I told you they were a handful, and they were testing to see how far they could go. I made it very clear last night after my mom brought dinner; they had gone entirely too far. I doubt you will have any trouble out of them again."

Second to None

"I hope you weren't too harsh on them. They are only children, and it is my responsibility to—"

Wyatt stopped her again. "This is a working cattle ranch, Charlotte. There are loaded weapons, horses, wild animals—plenty of things that could seriously hurt any of the children who live and play here. Obedience is non-negotiable. You told them to play outside; they disobeyed. When they choose to disobey, there are consequences." Wyatt let out a long breath and raked his hands through his hair. "I wanted to be a father for so long; having my boys is a dream come true for me. I get to teach them to ride, rope, and whistle. And I always hate having to discipline them. But it's important to me that they understand that. The rules are established because we love them and want to keep them safe."

Charlotte nodded and folded her hands in front of her waist. "I heartily agree," she said, nodding again.

Wyatt stood and snatched a worn cowboy hat from a long peg by the back kitchen door. "Oh, and Molly said to tell you she stocked the deep freezer in the garage with fudge pops. Apparently, the boys are nuts for them. She said you could use them at your discretion." He gave her a slight smile before whisking out the back door with a quiet "Have a good day."

Charlotte let out a sigh of relief, delighted to still have a job. She turned and checked on Logan before slipping into the kitchen to prepare breakfast for the boys. It would be a good day, she promised herself. She took a deep breath and allowed herself a moment of hopefulness. It was definitely going to be a good day.

And it was a good day. And so was the day after that and the day after that. Molly had been right about the fudge pops. Just the promise of one before nap time was enough to ward off the temptation of bad behavior. By the end of her first full week, Charlotte too was becoming more relaxed and familiar with the boys' unique quirks. She learned that Robert hated being called Bobby by his cousins and hated crusts on his sandwiches. James didn't mind the sandwich crusts but refused to nap like the baby.

To accommodate the required resting period, Charlotte and Robert constructed a blanket fort in the upstairs playroom each afternoon after lunch. Charlotte would then collect a stack of picture books, and the three would snuggle down under the fleece cover of their fort while she read. By the time she'd read only five minutes, James was usually snoring softly, and Robert would follow a few minutes after.

Second to None

On the first day of her second week, a soft winter rain fell all morning. Long fingers of light mist had made the ground sodden and impossible to allow the boys to run off their extra energy. Charlotte found herself on her fourth picture book with both boys stirring restlessly around her. She stopped in the middle of a word when she heard the back door close downstairs and a familiar man's voice boom out.

"Anyone home?"

"Uncle Ian," the boys cried in unison. Their faces cracked into wide smiles, and Charlotte, too, found herself smiling at the prospect of seeing him again.

In a flash, they were down the stairs to tackle their uncle. Charlotte laid back against the pillows of the fort and let herself rest. The boys were safe downstairs with Ian, and Logan was napping in his crib across the hall. The baby monitor would inform her if he woke. She was going to take a few well-earned deep breaths. Two active boys cooped up inside all day had nearly worn her out. She'd barely managed to let out two long breaths of air when the sound of small feet, followed by a pair of large boots, pounded toward her.

"See, Uncle Ian? See?" Robert said excitedly. He pulled Ian's wrist toward the fort. "See, we built it, just like I said. Isn't it cool?"

Ian knelt before the fort and pulled back the Star Wars blanket that was used as a door to see Charlotte's deep coffee eyes staring back at him. "Go in, try it, Uncle Ian," James urged, pushing him forward with tiny thrusts and grunts.

Charlotte slid to one corner and patted a pillow beside her. "I was just about to read a story about a bear hunt," she said.

"Would you like to go on a bear hunt with us, Uncle Ian?" Robert begged.

Ian didn't miss the playful grin that spread across Charlotte's lips. He was trapped into bear hunting whether he wanted to or not. And she knew it.

"Of course," he said good-naturedly. Ian listened with rapt attention to the accented lilt of her voice as she read, and he and the boys pretended to go around, under, and over the obstacles she described in the book.

The rain patted harder against the window. Charlotte looked over and caught a glimpse of a rare smile across Ian's lips. It wasn't the first time she'd seen him smile. He'd always seemed to smile or laugh when he was with Midge or Wyatt and the boys. He'd seemed more relaxed lately, especially around her. They'd even managed to enjoy a few pleasant conversations over dinner. His friendship, such as it was, made life seem more bearable on the ranch. There was still a great deal she needed to learn. And she was thankful the tension between them had eased. There was an unspoken truce ending the tiny battle that had begun after her first day. More than she wanted to admit it, she was thankful to have his friendship.

Swaddled there in the cozy warmth of the blankets, happy and laughing, she let her heart savor the moment. She let the images and sounds roll around her mind like a good wine that soaked into her tongue. She wanted to remember each word, every sound, and the expressions of wonder on the faces of the boys. But mostly, she wanted to remember Ian's smile.

When Charlotte read the climax of the story, announcing the coming of the bear, Robert and James stood abruptly, pushed two of the blankets away, and ran squealing and laughing from the room. Charlotte found herself alone with Ian encased in a soft, dilapidated teepee.

Charlotte's mouth opened, and she let out a warm laugh. She looked over and saw Ian too was laughing. Then, he looked into her face and suddenly stopped. His gaze instantly warmed, sending pinpricks of heat over Charlotte's spine. His smile faded slightly, but she could tell he was happy.

His fingers reached out and plucked a stray strand of hair from over Charlotte's eye, and he let the tips of his fingers trail down the soft curve of her temple, her cheek, and then her jaw. Charlotte's breathing stopped. Her heartbeat quickened. Her body relaxed as he leaned closer to her. Their eyes began to drift closed as he touched her chin. She could feel his breath against her mouth. He only had to lean just an inch closer—

"Uncle Ian!" Robert said, snatching the cocoon from around them and flinging it over his shoulder. "Logan's awake. That means it's time for fudge pops. You want one?"

Ian's hand and body snapped back. "None for me. You can have mine."

Robert's face went alight with excitement. "Can I? Miss Charlotte, please?"

"I'll split it between you and your brother," she said, unfolding her legs and standing up. She managed to dismantle the fort with a few quick flicks of her fingers. "You boys fold up all the blankets and put them away. I'll get the baby and the ices."

The boys immediately set to work while Charlotte walked sedately across the hall and scooped Logan from his crib. He'd only begun to fuss, and Charlotte suspected it was the squealing from the bear hunt more than his desire for a bottle.

"Hello, little man," she said, kissing his forehead. "I'm so happy to see you awake. Now, tell me truthfully. No fibbing, now. Did your brothers wake you, or are you sincerely hungry?"

Logan gave a loud whimper and then opened his mouth to let out a tiny, helpless wail.

"I can change him if you want," Ian said from the doorway.

"Thank you, Mr. McGuire. I can get a head start on warming his bottle and getting the boys their snack."

Ian stepped closer and held out his arms as Charlotte gently laid the fussing infant into his hands. Snuggled in his oversized arms, Logan looked even tinier—like a newly hatched caterpillar nestled in the leaves of an oversized flower. It always surprised Charlotte how tenderly Ian's large, clumsy-looking hands managed to be so delicate with the newborn. There was obviously more depth to him than the brisk boarish side she managed to see so often. And yet, not as often now as when she'd first arrived.

"Charlotte," Ian said. He swayed back and forth, soothing the baby a bit. Charlotte turned from the doorway and raised her brows in response.

"I suppose I'm the one who owes you an apology now," he started. "For underestimating you. You seem to be covering things a little better now."

Charlotte couldn't reply. She simply nodded, turned, and left without a word. She had felt sure he was going to apologize for wanting to kiss her. Her mouth had gone dry instantly at the idea. But she would have assured him that there was no need to apologize. After all, she'd wanted it too. Although she'd never admit that to him.

A cloudless sky boasted a bright winter sun the following day. Charlotte could feel the warmth of it on her face as it shone in through the stained-glass window of the small country church where the entire Hampton family worshiped. It seemed impossible to believe the temperatures would scarcely reach the freezing mark that afternoon. The sun felt so warm until she stepped outside. Charlotte found her teeth clacking together in the few steps it took to get from Midge's truck back into the house after the service. After a large family meal, to which Charlotte was invited, Ian set a blazing fire in the hearth at Midge's house. It did wonders to warm her. The house, which thundered with the sounds of the many

Hamptons just an hour ago, was now silent and still save for the crackling of the logs.

Charlotte slowly paced in front of the fire. "Mrs. Hampton," she started. There was no reply. "Midge," she called again. "I wonder if I might borrow your car this afternoon. I need to venture into town later."

Midge was curled up in the corner of the well-worn sofa, a folded magazine in her lap, and her eyes closed.

"Midge?" Charlotte said again. But there was no answer apart from the soft breathing of a sleeping matriarch.

"I can carry you into town if you need to go," Ian said. His massive frame filled the doorway of the living room. His arms were loaded with firewood.

"Oh, I don't want you to go to any undue inconvenience," she said. The truth was, Charlotte needed to go alone. If Ian was with her, she wouldn't be able to keep the appointment she'd arranged. An appointment she didn't want the Hamptons finding out about.

"I'm headed that way; it's no trouble." Ian laid the logs into a neat stack and dusted his hands clean. "Just let me grab my coat."

Charlotte swallowed and nodded. She would have to agree to let him take her. What else could she do?

Refusing his offer made her look suspicious. Drawing suspicion to her could provoke someone to look into her past and her more closely. And that could not happen. Besides, she didn't mind being alone with Ian as much anymore.

Ian skipped up the stairs for his coat. His heart beat a little faster at the idea he'd get to spend the afternoon with Charlotte tucked into his truck beside him. She'd become more comfortable around everyone at the ranch and was finding her place. And he had to admit that she actually fit in—snobbery and all. She was funny and usually managed to make him laugh while they ate dinner together. It didn't escape his notice that Midge had taken to eating either extremely early or rather late, forcing the two of them to eat alone together each night. Not that he'd minded it.

Ian hopped down the stairs to see Charlotte nervously tugging at a strap on her tote bag. She was once again wearing gray wool pants, a cashmere sweater, and that thin black coat. Her fingers never had gloves. The woman had to be freezing.

"Is that the only coat you have?" Ian asked as she slid into the seat of his truck beside her.

Charlotte nodded, her shoulders shaking from the cold. "It's fine for the cold but does nothing to block that wind. It's like a thousand razors."

"Don't you own any jeans?" he asked. In all his life, Ian had never known a single woman who didn't own a pair of jeans. And how was it that a nanny could afford these designer wool and cashmere clothes anyway? He knew what Molly and Wyatt were paying her. It wouldn't afford that.

"No," Charlotte said, a hint of disgust clouding her brow. "This is the second time you have commented on my attire, Mr. McGuire. You find my vestments unsuitable in some way? I assure you that every nanny I ever had dressed in a similar fashion."

Ian laughed out loud at her as he pulled the car onto the highway. "First of all, my name, again, is Ian, not Mr. McGuire. We both work here. We're equals. And if I can call you Charlotte, you can call me Ian. Second, you need to lighten up on the ten-dollar words."

"I beg your pardon?" Charlotte said, obviously affronted. "I was unaware the use of an educated vocabulary was offensive."

"See, that's what I mean. 'The use of an educated vocabulary,'" Ian mocked in a high-pitched tone. "Who talks like that?"

"I do," Charlotte said.

"Well, you sound like a snob," he said. He remembered the first time he'd called her that. And really, she wasn't. She was just from a completely different world, he realized. When he saw her reaction to the word, his heart squeezed. He'd hurt her feelings, and he hadn't meant to. "I'm sorry. I didn't mean any offense. But when people talk like that, it feels like they're trying to prove they're better than everyone else. I get it; you're smart."

The last part he meant. She was smart. She knew the answers to every single one of Robert's questions without having to Google a single one. *Why was grass green but the sky blue? What happens to dogs when they die? Can it snow up? What makes you burp? How loud do lions roar?* She was constantly pointing out interesting facts about nature to the boys, and she spoke to Logan in fluent French and Italian.

Charlotte crossed her arms over her chest. "Lottie," she replied simply in a quiet voice.

"What was that?" Ian asked, not quite sure what she meant.

"I prefer not to be called," Charlotte cleared her throat, "that is, I mean to say, call me Lottie. All my friends and family do."

"Lottie?" Ian repeated. The nickname suited her much better than Charlotte. "I like it. Well, where is it you needed to go today, Lottie?"

"I'd like to see about finding some tea," she said. "And I . . ." she paused, chewing on her lip. She seemed to be choosing her words carefully, Ian noticed. "I have an appointment on River Bend Street."

Why would she be nervous about an appointment downtown? He couldn't recall what businesses were on River Bend Street, but wherever she wanted to go, she had to know it was no business of his. Right?

"OK. I can drop you off on Main, and once you finish up your appointment, you can walk back. I think there's a coffeehouse that sells tea. I can meet you at Michelangelo's Pizza later for dinner if you want."

Lottie's chin bobbed up and down. "Thank you. That would be lovely—I mean, fine."

"Better," Ian smiled again.

Ian parked in front of the hardware store. "River Bend is the next block over. That's the coffee shop." He pointed in one direction down the street. "And that's Michelangelo's." Lottie's eyes followed him as he directed her. She pulled her coat tighter around her neck and started walking in the direction of River Bend. As she walked, Ian noticed she glanced over her shoulder several times. He dismissed his suspicions again. She's just making an effort to remember her route, surely. She almost looked as if she was searching for someone or scared of something, though. Was she nervous? Ian's mind raced with possible scenarios.

Perhaps it was too many years serving in special forces, but Ian couldn't stop rising suspicions. He liked Lottie. But there were too many things that were just not adding up. She wore expensive clothes she said her own nannies wore. She grew up with nannies? Her ten-dollar words certainly gave away her elite education. So what was a highly educated woman with money doing working as a nanny in a nowhere town in Oklahoma? Ian shook his head. Whatever it was, he needed to find out about it before he let her get too close to his family. Then, before he even realized he'd moved, his feet were following silently behind her.

There were lots of things being an operator had taught him. He learned how to clear a room of combatants, interrogate a suspect, and field strip an M-4. He also learned how to follow someone without being seen or heard. Ian traced Lottie's steps down River Bend Street to the front of the Horse River Bed and Breakfast. He assumed a post across the street where he could easily see into the oversized Victorian paned windows across the front and along one side of the inn.

Seconds after entering, Lottie found her "appointment." He was an older man in a camel-colored wool coat. Dark swaths of black cut canyons of color through an otherwise gray head of thick hair He had the same European look about him as Lottie. But the two looked nothing alike. Lottie flew into his arms and embraced him. He held her for several long moments.

So, apparently, Ian thought to himself, these two know each other. Were they lovers? She hardly seemed the type to sneak off to a rendezvous with an older man. And, as far as he knew, she received no phone calls or letters from anyone. That suddenly seemed odd to him now too. She'd mentioned her family and sister quite often. So why didn't they call or write? Ian made a mental note to check into that later.

He moved closer to get a better look. When he got sight of Lottie's face again, a large hand was removing a black leather glove and wiping a long stream of tears from her cheek. Seeing her cry with her face squeezed with intense emotion made Ian's fists clench involuntarily. He was uneasy with the idea of someone making her upset.

Of course, he didn't like it when anyone made a woman upset. Charlotte—Lottie, to him now—was no different, right?

Ian could easily see the two talking but couldn't make out what they were saying. He pulled his cell phone from his pocket and snapped several pictures of the two who had now taken a seat on a sofa in a small parlor.

Forty-five minutes later, Lottie left the hotel headed back toward Main Street. The mystery man she met dipped into a waiting town car and took off in the opposite direction. Ian quickly memorized the license plate—an unshakeable habit from his training. He knew if he traced it, it would only reveal the car was rented. When they'd gone, he strode up the steps of the white clapboard inn two at a time.

Behind the reception desk stood a tall, thin woman with a long beak-like nose. A pair of oversized glasses perched on the very tip of it. She wore them tethered to her neck with a strand of pearls. Tight curls in an unnatural shade of reddish pink created the illusion of fluffy cotton candy around her head. She offered Ian a large smile showing off huge white teeth and an expanse of fleshy pink gums.

"Good afternoon, sir. May I help you?" she said in her most genial nasal tone.

"Yes, I'm looking for a business contact of mine who said he was staying here. An older man, distinguished. I think he was meeting his niece here a little while ago. I hope I didn't miss him."

The woman nodded and gave Ian a sad look. "I'm afraid you did. They actually left just a few moments ago. But he's not a guest with us. He just ordered two hot teas and waited for his—niece, did you say?"

"I'm guessing he paid cash for the tea?" Ian asked expectantly.

"Yes, sir, a fifty-dollar bill. Told me to keep the change. Said I made the best Earl Grey tea he's had on this side of the pond."

"The pond? He spoke with an accent? British, right?" Ian said, pleased he hadn't missed his guess the man was European.

The teeth and gums reemerged as she smiled at Ian again. "Oh yes, sounded just like James Bond." She let out a nervous, girly titter.

Ian swore she said that name with a sort of swooning sigh.

"And so handsome. I wish he was staying here. A single gal would love to have a chance to get to know a gentleman like that." She sighed wistfully. "You know what I mean?"

At this, the woman behind the desk, whose name tag said she was Carole, wagged her eyebrows and began to look Ian up and down. She bit her lower lip and slowly slid the giant orbed lenses from her nose. Her bony fingers gave her helmet-shaped coif a soft fluff as she stared Ian up and down. He suddenly felt as if he were losing every stitch of his clothing inside her imagination. It was time to go.

Ian thanked the attendant and set off back toward Main Street. His mind buzzed. Yesterday, Charlotte Poole was his sister's nanny and a friend of sorts. Today, Lottie was a mysterious, affluent, well-educated woman who may be posing as a nanny to meet with some sort of European aristocrat? Lottie Poole was becoming more and more intriguing by the minute.

Back on Main Street, Ian waited outside the coffee shop. He could see Lottie fingering through tins of tea, sniffing several varieties before settling on her choice and making her purchase. She emerged a few minutes after he arrived carrying a small brown bag.

"Did you find what you wanted?" he said, announcing his presence.

Lottie smiled at him. "I was pleasantly surprised. They had my favorite."

"Earl Grey?" Ian guessed, remembering what Carole had said back at the bed and breakfast.

"Ceylon," Lottie replied. "The good stuff is a bit harder to get back home. I didn't think they'd carry it here."

"Oh, and where is back home?" Ian asked innocently. She steered them in the direction of the Italian eatery.

Lottie smiled and seemed to ignore his question. "Ian, I wonder if you would help me with something else."

Ian quirked a brow. He made a permanent notation in his memory at the way she evaded his questions. But he was pleased she'd called him by his first name. "Sure, since you called me Ian."

"Contrary to what you may think, I truly do want to fit in on the ranch. So, where does one go to purchase jeans?"

Ian stopped in the center of the sidewalk and gave careful consideration to Lottie's question. She didn't know where to buy jeans? How was it possible that a woman, any woman, didn't know where to shop for anything? Wasn't there a shopping gene inside every girl's DNA? Had Lottie been raised under some sort of European rock?

"They don't have stores in London?" he asked. His reaction was genuine. But he was also trying to round back to his question about her home. Lottie had been quiet about the details of her life. Now that he reflected upon it, she often avoided or deflected questions about her past, her home, or her upbringing. Maybe he should just come right out and ask her what he wanted to know. Of course, this way was less likely to force her to lie if she was indeed hiding something. It was good old-fashioned psychological operations at its finest.

"Of course they do," she answered. "I meant, here. Certainly, I wouldn't expect to find Harrod's or Marks and Spencer's around the corner."

"No," Ian said. If this woman was trained to evade questions, she was trained well. Perhaps she was some sort of government employee? CIA, NSA possibly? He'd get John to look into her. The thought reminded him of the last time he'd worked with those guys. They'd been sent home on leave—to try to escape their jobs and heal from the wounds from the IED explosion. But somehow, the mission managed to follow them home.

A known terrorist, who'd tried to have Ian's special forces team killed in Afghanistan, made several attempts on Preacher's life. The result had been the end of Moseldek Kaymar and, sadly, the murder of John's father.

He began to wonder if he was the next target of attack. If he were, Lottie could be here from his own government to lend a hand and protect his family. If she was listed anywhere in a Department of Defense roster of employees, his best friend would be able to find her.

"But there is this—" Ian let the speculations of his mind rest. He guided Lottie into the OK Resale Shop. In just a few minutes, Lottie chose several pairs of jeans, a warm coat, a knitted toboggan, and several long-sleeved t-shirts.

"I'll be better able to keep up with the boys outside in these," she said. She patted the bulging plastic bag in her arms. Ian stopped by the truck, tossed the bag inside, and was ready to head across the street to Michelangelo's for a beer and his favorite sausage and olive pie when he noticed Lottie staring in the window of a leather shop storefront.

"Aren't those gorgeous?" she said, pointing to a pair of handcrafted leather boots. Tiny cardinals were embossed along the tops with delicate trees of colored leather striping down the sides and across the rounded toe of the boot. Hand-stitched flowers and leaves adorned them, held together with stitches so small, it seemed no human could have made them.

"I know these people," Ian said causally. There was something about the girlish way she ogled the boots, like they were a much-desired Christmas wish, that made Ian's heart feel a little lighter. "Gunther Brody owns this shop. His daughter, Elsbeth, just started making boots."

"Why don't we go in?" Ian went on while Lottie continued to stare. "I can say hello to my friend, and you can get a closer look before you start drooling on the glass."

Lottie gave Ian's arm a playful slap, and the two went inside. The aroma of leather goods perfumed the air in an overpowering wash of rich, buttery luxury. Saddles and bags of every description lined one side of the shop. Rounds of belts and baskets of gloves dotted the center of the small store, and on the right, wooden shelves filled with handmade boots floated from the floor to the ceiling. Ian watched as Lottie drifted toward the boots, carefully fingering the fine leather craftsmanship of each shoe.

A little silver bell tinkled above the door as they entered, calling a young, petite brunette. She skipped out from behind a thick leather curtain separating the front of the store from the back.

"Hey there, Mr. McGuire. What can I do for you?"

"Elsbeth," Ian greeted the girl with a nod. "This is Lottie Poole." He used his thumb to point to Lottie, who was now halfway to the first pair of boots on a shelf. "She's nannying for Wyatt and Molly. She needs a pair of boots for the ranch."

The girl smiled and nodded. "I heard." Lottie looked over her shoulder at the young woman. Her eyebrow rose with apparent curiosity.

"I'm friends with Brandon Hampton. Well, a bit more than friends, I guess," Elsbeth answered Lottie's unspoken question. "He told me there was a real British Mary Poppins living on the ranch taking care of Molly's boys." Elsbeth offered Lottie a sympathetic look. "I've sat for them a time or two. You sure have your hands full."

Lottie smiled. "Indeed," she said, giving the girl a knowing smile. Turning back to the boots, she asked casually, "Are these European sizes?" Lottie gestured to a number on the bottom of one of the boots.

Elsbeth answered they were and walked over to help Lottie choose a pair to try on. Ian watched as she slid her slender feet into the boots. She stood and twirled. She bounced up on her toes and then walked back and forth in them. He could tell she loved them at once. Every woman who tried on Elsbeth's boots did. The leather was as soft as butter, and the soles were made to hug a person's foot, supporting every inch gently. They were the most comfortable boots Ian had ever worn. Of course, his were just plain black with a subdued American flag at the top. No trees or flowers or any of that other girly crap.

Lottie picked up the price tag, and her mouth fell open. "Two hundred?" she nearly choked. "Dollars?"

Elsbeth nodded. The boots were on the high end for the small Oklahoma town, but they were one of a kind and handmade. And Elsbeth knew it.

"They are beautiful. I truly adore them," Lottie said, slipping them off easily and laying each one gently back in its wooden box. "But I simply can't—"

"We'll take them," Ian said. He slapped his credit card on the counter. The desire to please her, to make her happy, was unexpected and overwhelming. More than anything, at that moment, he wanted to preserve the look of sheer delight on her face. It almost felt as if his own happiness depended on hers. It was a ludicrous notion but one he was helpless to avoid. The moment the words to buy the boots left his lips, he was glad he'd done it.

"Mr. McGuire," Lottie started. Ian gave her a scowl. "Ian, I can't accept such a—"

"You need boots," Ian said simply.

Elsbeth ignored their argument, plucking up the credit card before Lottie could change Ian's mind. She happily rang up the sale and swiped his card.

"Besides, if I'm going to leave you on the side of the road to walk back to the house from Molly and Wyatt's place, the least I can do is see to it that you have proper shoes."

He gave Lottie a wink and watched her face flush a deep rose.

"You're most considerate, really, but—" Lottie started to protest again.

"No more ten-dollar words." Ian took the wooden box under his arm and started for the door.

"Tell your dad I said hello," he called back to Elsbeth. "And I'll be sure to tell Brandon I bumped into you today."

"Thanks. Enjoy the new boots. And good luck with the boys, Lottie."

Across the street, Lottie and Ian sat down at a small table at Michelangelo's Pizzeria. It was a typical American restaurant with pool tables and dart games in the back. It had a long bar, lined with stools where men and women of all walks of life were glued to some sort of sporting event—no, make that three different sporting events—on one of a half-dozen oversized TV screens.

A tall, thin woman wearing a skintight t-shirt and low-waisted jeans came up to the table and squatted down beside Ian.

"What can I get for you, hun?" she asked, giving Ian a bright smile.

Ian cast Lottie a playful look. "Do you trust me?" He gave her another wink.

"Okaaayy," she cautiously replied.

"Good enough." Ian turned to the waitress, who clicked a tongue piercing on her front teeth.

"We want a large pie with sausage and olives and a pitcher of Cowboy IPA."

The waitress scribbled on a tiny spiral notepad, nodded, and left.

"I figured since you like Ceylon tea, you'd like a more bitter-tasting beer," Ian said, stretching a leg out on one side of the table. "If you drink beer. It goes well with pizza, at any rate."

"You know tea?" Lottie asked. She made no effort to mask her surprise.

"I spent some time traveling. Tea is a kind of universal beverage. I pick up a little here and there every place I go."

"What's your favorite then?" Lottie asked. The waitress plopped a foaming pitcher of amber liquid on the table and two frosted pint glasses. Ian poured them each a pint while he replied.

"I think the chai in Turkey is my favorite. It's strong and has a nice mellow flavor. I like Iraqi spiced chai too, but they use too much sugar for my taste. Indian tea is good. That's where I tried your Ceylon. I was in Sri Lanka a time or two."

"My, you certainly have traveled extensively." Lottie took a sip of the beer. She hummed her approval. "You were right. I do like it." She took another sip before continuing. "What took you to all those exotic locales?"

"My previous employer had interests across the globe," Ian skirted. He didn't want to talk to her about his life with the army right now. He felt good about her finally calling him by his first name and was still riding the high of making her happy with the boots. He didn't want to talk about killing and death. He wanted this feeling with her to last a little longer. He had no idea what it was, but he hoped it would last all night if it could.

Taking a sip of his beer, he replied simply, "What about you? You travel much?"

"My parents believed travel equaled education. I've been all over Europe mostly. Oh, and Australia. I loved Australia."

"Me too," Ian replied. "But if you ever get the chance, New Zealand is way better."

"Is there anywhere you haven't been?" Lottie asked, impressed.

"I have never been to Antarctica, China, or any of those islands in the South Pacific where they rent you the little hut that sits out over the water." He swallowed another gulp of beer.

"Me either," Lottie confessed, beginning to feel the effects of her beer on her empty stomach. "But I'd love to go someday if I get the chance."

Ian looked across the table at the beautiful woman smiling back at him. Who was she, really? He was beginning to let his earlier suspicions dissolve. More than likely, she was just a woman who wanted to keep her private life private. That wasn't a crime. And just because her family may have had money didn't mean she did.

Ian had a pretty good sense of people. And he trusted his gut. Tonight, his gut was telling him that Lottie Poole was just a woman he wanted to know better. He didn't have to suspect she was a part of any sort of subvert mission. He could allow himself to just enjoy the time of learning who she was. He had to let go of his past and that life of always looking over his shoulder.

The two enjoyed another hour of easy conversation while they consumed the entire pizza together. They talked about travel and beaches and hotels they loved. They talked about books. Ian considered himself to be a pretty well-read person, but Lottie had more great reads to recommend and seemed to know everything about classic literature.

Before he realized it, they were standing in the hallway at the top of the steps in Midge's farmhouse. Ian stood in front of his bedroom door and Lottie in front of hers, her arms full of the purchases she'd made that day. Her face was shining, and she smiled with such genuine affection, Ian couldn't help but smile back. Her joy was infectious.

"Thank you for today," Lottie said. "And the boots. That was incredibly generous of you."

"No more ten-dollar words. I'm tired. Good night." Then, without even knowing he was going to do it, Ian stepped forward. He reached out, tipped her chin up, leaned in, and deposited a soft kiss on Lottie's lips.

It took two full heartbeats for the act to fully register in his brain. He stepped back to see his own shocked expression reflected on Lottie's face. Where the hell had that come from? Mumbling something that sounded a little like "good night," he made a hasty retreat.

Ian closed the door of his bedroom behind him. What on earth possessed him to kiss her? He couldn't imagine. Yes, she was pretty. OK, she was more than pretty. She was beautiful. And, of course, he would want to kiss her. Who wouldn't want to kiss that sweet mouth with those blush-pink, full lips? But he'd just reached out and kissed her. He'd kissed her, and she'd let him. But he didn't think she'd kissed him back. Did she? She didn't push him away, though. That had to be something. Next time, he'd kiss her like he truly wanted to—like he had wanted to under the blanket fort a few days ago. If there was a next time.

Across the narrow hallway, Lottie laid in bed and let her fingers brush along her lips where Ian kissed her. It probably meant nothing. It had to. She was only here for a few weeks. Molly was supposed to be home from the hospital in a day or two. And, as soon as she was well enough, the Hamptons wouldn't need her anymore. She had to keep moving. She couldn't settle down. It was too risky.

She tried not to think about Ian. About his firm lips. His tender fingers. The way he touched her. The feel of him. The way he smelled of soap and hay and winter air. And the more Lottie tried not to think of kissing Ian McGuire, the more her mind filled with images of him.

CHAPTER FIVE

Charlotte sat bolt upright in her bed. Something had woken her. What was it? Her heart was pounding. Her skin was slick with perspiration. She tried to slow her breathing, but it came only in gulps and pants. Her mind raced to find an explanation. Perhaps she was just having the dream again. No. This time, she'd heard a sound too, hadn't she? She held her breath and strained to hear it again, but there was nothing now.

The moon was still high against a black curtain of night. Then she heard it. The sound hadn't been from a bad dream. It had been real. And it had scared her so fiercely that she'd woken with a jolt. Her hands began to tremble.

The downstairs screen door tapped shut. That was the sound that had awoken her. Lottie checked her watch on the bedside table. The bright green backlight showed it was barely after two. No one would be up at this hour.

Oh, God, he's here! The notion ran briefly through her mind, pushed panic and fear through her body, and nearly brought her to the brink of hysteria.

She took a few deep breaths and gathered as much courage as she could. On shaking legs, she walked to the window and peered out into the starlit sky. There was a soft yellow light coming from inside the barn. She could see it clearly from her bedroom window. Lottie watched as the dark silhouette of a man approached the large side door. He slid it open, looked around himself, and then slipped inside, sliding the door closed behind him. Lottie's blood froze. She twisted her body to move out of the view of the window in case she could be seen. Her heart began to pound, forcing the veins in her neck to throb in a steady staccato of alarm. Had he actually found her?

Ian and Midge may have heard it too. Someone could be inside the house. And that someone may be . . . him. Lottie forced her mind to cease its terrifying speculations. Common sense could prove there was no way he could have found her out here. She'd been careful. Until she'd been forced to go into town for that meeting. Ugh! She knew that had been a mistake. She took a deep breath.

Lottie tip-toed into the hallway and tapped softly on Ian's door. If there was someone in the house, she didn't want to alert him to her presence. She had to keep quiet. Although she was certain anyone within five feet of her could hear her heart pounding. There was no answer. Her heart racing, she turned the handle slowly, grateful the mechanism turned smoothly.

Pushing the door open, she could see Ian lying in bed with his back turned toward the door. The outline of his massive form was highlighted by a faint silver glow of moonlight peeking through tiny openings in the blinds that covered his window. She crept to the edge of the bed and reached her hand toward the sleeping figure, her arms trembling violently. If she'd put this family in danger, she'd never forgive herself. Her hand hovered inches above his shoulder. Before she could even touch it, Ian's voice muttered.

"You better have a good reason for sneaking into my room at this hour of the night." Lottie jumped back, covering her mouth to stifle a scream. She thought he was asleep.

He rolled over to look at her. Lottie caught only a flash of something lying against his chest. The dim light from the window unable to give her a full view of what it was.

"What's wrong?" His voice was a rumble, edged slightly with irritation and the last remnants of sleep.

"I heard a noise. I think someone may be in the house," she stuttered in a whisper, her eyes wide.

"I doubt anyone would be out here in the middle of nowhere robbing this place. I'm sure it's nothing." He tossed the covers off of himself and sat up slowly. He was in a pair of long, dark flannel pants, his chest bare. Lottie now noticed the metallic object she'd seen a glimpse of earlier was a large caliber pistol gripped in his hand.

"You have a gun?" she exclaimed in a sort of shouting whisper. She wasn't yet still certain someone was in the house, and she didn't want to set off any alarms—yet.

"Someone was sneaking into my room," Ian explained coolly. He laid the pistol on the bedside table and clicked on the light. A soft yellow glow flooded the space around them, leaving cones of dark shadows tucked into the corners.

Ian stared into Lottie's face for several long seconds. She stood before him in her pajamas, barefoot. Her blond hair had escaped the loose braid she'd put it in to sleep. Her body shivered, and her shoulders were shaking so hard she knew he could see it.

"Geez, something did spook you." Ian stood and slid his feet into a pair of soft leather slippers set next to the bed. Lottie's legs began to quiver, her knees trembling to keep her body upright. She'd never been so terrified in her life.

Lottie nodded, tears dancing at the back of her eyes. "I heard someone in the house, and then I saw someone go into the barn," she whispered. She clutched at the front of her pajama top, gathering the fabric tight in her fingers. Ian reached for her hand and loosened her grip. His hands were steady and warm.

"Hey, it's all right, Lottie. It's probably nothing. But I'll go check it out, OK? Just stay here," he said soothingly. She was grateful he was calm. He didn't seem to be alarmed. Perhaps it was just her dream again—amplified by her imagination. "I'll be right back. Try not to worry."

Lottie nodded like a bobble-head doll, hugging herself and willing back tears. She was not going to cry. It was bad enough she'd woken Ian in the middle of the night. She wouldn't take away whatever shred of dignity she had left with hysterical tears on top of everything else.

"Hey," he said as he reached the door. Ian's voice was low and even in a way that instantly stilled the most violent of tremors that shivered through her body. "Everything is going to be all right, I promise."

There was something about hearing those words from his lips that made her believe he would make them true.

Ian slipped on a sweatshirt hanging on the back of a chair near the door, grabbed the pistol he'd laid down earlier, and slipped out into the darkened hallway. As he left, Lottie extinguished the lamp and tucked her body into a corner. She hugged her arms tight across her chest, closed her eyes, and prayed he hadn't found her.

Ian walked quietly down the stairs and through the house. It was empty and still. The front door was bolted. The back door was unlocked, but that wasn't unusual. This far away from civilization, the worst that could happen is the barn cat could slip in and find a warmer place to bed down for the night. He stepped out onto the back porch and looked toward the barn. There was an odd light coming through the cracks between the wooden planks in the door. A flashlight, maybe? Ian walked carefully through the shadows to the door and silently peeled it back.

"Please," a woman's voice pleaded from somewhere behind a load of square hay bales that had been delivered yesterday. The source of the light emanated from the same place as the sound. "Ow, stop!" it said and then let out a soft, muffled shriek. Ian leaped forward and came around the side of the hay bales, his gun drawn.

The woman's voice he heard was attached to a petite brunette. A naked petite brunette. A naked petite brunette he knew. Elsbeth. He could only see a portion of her face in the dim light, but he knew it was her. Her eyes were closed, and a pained expression was masking her face. A naked man was lying on top of her, propped on his forearms, her knees spread around his waist. The couple was clearly engaged in humanity's age-old mating ritual. Ian cleared his throat to announce his presence.

Elsbeth's eyes popped open, and she screamed. The man lying naked on top of her turned around. Even before he completely turned around to face him, Ian knew who it was. Brandon's eyes grew wide as he peered up at Ian, a black .45 caliber pistol pointed at his bare behind.

Ian quickly dropped the gun and spun around, turning his back to the pair. He didn't give a damn about Brandon's pride, but poor Elsbeth deserved what little dignity he could spare her. Damn kid. What the hell was he thinking?

"Get dressed," he said gruffly. He took a few steps into the shadows to give the young lovers a bit more privacy. Stuffing an unsatisfied and quickly fading erection into his jeans, Brandon approached and stood facing Ian, who kept his back to a quickly dressing Elsbeth.

"Ian, man, I'm sorry. We were trying not to wake anyone," Brandon started, his face a shocking crimson.

"What the hell are you doing out here in the middle of the damn night?" Ian said, then waved a hand. "I mean, I can clearly see what you were doing, but damn it, son. You couldn't find a better place than a freezing cold barn at two in the morning?"

Brandon blushed again. "Where would you suggest? At my house with seven other sets of ears to hear us? Some cheap motel?" Brandon pushed his fingers through his hair. "I live in the middle of five thousand acres, and there's no privacy," he whined.

He glanced over Ian's shoulder. Ian twisted to follow his gaze. A shame-faced Elsbeth was stuffing her arms into her coat and slinking toward the barn door with shocking speed.

"You two meet out here often?" Ian asked. Brandon stepped around him and gathered his shirt to slip it on.

"No. This was the first time," Brandon murmured, clearly frustrated. "And the last, thanks to you. I'll never get her to agree to . . ." Brandon let his voice trail away.

"You mean, this was the first, first time?" Ian asked. He turned to face Brandon, the realization of the significance of the event finally taking root. He noticed Elsbeth had fled the barn. Brandon nodded.

"Sorry, man." Ian shook his head. "For her or for both of you?" When Brandon didn't answer, Ian asked again. "Both of you, then?"

Brandon only nodded, a pink stain beginning to flush against his cheeks.

"Do you love her?"

"I suppose so," Brandon shrugged. He was clearly embarrassed by Ian's line of questioning.

"You take that sweet girl's virginity and give her yours, and you better be a bit more certain," Ian warned. His voice was taking on a more authoritative tone than he'd planned.

He looked around the hay bales to see the flameless candles, scratchy wool blankets, and cell phone piping out a country love song propped up on its side. It was an amateur's attempt at romance. Still, it was a far cry from the twin bed in Tiffy Morgan's college dorm room. There was nothing romantic about his first time either. At least Brandon was making an effort. It was more than he'd done.

"And I suppose the condoms are in your pocket?" Ian said. He raised one eyebrow and cast Brandon a questioning stare. He didn't need to answer. Ian could see the truth in the deepening cherry stain that now flamed over his cheeks. Damn it; someone needed to talk to this boy.

"She said she had that handled," Brandon said. "Look, are we seriously going to discuss this right now? I don't need to explain myself to you. I'm twenty-one years old. I'm a grown man. I can have sex if I want to."

"All right then, grown man," Ian started. "Next time, plan your business a bit better, and don't scare the nanny half to death sneaking through your grandmother's house to play slap and tickle with your girlfriend in a dusty barn." Ian groaned. He stuffed the pistol and his hands into his sweatshirt pockets and strode toward the barn door. He passed Elsbeth leaning against it, tears streaking her face.

"I deeply apologize for disturbing you tonight," Ian said to her softly. She jumped at the sound of his voice. "I am truly sorry if I embarrassed you." Ian said nothing more, just turned to leave. Better to leave them with what dignity they had left.

"Mr. McGuire," Elsbeth called out in a weepy voice. "I know you and my father are friends, and—"

Ian stopped her with a raised hand. "You and your grown man there are both consenting adults," Ian started. "I don't see a need to tattle to your father about something that's not any of his business or mine."

Elsbeth gave him an appreciative look. "Thank you," she said as Brandon appeared at her side.

"Brandon will be taking you home now," Ian said, the subtilty of the command not lost on Brandon. He shot Ian a sideways glance.

Ian shook his head and grinned to himself as he watched the two walk away. He saw Brandon draw Elsbeth close to his side and rub her shoulder. If it wasn't love he felt for that sweet young girl, then it was the next best thing.

When he reached the top of the stairs, Ian stuck his head into Lottie's room to tell her the suspected prowler turned out to be Brandon, but her room was empty. The bathroom door was open, and the light was off; she wasn't in there. He walked into his room and didn't see her immediately. Out of the corner of one eye, however, he caught a flash of the bright gold of her hair.

She was sitting in a corner, hugging her knees she'd drawn up tight against her chest. Her body trembled violently, and tears streaked her pale face. She rocked back and forth. It was an automatic reaction people made when they needed to soothe or calm themselves.

She must be really freaked out. What on earth had terrified her? This kind of reaction wasn't just some noise she heard. This was the result of a deep-seated fear or some kind of trauma. He tucked the pistol back into the top drawer of the bedside table before kneeling silently in front of her.

"Lottie," he whispered softly. Despite the fact her eyes stared right at him, he got the sense she wasn't even seeing him sitting right in front of her. She was in shock. From a noise? No. From something else. He called her name softly again. The last thing he wanted to do was frighten her even more.

She blinked that time and then seemed to focus more clearly on him. "Everything is OK. You're safe." Ian extended his hand to pull her up. Lottie rose to her feet, her trembling knees giving out under her. Ian easily swept her into his arms, carried her across the room, and sat with her on his lap on the edge of his bed. Lottie buried her face into his neck, clutching his sweatshirt in a tight fist, and wept.

Ian let her cry. Her hot tears splashed against his skin. Who had done this to her? Whoever it was, he wanted to beat the life out of him. When the tears finally began to slow, he whispered to her.

"Shh, you're safe," he repeated again and again. He stroked her hair, which had now come undone from its braid completely. The silken strands smelled of shampoo and the scent of fear mixed with sweat. That was an odor he knew only too well.

"There's nothing to be scared of." Ian soothed and petted her. It took several more minutes before Lottie finally began to stop trembling, and her tears dried. He held her tight, trying his best to comfort her. Why did her trembling affect him so deeply? He should be shooing her out of his room and into her own bed so he could get some sleep. But he could not let her go. He needed to hold her. He needed to know she was all right. He needed to make it right. The need was unexplainable and unassailable. It was unsettling.

Ian never confronted an enemy he couldn't overcome. Until now. This need for her was commanding him, and he was powerless against it.

Lottie sat up and stared into his face with swollen, red-rimmed eyes. Ian wiped the tears from her cheeks with the pad of his thumb.

"Are you OK?" he asked after several long moments of silence. Lottie had a faraway look on her face again. She shook her head weakly.

"Was . . . was there s-s-someone there?" she asked. Her voice sounded as if she was terrified to hear the answer. "I . . . I thought I heard s-someone s-scream."

Ian drew her head back onto his shoulder and gently kissed the top of her head. "It was just Brandon and his girlfriend in the barn. I scared them. That's all it was. You're safe, Lottie. I've got you."

"You're certain?" Lottie asked. Her voice shook, but Ian thought she sounded a bit less terrified now. "There was no one else?"

"No one," Ian said with certainty. "I checked the barn and the house."

Lottie finally let out a quivery breath she'd been holding. "Thank you," she said. She gave his cheek a soft, chaste kiss. Lottie climbed out of Ian's lap, but he kept a firm hold of her hand and forced her to sit beside him on the edge of the bed.

"Will you be all right if I leave you here for two minutes?" He spoke softly and slowly. Lottie nodded once.

Ian held up two fingers as he repeated, "OK, two minutes." He slipped out into the darkened hallway. Exactly two minutes later, he re-entered the bedroom door carrying two glasses and a bottle of some sort. He put the two glasses on the bedside table and poured an inch of dark amber liquid into each.

"Here," he said. He handed one of the glasses to Lottie. "Drink this."

Lottie accepted the glass and sipped the contents. She coughed and sputtered.

"What is this?" she asked in a rasp.

"Whiskey," Ian said. "Good whiskey." He downed his dram in a single gulp and poured himself another. "You seem like a white wine kind of a woman to me," he said. He sat down beside her and let his hand lay softly over one of hers laying on her leg. "But I thought your nerves might need something a little stronger."

"Thank you," Lottie said weakly. She took another sip.

Ian noticed her hands were still trembling, but the shivering had stopped. The demand of the universe to restore Lottie's happiness commanded him again—just as it had in the leather shop. And now, it was compounded with the necessity to protect her.

Thinking back, he realized it had been Lottie that had started all of this that rainy afternoon in the boys' blanket fort. She'd warmed his heart. In that brief moment with her surrounded by clouds of fleece and laughter, he felt true, genuine peace. The peace and happiness he'd been looking for all this time. And ever since, he now realized, he'd been hoping to find it again. And he had. In the leather shop. During the dinners they shared. Over pizza at Michelangelo's. And even right now. And he needed to keep its source safe.

"Something really scared you tonight," Ian said. He took a tiny sip from his glass. "Want to tell me what it was?"

Lottie's spine straightened, and she sipped on her whiskey again. "It was nothing," she said. Her words tumbled out a bit too quickly for them to be believed. She sipped again. "The overreaction and imaginings of a silly woman, I suppose," she said.

"I've seen hysterical women before," Ian said. He leaned forward to rest his forearms on his knees. He twisted his head and looked up at Lottie. "And I've seen true, genuine fear. You call it what you want, but you were honestly afraid of something or someone tonight. What was it?"

Lottie took the last sip of her whiskey and leaned over to put her glass on the edge of the bedside table. "Who would I be afraid of?" Lottie said, her voice quavering.

Ian couldn't be sure, but he would swear her eyes said she was trying desperately to hide something.

"I'm more embarrassed than anything right now."

Ian sniffed. "Well, that would make two women I embarrassed tonight then. That could be a record for me." He decided to let his questions drop for now. She wasn't going to tell him.

"Two women?" Lottie's brows knit in confusion. "You mean the girlfriend? Was it Elsbeth from the leather store?"

Ian lifted his glass to his face and waggled his eyebrows.

"Oh," said Lottie, and then realization dawning further. "Oh!" She allowed herself to laugh slightly at her fear. "So all this time, I think he's found me, and it was just some randy bloke shagging his girlfriend in the barn?" Lottie's laugh turned into a hiccup. The whiskey had done its job, Ian noted.

"You thought it was who? Who found you?" Ian probed again, hoping perhaps she'd open up to him. But Lottie just waved a hand and leaned over to rest her head on the pillow on Ian's bed. He knew she was exhausted. Adrenaline did that to people. The high and then the ultimate crash. He'd seen it—hell, he'd experienced it more times than he could count.

Ian gently teased. "You're a cheap date." His words were too quiet for Lottie to hear. Or maybe she did hear him but was too content to protest. "One whiskey, and you're crawling into my bed." He shook his head.

Ian downed the last swallow of whiskey and added the empty glass to the space next to Lottie's on his bedside table. When he turned to look back at her, her eyes were closed. She was asleep. Ian guessed she'd probably wake up in a few minutes when the initial reaction to the whiskey wore off and trot off to her own bed. With that thought, and a heavy weariness seeping into his own bones, Ian stripped out of his sweatshirt and shoes and climbed into his bed next to Lottie.

His dreams that night were filled with images of her. A curtain of long blonde hair draped around their bodies while he made love to her. Her head thrown back. Her hips grinding over him. Soft mewls and moans of pleasure purring from her throat. Her deep chocolate brown eyes staring into him. A smile stretched across her face. Then music.

Ian's eyes blinked. The music was coming from his phone. Damn, it was 4:00 a.m. already, he cursed silently. He turned to reach for his phone only to realize that a soft, warm female body was curled up to his side. Ian stretched for his phone and managed to silence the alarm, which, thankfully, hadn't woken Lottie. He shifted uncomfortably, the painful erection he'd woken with demanding to be satisfied.

Carefully, he peeled himself from around the beautiful sleeping woman at his side and slipped into the bathroom to get ready for work. When he returned from the shower, dressed and ready for a day on the ranch, Lottie was still sleeping peacefully in his bed. She'd curled herself around his blankets, looking like a blond burrito wrapped in his down comforter.

Ian sat down on the edge of the bed and gently stroked her hair. She had such beautiful hair. She'd spent the night in his bed, too scared to return to her own room. The question of who or what she had been so afraid of last night still bothered him. He wanted to know. But more than knowing what had frightened her, he needed to know she trusted him. He wanted her to trust him. He smiled at that thought. He wanted her trust because he wanted her. She was the source of his long sought-after peace.

His fingers brushed over her cheek; the soft creamy flesh felt like velvet. He was glad that she'd come to him, though. He'd liked holding her, easing her fear. For the first time in a long while, he was ridding someone's life of fear, not causing it. It was an intoxicating feeling. One he'd like to get used to. Lottie let out a little purr of pleasure at his touch. She snuggled deeper into his comforter as Ian slipped silently from the room and down the stairs.

CHAPTER SIX

Lottie felt so incredibly cozy. She didn't even want to open her eyes. But her father and Maisie would be waiting for her to have their breakfast, and she wanted to see if Maisie's new roses were blooming yet. Lottie let her eyelids flutter gently open, the last images of her dreams of home and her family blurring over into the new day. Small slits of bright sunshine sparkled in her eyes. She stretched languidly and blinked slowly, allowing her body to ease into wakefulness. She couldn't remember the last time she'd slept so well and woke so refreshed.

Glancing around the room, she suddenly realized she was not at home. She was not even in her room at the Hampton farmhouse. She was in Ian's room. Oh, God! A flood of memories from the night before washed over her like a tidal wave—fright, anger, embarrassment, the thick-headed dullness of the whiskey.

"No. No, no, no, no, no!" She sat up and looked around. And the whole disastrous night had ended up with her in Ian's bed! This was not happening. If the family found out she was waking up in his bed—

She stopped herself before her mind could finish the end of the nightmarish notion. The sheets beside her, thankfully, were empty. At least there was no Ian in bed beside her.

She glanced at the clock beside Ian's bed. It was after eight. Way after. Oh, good Lord. She was so very late. She burst into the hallway and through the open door of her own room to pull on a pair of jeans and a sweater, her skin tingling with another rush of adrenaline. She was stuffing her feet into her boots when a soft knock at her door made her jump. Ian's broad frame filled her doorway.

Wearing a dark blue flannel shirt, worn jeans, and the most endearing Cheshire cat smile she could imagine, Ian's eyes eased over her body. God in heaven, she must look a fright. Too embarrassed about her behavior, Lottie lowered her eyes. She couldn't meet his gaze. What in the world had she been thinking last night? She'd heard a silly noise and then jumped like a scared rabbit into Ian's bed. Her father would be horrified. She was ashamed.

"Good morning," Ian drawled. He offered her the mug. "I made you some tea. Strong. Milk and honey, right?"

Lottie took the tea gratefully without meeting his glance and murmured something that sounded sort of like, "Thank you."

"You're welcome. How are you feeling this morning?" Ian asked. His tone didn't carry a hint of mockery. His words carried no effort to deride her for her absurd notions that had him traipsing around the ranch at two in the morning. Lottie inwardly rolled her eyes at herself. How could she have, for even one moment, thought he'd found her here? In the bright light of day, her fear seemed improbable at best.

Lottie would pretend she didn't hear the genuine concern in his voice. She'd ignore the care and compassion with which he spoke to her. She was also determined not to remember the tender way he spoke to her last night. Even though she cherished it.

"I'm terribly behind my time," Lottie answered. "Why didn't you wake me? Molly just getting home from the hospital, and I'm showing up hours late. You should have woken me."

"Hey, take it easy. Midge wanted to take the morning shift. I happened to know you didn't sleep well last night.

I thought you might like a little rest before being set upon by my heathen nephews."

And now he was considerate and helpful. This could not be born. Disliking him was the only way to stay detached. And she needed to be detached. Because she had to leave. Liking him would make that too hard.

"Hey, look at me," he pleaded.

Lottie tried to meet his gaze. She just couldn't do it. She was too humbled. And the more she remembered what she'd said last night, the more horrified she became, knowing how close she'd come to revealing too much. But she was more embarrassed by the fact that she'd enjoyed waking up in his bed. The most humiliating part of it all was that she wanted more than anything for him to hold her again, to whisper to her the way he'd done last night, and lay beside her while she slept. No, she could not have that. She can't want that.

"Could you just please take me to the boys?" Lottie asked impatiently. She raked her hair into a tidy ponytail.

Ian let out a sigh. "Sure, c'mon."

Lottie remained mute as they crunched down the gravel lane to Wyatt and Molly's home. She was grateful Ian didn't try to get her to talk. She hardly knew what she would say. When they parked at the drive, Ian turned the truck off and started to get out.

"Where are you going?" Lottie asked, nervous fear edging her voice.

"I need to talk to Wyatt about something," Ian said simply. Lottie gulped. Was he going to tell Wyatt about last night? What would happen to her when the family found out she'd slept in Ian's bed? She'd be sacked for sure. Molly had been released from the hospital only the day before, and she would still be needed for at least another week or so. She didn't want to lose her job here. As it was, it would be hard enough to leave the Leaning H when the time came. This family had welcomed her as one of its own. Their warm, friendly nature had made leaving her own family a bit easier. She felt she belonged. And she wasn't ready to leave. She would have to go soon enough. And she didn't think she'd find this at every assignment she took in the future.

The two entered the house together. Lottie could feel her cheeks flush a bright crimson at the touch of Ian's hand on her back as they walked inside.

Ian hugged his sister and kissed her cheek. Molly had a warm, friendly smile. A halo of short, dark curly hair framed her heart-shaped face. She had the same dark eyes as Ian, and they shared the same chin. She was sitting at one of the kitchen barstools stirring a spoon in a small bowl.

"You look good, babe," Ian said. "How are my boys?"

"*Your* boys?" Molly said, her tone dripping with sarcasm. "They're good. Thanks to Charlotte."

"I need to talk to Wyatt. Do you know where he is?"

"In the garden around back," Molly answered. "It seems my winter greens are feeding more deer than our family."

Lottie loved how close Ian was to his sister and with Wyatt. One day, she'd have to hear the story as to how that relationship was born. Ian and Wyatt acted more like brothers than they did brothers-in-law. In fact, in many ways, it seemed Wyatt was closer to Ian than he was to either Kip, Timothy, or Mattie.

"Thanks. You look beautiful, sis." Ian kissed her forehead, then left, headed, no doubt, to the garden.

Molly slipped off her stool and started spooning oatmeal into two small bowls at the kitchen island.

"Good morning, Lottie," she called out cheerfully. She made no mention of how late Lottie was. Nor did she mention how she knew to call her by her nickname. The two had talked nearly every day since she'd arrived to care for the boys. Molly wanted to know everything about the boys: what they had eaten, how they'd slept, and all the sordid newborn details of Logan's dirty diapers. Molly was a good mom, and Lottie knew she wanted to know all intricacies of their day because she missed them so terribly.

Each time they chatted for one of their daily reports, Molly had called her Charlotte. "Midge just left. And you're just in time for a second breakfast. I swear I'm raising a family of hobbits," she laughed. She slid a bowl and spoon in front of James. He and Robert had lazily joined the two women.

"Mrs. Hampton, I am terribly sorry for my tardiness. It won't happen again," Lottie said. She gave each of the boys a kiss on the tops of their heads as a greeting while they spooned oatmeal into their mouths.

"Don't worry about it at all. Logan had a good night last night, so I got to sleep a little, and Midge was here early this morning to help with the boys. I think she's been missing them."

Lottie wasn't paying attention. She was rehearsing what to say later when Molly and Wyatt questioned her about why Ian had woken up this morning with her in his bed. So whatever Molly said after Midge coming over, she'd missed it.

"Lottie?" She snapped back to the moment. Molly was looking carefully at her. Lottie had seen herself in the mirror this morning. She knew how she looked—dark circles ringing her eyes, and her hair was undone and barely looked brushed. In a word, she looked completely frazzled. "Are you all right? Ian said you had a bad night. We have worked you too hard, haven't we?"

Lottie offered a reassuring glance. "Not at all. I'm fine," she replied automatically. She was anything but fine. Sharing a bed with Ian had given her the most peaceful night's sleep since she'd left home. Her heart was getting too attached to this family and much, much too attached to Ian. She considered him a friend. It had been a long time since she'd enjoyed the companionship of a true friend. And she'd never had one as sexy as Ian McGuire in her life either.

"Why don't you sit down with me a minute?" Molly said. She took a seat in a small gathering room off of the kitchen. A warm fire was crackling in the hearth. Logan was asleep in his bassinet beside the chair where Molly sat. Lottie gave a look over to the two boys who were finishing their oatmeal and sliding down from their stools at the bar. "Don't worry about them. They'll go play. Please, sit with me."

Lottie sat and let out a long, silent breath. There was something calming and friendly about Molly's eyes. They were the exact shape and color of Ian's eyes, hooded by the same dark brows. The same ones that had stared warmly at her under the blanket fort. The same eyes that had looked at her with tenderness last night while she cowered in fear in his bedroom. And there was something inside Lottie that wanted more than anything to unburden her heart about what had happened. She could never tell the Hamptons the whole story, but she could at least rid her soul of this secret.

"I thought I heard something last night. In the barn. I suppose I am just not used to the sounds of the ranch at night, and . . ." Lottie began nervously. Her words came fast and seemed to run together in a rush. It would be better just to get the truth out in the open and accept whatever consequences would fall. "I hadn't intended for anything to happen, I swear it. But there I was, and I don't know, I thought maybe it could be . . ."

"Hey, Molls? Oh, morning, Charlotte," Wyatt said as he and Ian strode in through the back door. Their unexpected arrival broke the spell that had come over Lottie. She had just been about to tell Molly everything. Her hands were shaking. What had she been thinking? She couldn't tell anyone. For them to know would be to put them in danger too. And while she hated to admit it to herself, she had truly grown to love this family. And she could never do anything to put their lives at risk. Lottie eased into the kitchen for a glass of water while Wyatt knelt beside Molly in the chair. He took her hand, kissed her knuckles, and spoke softly to her.

"I think I've got a plan for fencing in the garden. Ian and I are going to get some supplies, and we have some other things to do that will keep us in town all day. I'll be home in time for supper. Will you be all right?" Molly nodded. "And you'll call me if you need me?"

"I'll be fine, Wyatt. Stop fussing. Go do what you need to. Lottie will be with me."

Wyatt leaned over and gave his wife a kiss. Lottie couldn't help but notice how in love the two of them were with one another. She smiled at seeing their affection. It was a life, a love she could never know.

"Yuck!" came the voice of a completely disgusted three-year-old waving a TV remote in one hand. "How can you kiss a geel, Daddy? They has cooties," James spat out.

"Exactly," Ian said. He rushed to the boy in two long strides. He scooped him up into his arms. "It's so yucky, right?" Ian said. He tossed James into the air, who giggled his agreement.

"We better not look then." Ian set to tickling the little boy in his arms, who arched and nearly squiggled right out of his grasp.

"Keep your eyes closed," Ian warned, laughing and tickling James, who cackled like a hysterical bird. Lottie found herself smiling and nearly laughing herself, watching him with his nephew.

"They're not done yet." The cacophony of James' laughter echoed in Lottie's own throat.

"All right, let's go," Wyatt said. He and Molly were now both laughing so hard themselves that kissing was impossible.

"Whew, you're saved," Ian said with dramatic emphasis. He dumped the giggling boy onto the floor. James scrambled to his feet and then tore down the hall, no doubt to make a full report to Robert.

Ian turned and caught Lottie watching him and James; her mouth spread into a wide smile. Their eyes locked. Lottie immediately turned her gaze from his, straightened her spine, and began to study something on her sleeve.

Despite how happy his lighthearted manner with the boys made her feel, she was still too embarrassed to look him in the eye. And she worried that her glances might give her heart away to everyone in the room. That could not happen. She was here to work. She was here to hide. She was here to keep her family safe. She had to remember that above all else.

Ian was by her side near the sink in a few long strides.

"Listen, if you're staying with Molly all day, I can drive you to Midge's when we get back," Ian said. He reached out to gently touch the edge of one slender pale finger resting on the counter. Lottie could feel the gooseflesh rising from the spot where he innocently touched. It crept up her arm, her neck, and over her scalp in a tingle she instantly loved and craved more of.

"I can find my way back. You needn't feel you must look after me, Mr. McGuire," she said a bit more coolly than she'd intended. She looked up at him then, an apology in her eyes, if not on her lips.

"I see, so we're back to Mr. McGuire now, are we?" Ian gave a sigh and stroked his finger lightly over hers. The gooseflesh worked its way into her stomach, where a thousand butterflies took flight into her chest. The beating of their fluttering wings accelerated the beat of her heart.

"Would you have dinner with me tonight?" Ian asked softly.

"Dinner?" Lottie gulped and willed her heart not to thunder with excitement as his low, honeyed voice compelled her to agree.

"I thought I'd pick up some steaks while I'm in town. Is that OK?"

Lottie gave a pleading look of utter indecision. Her heart desperately wanted to have dinner with him. But her head cautioned her. The more time she spent with Ian, the more she was going to fall in love with him. It was probably too late for that already.

"We have to eat, Lottie. C'mon. It's just dinner."

In the end, her heart won out, and she consented. The butterflies picked up their dance with the promise of more heart-pounding moments with him to come later that evening. He lifted his hand, which had been resting casually next to hers, and walked out of the door behind Wyatt.

Lottie felt dizzy. This could not be happening. She could not be developing any feelings for Ian. That was not part of the plan.

"Lottie?" Molly's voice was playful as she repeated the nickname only Ian knew about. "Is that what you like to be called? Ian called you that this morning when he phoned to say Midge was coming early. I hope you don't mind."

Second to None

"Not at all. All my friends and family call me Lottie. I'd like for you to as well," she lied. She'd like for them to call her Nanny Charlotte. She needed the reminder of her proper place and how temporary life at the Leaning H Ranch was going to be. Maybe then, her heart wouldn't grow so attached to them all. Because right now, all her efforts to distance her heart from this family were failing.

"Would you sit with me for a little while?" Molly asked, gesturing to the armchair positioned beside hers in front of the hearth room fire.

"I should probably see to this oatmeal before it sets," Lottie said nervously. "You could pave whole avenues with dried oatmeal, and—"

"Lottie," Molly said, her voice kind but more firm this time. "Come and sit down, please."

Lottie nodded and did as she was asked, being sure to bring another full glass of water with her. Something in her gut said she'd need it.

"You had started to tell me something before the guys walked in," Molly began calmly placing a pacifier into Logan's mouth. "About last night. You heard a noise in the barn?"

Lottie took a sip of her water. "It was silly, actually. I suppose I'm just not used to the sounds on the ranch. I heard something, and I woke Ian to have him see about it, and I suppose I was just terribly frightened. And he was gone for a while, so I just thought—"

Molly interrupted, "What was it?"

"What was what?" Lottie said, pulled from her nervous ramblings.

"The noise you heard?"

"Oh," Lottie waved a hand. "Just Brandon and his girlfriend in the barn." As soon as the words left her lips, she slipped a hand over her mouth. She shouldn't have said anything. If Brandon's parents found out, they'd probably be angry with him. It didn't matter how old he was.

Molly gave a smile. "It was Elsbeth, wasn't it? I had a feeling about those two," she said. "You know, he was barely in high school when I married Wyatt and moved out here. It's so hard to believe he's old enough to fall in love."

"Yes, well . . ." Lottie said. "About your brother."

"Lottie, I can't imagine what on earth you're worried about. A woman hears a noise in the middle of the night, you naturally go and wake up the man who always has a gun."

"He always has a gun?" Lottie said, swallowing hard. She hadn't thought to ask why he'd had the pistol last night. She was just thankful he'd had it. Just in case her desperate imaginings were actually true.

"Of course. The nature of his former life, I suppose. Lottie," Molly started. Lottie could see that she looked nervous about what she was about to say. She gave her a slight nod to indicate she should continue. "Did my brother . . . that is, he didn't try to . . . he was a gentleman last night, right?"

Lottie looked horrified at the idea of what Molly was insinuating. "Of course. He was very kind. More than I deserved."

"Well, I just couldn't help but notice how uncomfortable you seemed to be around him this morning, and, well, I just wanted you to know that if you needed me to speak to him, or if he had done or said anything to make you feel uneasy—" Lottie cut her off.

"Your brother is a fine man. I find it near impossible to believe that he would ever take advantage of a woman in any way."

Molly grinned. "No, he wouldn't. But I just couldn't think of any reason why you'd act as if—"

A realization dawned on Molly's face. Her eyes widened, and her jaw went slack. "Oh my God, something *did* happen between you two last night."

"It was all very innocent, I assure you," Lottie began to confess, her hands nervously tapping alongside her water glass. Her voice was panicked and strained, and her mouth worked to keep up with the words pouring out.

"I didn't mean to fall asleep in his bed. It was just that I was very upset, and he was so nice when he helped me to calm down because I was absolutely a mess, and then there was that bloody whiskey, and I suppose that had a little to do with it, but then I woke up in his bed." The words came out in a long tumble. When she finished, Lottie inhaled sharply and prepared herself for what was to come. Molly would fire her for sure.

"Oh, I see," Molly said simply. Her expression was difficult for Lottie to read. She wasn't upset. That was clear. So what was it? Intrigue? If Lottie were forced to say exactly what it looked like, she would have guessed it looked rather like something she said sparked the memory of a great secret in Molly's brain.

Logan began to fuss, and she picked him up and rocked him gently in her arms. The babe hushed instantly. "Lottie, I know that you're not going to stay in Oklahoma for very long, but I think you should know that I suspect my brother is attracted to you."

"Oh?" Lottie tried to look as though the thought had never crossed her mind. But it had. No less than a thousand times a day. The endless strings of what-if thoughts ripped through her mind over and over again.

"Did Ian tell you he used to be in the army?" Molly didn't wait for an answer before she began again. "Well, it was really a lot more than that. The army controlled every aspect of his life. They told him when to sleep, where to live, what to wear. It was his past, his present, and his future. Outside of Uncle Sam, there was nothing in Ian's life."

"How so?" Lottie said, genuinely intrigued.

"They told him when he could love, who he could love, and who he couldn't."

"I see. He chose his career over relationships?"

"He didn't have much choice. Ian was never one for lots of girlfriends growing up. I think I can count on one hand the number of women he's ever been with." She mused. "I think of him as a serial monogamist. Ian was a very good soldier. And even though he convinced himself he was happy with that life, he wasn't. He may have been in the beginning, but toward the end—he'd grown to dislike the man he was becoming. It was very hard for him. Hard for him to stay and hard for him to imagine life as anything other than a solider."

Molly let a long silence stretch out before she spoke again. When she did, her voice sounded reluctant to disclose that secret she'd been harboring in her mind. "Just now, when he looked at you in the kitchen, I saw that little spark he used to have when we were kids. I haven't seen that in a very long time, Lottie. So, just in case you were wondering about him, I wanted you to know. He's not perfect. But you can trust him."

Lottie suddenly felt warm. Her cheeks flushed, and she gulped the water in her glass to quench the fire that rose in her belly. *You can trust him.* Oh, if only she could.

"Why me?" Wyatt scowled across the bench seat of his red pickup truck at Ian. The two were on their way into town to purchase lumber for Wyatt's garden project. "He has a father to explain the birds and the bees to him. For Christ's sake, he's twenty-one years old. I'm sure he knows what parts go where."

Ian shook his head. "His father can tell him about the mechanics of sex, but he isn't going to tell him how to make love to a woman, Wyatt. You should have seen it. It was awkward. He had her naked in that freezing cold barn on a horse blanket. Besides, I don't think they're ready."

"Well, that's not any of our business, is it?" Wyatt said. He jabbed the indicator stick and turned into the hardware store parking lot.

"You're right. I'll just go talk to Kip. He's even-tempered and patient," Ian said sarcastically. "I'm sure once I tell him I caught Brandon and his little girlfriend in the barn with no condoms about to throw down and do the haystack hula, he'll be totally fine and not be the least bit upset."

"Stop it," Wyatt said half-heartedly.

"He'll be in the absolute best frame of mind to discuss the finer points of intimacy with his son."

"You've made your point," Wyatt said, his jaw clenching slightly.

"And Brandon will just be thrilled to discuss all of that with his father."

"Damn you, Ian," Wyatt interrupted.

"So you'll talk to him?"

"Why don't *you* talk to him?"

"He doesn't want to hear from me, I promise you," Ian said. He looked out the window at the low gathering clouds. "I have very old-fashioned notions about sex."

"Old fashioned?"

"Yeah. I'm no saint, man. But I don't typically advocate hopping into bed on the first date. I think you should be married to her, ideally. If not, you should be prepared to propose. I mean, love her that much. Sex means more to me than just getting off."

Wyatt raised an eyebrow at Ian. "And that, my dear brother-in-law," Wyatt said, thrusting the gear shift into park, "is exactly why you're the perfect man to talk to him."

Ian shook his head. "C'mon, man. You're his uncle. You're family."

"Exactly. No one wants advice on how to take a girl's virginity from their uncle. You're the single guy. And I trust you."

Ian scrubbed his face with his palms. "Ugh! Fine. But you owe me, big. I'm going to go across the street to the drugstore to get him some condoms. You get what you need. I'll meet you back here and help you load up."

"Sounds good. I need to go by the vet clinic and the store after. You wanna grab some Puffy Taco for lunch?" Wyatt stifled a laugh, satisfied he'd won the argument with Ian.

"Sure," Ian replied. He wrenched open the truck door and walked across the street and into the drugstore.

Standing in front of the FAMILY PLANNING section, Ian grabbed a package of condoms and some lubricant. Maybe he should grab some for himself. Visions of Lottie from his dream the night before came flooding back to his mind. He pictured her beneath him and then lying beside him naked with her long golden hair spread out like a blanket. Ian sucked in a deep breath as he felt his body begin to respond to these thoughts. He pushed them from his mind with a sigh. He would only be able to dream about having her back in his bed. He couldn't even get her to look at him this morning. He grabbed a pack for his bedside table anyway.

On his way to the cashier, he also grabbed a couple of soft blankets and a few more of the flameless candles he'd seen in the barn last night, along with an extra package of batteries. He carried everything up to the front and got in line behind a petite brunette. A familiar petite brunette. He rolled his eyes. Perfect.

Elsbeth turned and looked wide-eyed at the customer who'd stepped up in line behind her. "Um, hey there, Mr. McGuire," she said, her face instantly turning a bright shade of pink.

"Elsbeth," Ian said coolly. He silently prayed she didn't notice the particular items he was about to purchase. But his prayer, as it turned out, had fallen on deaf ears. Her gaze immediately scanned over the two boxes of condoms and lube.

"What's all this?" she said. She gestured to the items in his hands.

"Date night," Ian said causally.

Elsbeth let a smile crawl across her lips. "It's the nanny, right?" she whispered. "Good for you. I thought you two kinda liked each other that day you were in the shop. Don't worry. You keep my secret, and I'll keep yours." She gave him a conspiratorial wink.

It was Ian's turn to flush now. He opened his mouth and tried to stammer out an explanation but realized it was no use. He closed his mouth and shook his head. "It's not what you think—" he started. But Elsbeth turned away when the cashier called for the next customer in line.

She made her purchase and then bounced out with a convivial "Good luck" before pressing through the door. Jesus, and now he was going to have to explain that to Brandon as well. That wouldn't be awkward at all.

The winter wind picked up, pushing a crumpled newspaper and the remnants of last fall's crisp brown leaves through the street. Popping open the door of the truck, Ian shoved the bag from the drugstore into the back seat and plopped onto the seat beside Wyatt. The line inside the drugstore had been longer than he anticipated, and Wyatt had already loaded his supplies.

"What's the matter?" he asked Ian, who had a scowl affixed to his face.

"Elsbeth," Ian muttered. "She was in the drugstore in line in front of me."

"And let me guess. She just happened to notice the king-sized box of condoms you had in your hand?" Wyatt snickered.

"It wasn't king-sized. And yes. She did," Ian shot back.

Wyatt erupted into a fit of laughter. "What did you tell her?"

"I said it was for date night," Ian said, crossing his arms over his chest. "I just didn't say who was going on the date. She assumed it was for Lottie and me. I let her go along with that."

"It's Lottie, now is it?" Wyatt teased, still laughing at Ian. "Maybe you should have gotten the king-sized box. You two could have split it."

"Can we just go get the damn tacos? I'm starving."

Wyatt continued his laughter while Ian brooded in the passenger seat until they pulled in front of the Mexican restaurant.

"Don't worry. We can stash everything at the fishing camp," Wyatt said, cackling again. "It's time he learned the Hampton family secret anyway."

"Fishing camp?" Ian quirked a brow as they walked to the front door. The delicious aroma of fried corn, roasted garlic, and cumin-spiced meat wafted through the breeze outside. Ian's stomach rumbled.

"Yeah, you know about the fishing camp, right?" Wyatt said. He held up two fingers to the hostess to indicate how many would be eating lunch. The two men were immediately ushered to a booth near the back of the tiny eatery. Ian shook his head.

"Ah, well, the first thing you should know is that the fishing camp has nothing to do with fishing. There's a nice lake on the south side of the ranch. The lake itself isn't part of the ranch, but we have water rights to fish there. You can walk there from my house in an hour or so."

Wyatt folded up his menu and looked across the table at Ian, who was already tearing into the chips and homemade salsa laid out on the table.

"Buenos días, señores," a plump waitress said under her breath. "What jew have?"

"Just a water to drink and four puffy specials with extra sauce for me," Wyatt said.

"The same. And a side of jalapeños, please," Ian echoed. "And he's paying." He pointed an accusing finger at Wyatt. At that, the waitress looked up. Ian watched her tired face spread into a smile.

"Jew paying today, Doctor Wyatt?" she smiled wide.

"Sure, Maria. Give me the tab." She nodded and left the table.

"So about this fishing camp," Ian said, returning them to their previous conversation.

"Yeah, so when Kip and Susan were first married, they didn't have a whole lot of money. Kip was only eighteen, and both of them not even out of high school yet."

"Wait, Kip and Susan were married before they graduated high school?"

"Yeah, Brandon was a prom night baby. I thought you knew. Didn't matter to Kip though. He acted like he'd won the lottery when Susan told him she was pregnant. That's all that man has ever wanted, a yard full of kids and to work the ranch." Wyatt scooped up a mouthful of salsa onto a thin crisp tortilla chip and slid it into his mouth.

"The first year of their marriage was pretty rough," he mumbled with a mouth full of salsa. "Susan's parents disowned her. Kip was trying to work full time, go to school, build a house, and be there for Susan. Then the baby came, and it's up all night, work all day. We didn't think they'd make it. That's when Kip built the shack."

"What shack?"

"It's just a one-room little house. At first, it was pretty rough, but over the years, we've all added our little touches to it to make it more . . ." Wyatt stuffed another chip overflowing with salsa into his mouth, "Comfortable."

"Comfortable for what?" Ian said. He stirred lemon into the glass of water Maria placed on the table.

"Sex," Wyatt said, matter-of-factly. "I mean, it's not like we can just slip into town for a date with our wives," he said. "We live an hour's drive away. And then there's the matter of finding babysitters for that long. So we have the shack."

"A sex shack?" Ian said. "Are you serious?"

"Absolutely. A husband says he's taking his wife fishing, and no one thinks twice about it. We sneak off and—" Wyatt winked. "Maybe just a quickie, maybe spend the night. Matthew and Ginny spent a whole weekend there once. Nine months later, Abigail was born." He shrugged. "Just sayin'."

"And everyone knows about this sex shack?"

"Fishing camp," Wyatt corrected. "And no. Just us guys and our wives. The kids and my mother are blissfully ignorant of its true purpose. And we intend to keep it that way." He wagged a fear of warning.

"And Brandon," Ian said. "You plan to let him in on this little Hampton man secret?"

"I suppose so."

"And you'll stash that stuff I bought there?"

Wyatt nodded and leaned back as Maria slid a large plate of fried tacos in front of him. "I'll show it to you. It's a pretty well-supplied location. There's wine, glasses, corkscrew, snacks, plenty of condoms, lube, candles, whatever you'd need to set the mood."

"And you took my innocent baby sister . . ." Ian swallowed. He looked sick at the thought, now unable to escape his mind. "Fishing?"

Wyatt started to laugh, then caught a glimpse of rage forming at the corners of Ian's eyes. "Whoa, man. After we were married. *After*. She is my wife, after all. What did you think?"

"She's my baby sister, Wyatt. I don't want to think," Ian said, waving his hand.

Wyatt laughed again. "We have three boys, man, the secret's out. I'm having sex with your sister."

Ian flicked a jalapeño pepper off of his plate and hit Wyatt in the eye with it. "Screw you, Wyatt Hampton," Ian said. Wyatt pulled seeds from his burning eye. His shoulders shook with laughter as tears from his burning eye ran down his face.

CHAPTER SEVEN

Lottie had already made her way back from Molly's long before Ian and Wyatt returned from town. It had been a wonderful day. Molly was feeling so much better. Her blood pressure had been normal all day, although the medications made her feel more tired than she would have liked. When she and the boys laid down for a nap, she'd sent Lottie home. Lottie called Wyatt, who assured her he and Ian were just a few minutes from the house, so she was free to go. To say she was grateful was an understatement.

Despite sleeping in that morning, she found herself bone-tired from chasing the boys outside for most of the day. It took only a few minutes before she fell asleep reading on her bed upstairs. She was awakened by the delicious aroma of beef fat cooking over an open fire. She tiptoed downstairs and saw Ian carrying a plate in from the back porch.

"I just put the steaks on. How do you like yours?" he asked, licking a drop of the marinade from his thumb. Lottie looked at him, watching more closely than she had in recent days. Molly was right. He did look happier. There was something in his eyes that had not been there the day she'd arrived. That awful day at the airport when she'd been so rude to him. Seeing what Molly had referred to as his "spark" and knowing it could be her that put it there made her smile.

"Medium well, please," she said. She wrapped an oversized cardigan tightly around her and slid onto a stool at the large island. "May I help?"

Ian shook his head. "No ma'am. Steaks are on, there's asparagus in the oven, and I bought the bread. Wine?"

Lottie noticed there were only two places set at the bar. "Is Midge out this evening?"

"Monthly pot luck and Bible study at church. You don't mind it being just us, do you?" Ian asked. He pulled a cork from a wine bottle with a satisfying pop. Lottie shook her head and proffered the wine glass sitting in front of her.

"Not at all," she smiled.

"Good. So tell me what you did today." Ian took a sip of his wine. He unrolled and re-rolled the sleeve of his flannel shirt. Lottie couldn't help but notice the way the muscles flexed and moved. The more she looked at him, the more she liked what she saw. She should stop looking, she scolded herself.

"Finger painting," she said, finally sipping her wine. It was a very good bottle. The grapes weren't too sweet, and there was a faint cinnamon and chocolate flavor that would pair well with the steaks. "Mmm. This is lovely," she said, swirling the glass. "You know tea and wine."

"Thanks. Finger painting, huh? I bet the boys loved that."

"They did. I found this long roll of white paper in a closet. Molly said it was used for some purpose when the house was being built but had no use now. We rolled it out along the length of the porch and painted the longest picture in the world."

"Is that right? The longest picture in the world. I can't wait to see it."

"Truly. It's on display at the Hampton Museum for a limited showing. You should get by to see it as soon as you can."

Ian couldn't hide his pleased expression. "I'll do that. You know, you're really good with them."

"They're good boys. A bit active, but I find boys just need more physical release than girls." Her face flushed at the double meaning of that statement. She hadn't meant it to sound so sexual. Although Freud would disagree if he knew the thoughts she'd been having of late.

Ian stepped closer to her, the smell of charcoal smoke lingering over his clothes.

"Is that so?" he said. He gently placed his hand on her back and rubbed in slow, small circles. Lottie's breath hitched. Her pulse quickened. Apparently, Ian graduated magna cum laude from the Sigmund Freud school of double entendre. "I'm going to check the steaks."

As the back door bounced shut behind him, Lottie let out the breath she'd been holding. Dear Lord, she liked him. She really, really liked him. Why couldn't he just have continued to be the overbearing, growling man she'd first met? Every time he touched her, looked at her, or spoke to her, her heart melted just a little bit more. She had made a plan. A plan to keep her family safe. She hadn't factored in falling in love with Ian McGuire. The problem was, he made it so easy. And she didn't want to fight her heart anymore.

———••●••———

Ian hadn't really needed to check the steaks. He'd just put them on. But this gorgeous woman was sitting right across from him in an empty house talking about how boys needed physical release, and he couldn't stand it. He needed the bracing cold winter air. Otherwise, he was going to seduce her right there on Midge's kitchen island. Images of exactly what sort of physical release he wanted were now swimming through his head. And they were beginning to tap on the zipper of his jeans.

He wasn't going to scare her off. He liked her. He really liked her. And Wyatt and Molly had given their blessing since she wasn't supposed to be an employee of theirs for much longer anyway. They'd both actually been pretty cool about the whole thing when he'd talked to them about it this afternoon. He suspected that Molly already knew how he felt. Her reaction had been too serene for him to think otherwise.

"Just about done," he said as the screen door popped closed behind him again. "So Wyatt told me this afternoon you won't be working for them much longer. Any idea where you'll be headed next?"

Lottie shook her head. "The agency will arrange for another position. But I'm going to request to stay in this part of your country if I can. It's so unlike where I am from. It's so interesting and new."

"How so?" Ian hoped she'd disclose more about herself. He was eager to uncover a bit of the mystery that seemed to cloud this woman.

"I lived near the sea," Lottie said. "There's salt in the air, a warm breeze that seems to never still, and the sound of the waves beating against the rocks."

"The sea, yeah, that's a long way from here for sure." Ian swirled the last swallow of his wine and refilled his glass. He added the last bit of the bottle's contents to Lottie's glass. "You must miss it."

"Aye, I do."

"I know. The ocean gets into your blood, doesn't it?"

"You were raised by the sea?"

"Virginia Beach. My father was a Navy SEAL. I grew up on the Atlantic Coast."

"So Molly has a love for the sea as well? And your parents? Are they still living?"

"Yep. I think they'll die in that little house they live in. My older sister, Shawna, lives there with her family too."

"I was unaware you had an older sister."

"She's about ten years older than me and twelve years older than Molly. We really didn't grow up together. She wanted to be a second mother to me more than a sibling.

And she pretty much disowned me when I joined the army."

"Really? Molly said you'd served with distinction. But your sister, Shawna, did you say, was not supportive of your career choice?"

"Sean McGuire wasn't a good father or a good husband. He wasn't home long enough to know how to be one. And he didn't want to be."

Lottie couldn't help but notice the way Ian's jaw clenched when he began speaking of his father.

"He never hit us or anything like that, but it was pretty obvious that we were tolerated and nothing more. Shawna blamed the navy for making him that way. When I joined up, she was afraid the same thing would happen to me. When I insisted I was going to enlist, she stopped talking to me."

"What a shame," Lottie said. "Truly."

"She doesn't keep in touch, so I'm not really sure what's going on in her life. Last I heard, she had a couple of kids and was married to a man who owned a carpet business in Fairfax, Virginia. We just don't talk." Ian's mood was shifting, and he didn't like it. "I bet those steaks are done. Hungry?"

"Starving," Lottie said. She plastered a wide smile across her face. "I hope you won't judge me too harshly for the indelicate way I am about to consume this entire meal."

Ian grabbed a clean dish from the countertop. "No more ten-dollar words, love. I've had too much wine to keep up." He gave the tip of her nose a tap with his finger and had the steaks off the grill and the table set in minutes.

He'd called her love. He knew he had. The use of the word wasn't an accident. She hadn't even cast him an unhappy expression. He would have bet his next month's salary that she was falling for him too. He'd planned this night out and hoped that by the end of it, she'd understand he was playing for keeps.

The two gorged themselves on Ian's meal in relative silence, the quietness punctuated only by occasional hums of pleasure as Lottie savored every morsel. When she took her first bite, she danced in her seat, shaking her shoulders. The movement sent a thrill through him that he instantly became addicted to. He'd wanted to see that look on her face again and again. For a very long time.

The steak was cooked to perfection, bearing a salty tang accented by the smoke of the charcoal fire. The asparagus was roasted with garlic and herbs that made the steak taste even better as the notes and flavors combined in their mouth between bites. Thick pats of butter slathered over the pillow-soft bread was the perfect way to soak up the strong flavors.

Lottie pushed back her plate with a satisfied sigh. Ian knew exactly how she felt. He was completely satisfied. Well, his stomach was, at least. Other parts of him were thinking of the dessert course later in the evening despite his best efforts to push them aside.

"I believe that was the finest meal I have eaten since I came to this country," Lottie said. She dabbed the corners of her mouth delicately with her napkin.

Ian had gone the extra mile to make this dinner great. He'd even begged Midge to use her good linen napkins and her best dishes. It paid off. Lottie seemed impressed and nearly joyful.

"My compliments to you, sir." Lottie raised her glass.

"It was entirely my pleasure. I'm happy you liked it."

"I more than liked it, Ian. It was wonderful. And I'm overwhelmed at your kindness. It was really just perfect." Her voice had been soft and her eyes sultry. When he went to reach for her, she stiffened. Her tone became brighter and more animated. "And now I must earn it. Let me clean up," Lottie rose and picked up two plates, but Ian stood quickly and put his hand over her wrist to stop her.

"Let's let these sit a while. I thought we could tackle a nice bottle of port I got on the front porch." Ian let his fingers slip around her wrist. His thumb instinctively made lazy circles against the place where he could feel her pulse quicken.

"I never could resist a good port."

They ventured out to the front porch where Ian had thick blankets folded on the wooden porch swing.

"The port is a Spanish twelve grape. I've never had one of these before, but the sommelier at the store talked me into it," Ian said. He pushed his way through the front door, carrying two tiny wine glasses, perfect for the port.

"Me either," she admitted. Ian handed her a glass before taking a seat beside her closest to the house. He spread a blanket over their legs. The air was quite cold, although the wind had died down considerably.

"It's very good," Lottie said, taking the tiniest sip of her wine. Ian's long legs pushed the swing into motion.

"Well, I'll be sure to let the sommelier know the next time I'm in the shop."

A small red bird flitted down and landed on a bird feeder near the fence at the edge of the yard. The wooden split rail acted as a border between what Midge was keeping as her yard and the hay meadow beyond.

"Look at that bird, Ian. Can you see her? She's beautiful. I don't think I've ever seen a red bird like that before."

Ian glanced around. "That is a him, actually. A cardinal."

"Oh, you can sex a bird at fifty paces, can you?" Lottie joked.

"I give you points for knowing that's about fifty paces, well done. But sexing is easy with those. They're cardinals. Male cardinals are that bright red. The females are more of a gray with a light red belly. But the bright orange beaks and black masks around their eyes are the same. If we're still, we should see her in a bit. They're always together."

Lottie sat motionless for several long seconds until another small bird settled on the fence beside the feeder.

"Oh, there she is," Lottie whispered. Ian leaned in very close. He could smell her shampoo and feel the heat of her skin on his. Lottie watched the bird with childlike wonder. It was as if Ian were seeing these creatures for the first time with her. It filled his heart. It was every bit as exciting as watching one of his nephews discover something new.

"Is that his mate then?" She asked, her voice still low so she didn't scare them away.

"Probably." He whispered softly next to her neck. "It's the season for them to be choosing now." He could practically feel the gooseflesh rising on her neck as his breath brushed against her skin.

"Will they mate for life?"

"Yes, and you rarely see them apart. They'll fly together, feed together, build their nest together. Raise their brood together. They live in that tree there," Ian said, pointing to a large oak tree several yards in the distance.

"Are they here only for the winter season? Will they be gone soon?" Lottie whispered.

Ian couldn't wipe the smile from his face. The joy that was overwhelming his heart was difficult to contain. And he was growing weary at trying to suppress it anymore. "No. Most people think they migrate, but they don't. That's why they stay here, I think. We're a good food source for them during the winter. Wyatt said Lizzy put that feeder out years ago, and they've always had cardinals in the yard."

Lottie watched as the bright red bird flitted to the fence and perched next to his lady. Their heads twitched, and then his head cocked to one side and their beaks touched. "Look, they're kissing." Lottie clapped her hand over her mouth. Her words were much louder than their previous whispers.

"Nah. He's feeding her," Ian said. "Feeding a woman and keeping her happy is how she'll decide if she'll stay with him as his mate or choose another bird."

"Well, don't settle too quickly then, lady bird," Lottie said to the bird playfully. "Otherwise, you'll find yourself falling for the first good steak dinner you get."

Ian beamed softly at her comment and took a sip of the port. It really was good. Fruity, but not too sweet. The wine store expert had made him look like a rock star tonight. He was more thankful than ever that he'd taken Wyatt's advice and gone there to get the wine.

The birds lifted into the twilight headed back to their tree.

"Oh, she didn't heed me," Lottie said. "There they go, off to bed together. And after only one meal too."

"Don't judge her too harshly. I had you in my bed after one shot of good whiskey," Ian teased. Lottie gave him a playful punch to the arm.

"Seriously, they remind me of my parents, though," Lottie mused. "Always together like that. Anyone could look at my parents and tell how deeply in love they were. Anytime they walked together, my father would take her hand. They were always stealing little kisses and looks from one another."

Ian set the swing into motion again since the threat of scaring the birds away was gone. "That sounds nice."

"It was. I remember staying up late one Christmas Eve to catch Father Christmas filling our stockings. I heard him in our drawing room, but when I went downstairs, he'd already come," Lottie said, giving Ian a knowing wink. "My parents were standing together in front of the tree. It was all lit up, and the rest of the room was lit only by the dying embers of the fireplace. My father lifted his hand and touched my mother's ear, then her jaw, and finally her neck. Then he kissed her. And that's when I saw him touch her breast. I expected Mother to brush his hand away, but she didn't. She let her head fall back and let out a long sigh. Then father went to kiss her again, properly this time. And I snuck upstairs. I was barely ten. I didn't know what happened between men and women. But I knew whatever it was they were doing, it was love that prompted them."

"Are they still that way?" Ian asked innocently.

"Not anymore," Lottie's voice became quieter. "Mother passed away a year ago from ovarian cancer. We were all selfish and wanted her with us. But in the end, it was a blessing for her body to have been released from its suffering."

Lottie felt Ian's hand cover hers, their fingers lacing together. He gave her hand a gentle squeeze. "I'm sorry, Lottie."

"Thank you. Maisie continues her work, so there's this little piece of her that lives on, I suppose."

"Who is Maisie, your sister?"

"Yes," Lottie said, smiling.

"And what work was it your mother did?"

"She was a botanist. Oh, no university ever officially claimed her to be one, but she was. When she and father married, he gave her a rose bush. He told her that he wanted to give her roses every day, and this way, she could have them. But this horrible storm nearly ruined the small plant just days after we'd put it in the ground. Mother nursed it and actually spliced what she thought was a similar plant into its stem. Without even knowing it, she'd hybridized a new species of rose. She was hooked. She created three distinct species successfully and then began her work on vegetable plants. That's what my sister works mostly on now. Her current project is some sort of tomato venture."

"That explains the ten-dollar words," Ian said, teasing. "You're happy when you talk about your mom. I can see it on your face. Is her marriage the kind you're looking for yourself?"

Lottie cut her eyes slightly at Ian. "I'm not looking for anything. I'm not even twenty-five yet."

"When's your birthday?"

"May. More than three months away."

"Wanna bet you're engaged before it gets here?"

Lottie laughed. "That's impossible. And what about you? You're what, thirty-eight?"

"Thirty-five!" Ian said, abashed. He was a bit taken aback that he looked so much older. Well, he had lived a lot of life in the last ten years. He supposed he should be thankful he only looked a handful of years older. He often felt ancient.

"How is it you're not married then? Don't desire to be leg-shackled for all eternity?"

"Quite the opposite. I'm looking for the right woman."

"My grandmother once told me you should never marry a person you can live with. You should wait for the one person you can't live without."

"That's good advice," Ian said. "And how will I know when I find this person?"

"I'm afraid there were no sage words of advice there. You'll just have to keep looking."

"I doubt I have to look very far," Ian said. Fire burned through him. He had no doubt the heat of it burned through his eyes and into hers. Their eyes met, and he held her gaze for several heartbeats.

"Is that so?" Lottie gulped. "How far and wide has your search been extended exactly?" He slid his fingers up toward her face, touching her cheek, then sliding down to her neck, and leaned forward.

"Ian, I—earnestly request you reconsider this—"

"Hush your ten-dollar words, love. I'm going to kiss you now."

Ian felt the heat of her breath against his lips. Then gently, slowly, he pressed his lips to hers. The moment their bodies touched, Ian felt a sting of electric shock through him. It echoed off of his heart and circled back around and around again like a star in orbit. He felt the hot touch of her tongue on the seam of his mouth, inviting him to open it to her. She tasted of wine and salt and Lottie. Her lips were soft and molded to his as they pressed their mouths together over and over.

Ian felt her hands clasp the back of his head and bring him closer. Her kisses burned him with a heat and hunger he could taste. His skin was fevered as he brought his hand to touch her cheek. He opened his mouth wider, determined to consume her with his desire.

A flash of light slid across his face. It felt as if it doused the fire with a flood of cold water. Ian broke the kiss and slid back away from her slowly on the swing. Lottie was breathless, her lips pink and swollen from his kisses. But she instantly regained her composure as she realized the reason Ian had pushed back so abruptly.

Her eyes cut over to see Midge's truck turn into the gravel parking area in front of the house. Lottie tried to push up from the swing, but Ian clutched her hand under the blanket and laced their fingers together before she could get up.

"Don't go," he whispered. "Please. I want you to stay."

Lottie settled back down next to him.

"Well, hello, you two. Nice night for a swing," Midge said. "I have leftover lemon pound cake if you haven't had dessert yet."

"I couldn't eat another bite. Ian fed me well tonight. Thank you," Lottie said. Ian just waved her off, then patted his stomach in mute agreement.

"Well, I'll just leave this inside on the counter. You two enjoy the swing," she sang out. She flapped through the bouncing screen door and into the house.

Lottie felt heat rush to her cheeks. Had Midge seen them kissing? Would she lose her position earlier than she'd planned if Midge told Molly what she and her brother were doing out there?

"I think I should go," Lottie said, looking down at her feet.

"I'd like it if you'd stay," Ian said softly, giving her hand another gentle squeeze. "And I'd like it if you looked at me."

"I look at you," Lottie said, lifting her head but not meeting his gaze. Ian crooked a finger and tapped her chin to force her to meet his eyes.

"Look at me, baby." Her eyes met his. "That's better. Don't worry. She didn't see us."

"No?" Lottie looked skeptical. "I'm not sure how she could have missed it. And she knows I had a bad night last night and covered for me at Molly's this morning because you asked her. What did you say to her? She has to wonder how it was you had that knowledge of how I passed my night? There's no telling what she thinks about what happened."

"You're embarrassed," Ian said. Why on earth should she feel embarrassed? That seemed an odd reaction to him.

"Lottie, you have nothing to be embarrassed about. I've seen fully armed, seasoned soldiers get spooked over shadows and cower in holes. Last night, you honestly heard someone in the middle of the night, and it scared you. There's no shame in that."

"No, but it was the bit where I woke up in your bed," Lottie said meekly.

"What, you've never woken up in a man's bed before?" Ian smirked. He pushed the swing into motion again. Lottie curled her legs up into the quilt.

"Never," she admitted.

Ian abruptly stopped the swing. "Seriously? Because you kiss like you've done that before."

Lottie shook her head. "That's not to say I am an innocent," she added defensively. "But I never spent the night with him."

"Him? There was only one?"

"I am not an innocent, Ian. But I am also no slapper either."

"Slapper?" Ian laughed. "What is that?"

"You would call it, um . . ." Lottie tried to think of the American word. "Slut? A loose woman."

"I like slapper better," Ian chuckled.

The two sipped and drifted back and forth on the swing for several long minutes in silence. Whether it was his persistence or the wine, Lottie finally let her head fall on his shoulder. He loved the feeling of her body close to his.

"Did you love him?"

"Roger? No. But I wanted to. In the end, he was just a boy who wanted a tumble with a girl. And I turned out to be a girl who wanted a boy to make her feel beautiful."

Ian stopped the swing and looked at Lottie. "You are beautiful," he stated flatly. Lottie gave him an appreciative smile and took another small sip of her port.

Ian kicked off and started them swinging again. "So did you break it off with him then?" he asked innocently.

"No. He left for a better job. I never heard from him again," Lottie said, thinking back to Roger's boyish good looks, flaxen hair, and thin, tight smile.

"He worked for you?" Ian asked. He was more interested in learning about Lottie's life before she came to work for Wyatt and Molly and less about this Roger.

"My father," Lottie said. "What about you? Who was it that captured you first?"

"My high school sweetheart," Ian said honestly. "Her name was Miranda."

"Did you love her?"

"I wouldn't have slept with her if I didn't. I even proposed to her."

At this, Lottie sat up and looked into Ian's face to see the truth of his words.

"You have been married!"

Ian grimaced. "No. She decided that my enlistment in the army was a bigger commitment than she was prepared to make."

"I'm sorry," Lottie said, and Ian could tell she'd meant it.

"She got married to one of my friends in high school. They bought a little house, had a couple of kids. She's happy. And I'm happy for her."

"And that started your foray into the romantic business of breaking hearts on five continents?" Lottie laughed at her little joke.

"Six," Ian corrected and lifted his glass to toast her. Lottie clinked her nearly empty glass against his.

"Cheers," she said. Lottie leaned back against the arm of the swing and stretched her legs out so that her toes were just touching Ian's thigh. Ian felt the tickle of her socked feet against his leg and thought about the calves and thighs hidden under the quilt. He dreamed of the black leggings and what she would look like as he slowly peeled them off of her.

"Ian," Lottie started shyly. "Thank you for what you did last night."

"You're welcome," Ian said and drained the last of his port. Lottie offered him her glass, but Ian shook his head. "I'm here if you need anything, Lottie."

She took a deep breath.

In her eyes, Ian could see a reflection of himself, but he saw something else too. The real Charlotte Poole lurked somewhere behind those chocolate-colored eyes. She was more herself tonight—shared more of herself—than she ever had. But she was holding something back. Ian wondered if it had to do with the man she met in town or the unexplained fear of someone who had plagued her the night before.

"I should go. Robert and James will be expecting me early tomorrow." Lottie's expression looked sad. Or perhaps, as she said, she really was tired. She stood to leave, but Ian grabbed her hand and held her still. He stood, keeping his eyes fixed on hers.

In one swift movement, Ian gathered her body into his arms. Without a word, he reached up and cupped her face in his hands and tipped her face to his. Then, he pressed his lips to hers in a single, long soft kiss. He had meant it to be a kiss of hope and promise. One she could carry with her to the place deep inside where she kept all her secrets.

Ian let just the tip of his tongue brush against her teeth and then her tongue, tasting the sweet heat of the port on her mouth. His grip on her chin tensed as he let himself delve deeper, exploring her and allowing her to taste and explore his mouth fully. Before finally breaking the kiss, Ian kissed her bottom lip again, sucking it into his mouth softly and then releasing it with a tiny nip that forced a shiver over her body he could feel beneath his fingertips.

"Lottie," he said finally, her face still gently cupped in his warm hands. "I'm here."

With those words, Ian released his hold on her, collected their glasses from the swing, and moved to the front door. He held the screen door open for her and waited while she walked in and floated up the stairs before letting it snap shut behind him.

Ian laid in bed later that night with the taste of Lottie on his lips. He rolled to his side and stared at the door to his bedroom. He imagined it opening, Lottie coming to him, wanting him as much as he wanted her.

He wanted to be inside her, to love her, and to know her. To solve every mystery of her. It was a desire almost too palpable for words. There were so many unanswered questions about this woman. So many things she wouldn't say. Things he now suddenly felt he must know.

He couldn't explain why he needed to know her secrets and why he couldn't stop wanting to touch her every time he was near her.

He rolled onto his back. Maybe he did know. Lottie was the source of the peace and light that permeated every part of him. She was the great beacon that filled him and satisfied him from inside his heart. He felt it every time she was near. It was her light that dispelled the darkness that had filled him for so long. It was her light that brought him peace. At that moment, Ian knew. He had at long last found what he had been looking for. He'd found the one woman he couldn't live without.

CHAPTER EIGHT

Lottie flapped a large fleece blanket over the long prairie grass that grew along the far side of the pond at Molly and Wyatt's home.

"I can't understand this weather," she said, scrunching her nose and looking up toward the warm winter sun. "One day, it's so cold and windy you think surely the world will freeze solid, and the next, it feels like spring is around the corner."

"Welcome to Oklahoma weather," Molly said with a slight chuckle. "If you don't like it, just wait five minutes. It will change."

Lottie laughed. "I believe that. Still, I'm thankful, for the boys' sake, it's nicer today. They need to run outdoors some."

"Yes," Molly agreed emphatically. Logan was wrapped in a long coil of black fabric that wound around Molly's torso, snuggled in a ball against her breast. It seemed the only place he was content these days. And it freed Molly's hands to be able to help Robert and James more. Lottie looked at the young mother and her children, a pang of jealousy pushing through her heart and then sadness. It wouldn't be long before Molly would no longer need her help at the Leaning H Ranch. And she would have to reinvent herself again in another town. With another family. That had always been the plan. Short-term assignments. Small towns in the U.S. and keep moving. But somehow, after meeting the Hamptons, that plan seemed like it would be harder to stick to.

"Robert, James, please don't go too near that water. I don't want you wet," Molly scolded. The boys each took a half step back from the edge of the pond and then a full step forward again. Lottie shook her head. The sound of footsteps behind her made her turn with a jerk. No matter how safe she wanted to feel on the ranch, she always felt jumpy.

"Brandon," Lottie said, shading her eyes to the sun to look up at the tall young man striding toward her. He was carrying some sort of a red plastic toolbox that looked to Lottie as if it weighed as much as he did.

"Hey there, Miss Charlotte, Aunt Molly," Brandon said, cordially offering the ladies, now seated on the fleece, a wide smile of greeting. "Uncle Wyatt said he needed my help with a project today. Know where he is?"

Molly smiled. "He and Ian are trying to construct some sort of fence to keep the deer out of my garden. They're around the side of the house. Just follow the sounds of saws and swearing," she said, snapping her fingers in the direction of Robert and James, who were now, once again, precariously close to the edge of the pond.

Brandon laughed. "OK, thanks." He turned his attention to the boys. "Hey, Bobby!"

Robert glared at him with an unhappy scowl. "Don't call me Bobby," he said to Brandon. "I'm Robert. Like my Grandpa Robert who died."

Brandon grinned. "OK, Robert," he said slowly. "I bet James could beat you to that tree and back," he said, issuing a challenge.

Robert glanced back over his shoulder at a small cluster of trees that stood several dozen yards away from where Molly and Lottie sat.

"I could too, Ban-den," James assured him.

"I know it," Brandon said, teasing.

"He could not!" Robert replied. He was insulted at the notion his three-year-old brother, who was still practically a baby, could ever beat him in a foot race.

"Well, I'll count to three and you run. Best seven out of ten wins."

The boys agreed instantly. Brandon called out, "One, two," then gave a long pause for dramatic effect, to which James lurched forward and started running. "Three!" He laughed as the boys ran up the small rise to the cluster of trees.

"Thanks for that," Molly said.

"Nan always used to do that to Wyatt and me whenever we needed to be distracted from trouble." He said as he strode away.

———··•··———

Molly had been right. It was easy to follow the sounds of wood-cutting and curses that led him to the south side of the house where Molly kept her garden. It wasn't as large as the one his mother kept, but it grew the best strawberries he'd ever eaten. Brandon set his toolbox down and called to Ian and Wyatt, who were arguing about a measurement.

"Somebody called for a professional?" Brandon laughed and started walking toward the two men.

Wyatt looked up and gave him a wave. "Yeah, when's he going to get here? I'm surrounded by amateurs."

Wyatt and Ian walked toward Brandon and stopped to bend down, lift the lid from a cooler, and draw two bottles of water from it.

"You doing a low fence with chicken wire on top?" Brandon asked, surveying their work. "Dad and I built one for Mom like this a few summers back."

"Yep. After we take a break. We've been at this for hours."

"You've got a lot done. What do you need my help with?"

"Some of the longer pieces of lumber. Just need an extra set of hands. You got some time?"

Brandon nodded. "I'm going into town later, but I'm free till six or so."

"Hot date?" Wyatt teased.

Brandon's cheeks tinted a slight shade of pink as he glanced toward Ian, who looked away and took a long draw of his water.

"I'm taking Beth to the movies," he said.

"Better than the barn," Wyatt interjected.

Brandon cast Ian a hateful stare. Ian only shrugged.

"Listen, Bran," Wyatt started. "There are places on the ranch you can take a girl for a little privacy."

At this tidbit, Brandon's ears perked up. "Oh yeah?"

"Yes. But before we tell you where that is, we want to talk to you about a few things first."

Brandon squirmed, uncomfortable with this vein of conversation.

"How long have you and Elsbeth been seeing each other?" Ian asked.

"About a year," Brandon answered.

"Do you love her?" Wyatt asked directly. He put his bottle of water down and stared at Brandon. "Tell us honestly, even if the answer is that you're not sure." A long silence stretched out.

"I'm not sure." Brandon sighed. "I think so. But I don't know."

"Are you prepared to marry her in the next few months if she gets pregnant? And raise that child and take care of the two of them for the rest of your life?"

Brandon shrugged. "I suppose I would if that happened."

"You don't sound convinced," Ian said. "But you want to sleep with her?"

"I do," he said, a bit over-enthusiastically. "I think she's convinced if we do, then . . ." Brandon looked up at his uncle and shook his head. The two men sat in patient silence. After several long moments, Brandon spoke again. "If we're sleeping together, then I won't leave."

"Leave?" Wyatt asked, genuinely shocked. "Where might you be going?

"I got a job in Alaska," Brandon said a bit more confidently now.

"Alaska?" Wyatt repeated. "And your momma hasn't been over here in a fifty-foot hover over you moving to the other side of the known world?"

"I haven't told them yet," he said a bit shamefully.

"Why not?" Ian asked.

"Dad relies on me. I was needed around here, until you came, Ian. Now that you're here and have a good handle on how things run, I can finally get my chance to get out of Oklahoma and off this ranch. Don't get me wrong." Brandon kicked a clod of dirt and watched the dust splash out from his boot. "I love it here. I do. This is my home. But I want to see more than the ass end of a cow before I decide if this is where I want to make my life."

"What's the job?" Wyatt asked.

"Working for Donovan Petroleum. Some kind of assistant for one of the engineers up there scouting wells or something."

"Hunting and fishing are great up there," Ian put in. "I think you should do it."

Wyatt shot him a glare. "Me too. It'll be hard not having you around. Your poor mother will cry her eyes out." Wyatt sighed. "But . . . you're right. You need to decide if this life is right for you."

"Tell the girl," Ian put in. "You're not staying, no matter what. If she still wants to sleep with you, that's between you two. But wrap your dick. No matter what assurances she gives you about birth control."

Brandon gave them a grin. He'd always been treated like a kid on the ranch. Usually by everyone except his Uncle Wyatt. But since he'd married Molly, and they started having kids, he was just a kid again, even to his favorite uncle. He didn't mind being able to talk about this with Ian and Wyatt. They were talking to him like an equal. Even if it was just to give him advice.

"A girl's first time usually isn't the most pleasurable experience, so go slow and make sure she enjoys it up to the part where she won't," Wyatt added.

"And your first time won't last long, so don't get any wild ideas that you'll be making love to her all night long. She'll be too sore to do it twice anyway, so just enjoy your five minutes while you can." Ian smirked.

"Five minutes? You're not serious," Brandon retorted.

Wyatt opened the cooler again, and this time took out three bottles of beer and handed one to Brandon.

"If that," Wyatt said. "I'd research other ways you could enjoy her before the big finish."

Brandon took a long draft of his beer and drawled. "I'm not half bad at the optional events," he bragged.

Ian and Wyatt laughed at that, and they raised their bottles and toasted. "Here's to the newest member of the Hampton men's fishing camp," Wyatt said with a wink.

"The fishing camp?" Brandon looked astonished. "You mean, all these years when you took girls fishing, you were up there . . ." Brandon broke off and shook his head. He should have guessed.

"There's not even a rod and reel at that place," Ian said. "I dropped off some supplies up there for you just in case."

"Supplies?" Brandon looked confused.

"Some more of those flameless candles, some lube, and a box of condoms. I hope you don't mind. I got the extra smalls. I figured they'd fit about right," Ian teased.

Brandon lifted his middle finger and gave Ian a scowl. "Screw you, man."

And it was at the exact moment they erupted into laughter that they heard Molly begin to scream. Her shrieking didn't stop, and she howled Wyatt's name over and over. Wyatt, Ian, and Brandon sprinted around the side of the house and looked toward the spot in the tall grass where she and Lottie had taken the boys to play. Molly was ankle-deep in the pond with a soaking wet James on her hip. Robert, also soaked up to his shirt, was crouched beside her, crying. A tiny black bundle was lying on the fleece blanket. But there was no Lottie. Ian scanned the grass where Molly was pointing and saw it. It was nearly invisible, just the tiniest hint of two black eyes and two erect triangles of fur listening from the top of the tall grass, crouched and ready to pounce.

"Damn. Look! Bobcat!" he yelled. He pointed to a tiny movement in the tall grass, not ten feet away from where Logan lay sleeping.

"Don't move, Molly," Wyatt screamed. He was halfway to the back door to get his rifle, only to find Lottie standing in the doorway with his 270 shouldered. Ian grabbed Wyatt by the arm. "If you spook her, she could miss and hit the baby," Ian said.

"Lottie," Ian said calmly. Lottie never took her gaze from her target. "Give the weapon to me, love," Ian said sweetly. He extended his hand slowly. "If you miss, you could hit the baby."

"I never miss," Lottie said, letting out a long deep breath and slowly squeezed the trigger. Ian's eyes instantly flashed in the direction of her shot to see the bobcat pouncing from the grass toward Logan and then being jerked away in mid-air by an invisible force. In a split second, it was unmoving and lay limp on the grass. Lottie rested the weapon beside the door and began to run toward Molly and the boys.

Wyatt picked up the rifle, and the three of them followed on her heels. Molly was already scooping Logan up and carrying him and James toward the house with Robert fast on her heels. Brandon grabbed Robert and carried him into the house with Molly. Ian, Wyatt, and Lottie continued running until they reached the place where the animal had fallen.

Lottie quickly examined the dead animal lying prone in a patch of damp crimson-stained grass. She leaned over and spat on him, snatched up the fleece blanket, then turned on her heel and strode purposefully back to the house.

"Jesus," Wyatt said, examining the size of the beast. "That thing would have killed Logan."

"How the hell did she make that shot?" Ian questioned aloud. "It was damn near four hundred yards."

"We'll need to cart this off," Wyatt said finally. "I don't want coyotes scavenging this close to the house."

Second to None

Brandon appeared breathless beside the two men and stood over the animal. "Your love is a hell of a shot," he said, giving Ian a hard whack on his back.

Ian's brow knit tighter. "My love?"

Brandon grinned. "That's what you called her. You said, 'Lottie, my love, give me the weapon.'" Brandon repeated Ian's quiet whisperings to Lottie, mimicking the high-pitched tone of a girl. "Everyone heard you."

"I was just trying not to spook her, that's all. Where'd she even shoot it? I don't see any blood on the animal, just the grass." Wyatt picked up the animal's head by the ear and saw where the round had gone through.

"Damn," Brandon said. "She shot it through the eye."

An hour later, the three men had done all they could to dispose of the animal. Wyatt found Molly rocking Logan upstairs in the nursery, sobbing. Brandon cleaned up the work that had been done in the garden and headed for home. He was finally ready to talk to Beth, and he needed a shower first. Ian wandered upstairs, where Lottie had Robert and James in the bathtub.

"Diddle, diddle, dumpling, my son John. Went to bed with his trousers on; one shoe off, and the other shoe on. Diddle, diddle, dumpling, my son John." Lottie's sweet soprano voice sang out from where she knelt beside the tub.

With each "diddle, diddle, dumpling," she would splash her fingers in the water and extract a furious round of giggles from both boys who would splash each other. Ian crossed his arms over his chest and leaned against the door jamb. It was a beautiful sight to see Lottie loving and caring for children. He couldn't stop himself from imagining what their boys or girls might look like. While he stood and daydreamed about her, the warm, peaceful feelings enrobed his heart once again. Despite the excitement of the afternoon, he'd felt his shoulders relax. Lottie was both scared rabbit and fierce tiger wrapped in a puzzle he couldn't get his head around. But he was pretty sure it was the unusual combination of these things about her that made her so attractive.

"Uncle Ian!" Robert exclaimed. "Did you see us nearly get eaten by the bobcat? And James fell in the pond."

"I didn't fall. I's pushed," James said, splashing water and sending a soapy wave into his brother's face. "By you!"

"You're soaking Lottie," Ian said, stepping into the bathroom. "Aren't you boys clean yet?"

"Yes, sufficiently," Lottie said, glancing over at Ian. He was unfolding a clean towel. "I mean to say, all clean."

Ian gave her a grin. "OK, boys," Lottie said. "Since you boys were so good, Miss Lottie has chocolate ices for you downstairs after you get your clothes on."

"You dess me," James said as Ian fiercely rubbed his hair with a towel.

"No, sir," Lottie said, rubbing Robert with the towel now. "You dress yourself. You're a big brother now, remember?"

"C'mon, I'll help," Robert offered. Lottie tied their towels around their necks like a cape and sent them running off to their room. She turned and set to mopping the puddles from the bathroom floor and draining the tub. Ian resumed his post, leaning against the door with his arms crossed over his chest.

"Ices?" he asked innocently.

"Yes. I've learned that I'm not above bribery. The boys behave, they get ices."

"I gathered that," he said. "But what are ices?"

"You know, those flavored sugared frozen treats on a stick. Surely you've had an ice before?" Lottie pushed a strand of wet hair off of her cheek.

"You mean a popsicle?" Ian grinned. "Yeah, I've had one before."

"Popsicle, yes. I forget that's what you call them here."

"Lottie," Ian said, standing straighter. His body nearly filled the door. He stopped her from passing through carrying an armful of wet towels. "What you did for my family today, I—"

Lottie held up a hand. "I am not as resilient as I may appear, Ian. Please let's not discuss this until later. Molly gets to be the only hysterical woman today. After all, they are her children, not mine."

She pushed past Ian and bounced down the stairs to find Robert and James dressed and eating chocolate popsicles at the bar. Wyatt scooped up the towels from Lottie.

"Lottie, I can never thank you enough for today," he started. But Lottie held up a hand.

"Please, let's not talk about it now," she said, gesturing toward the boys. "I'll start dinner now if you'd like."

"No, I'll take care of it tonight. You go on home and enjoy the rest of the day. And tomorrow. I'm going to take Molly and the boys to the cowboy museum. I think a day away from the house would do her good."

"As you wish. Enjoy the museum. And let me know if there is anything I can do for you or your family."

"I'll drive you back," Ian volunteered. "Just let me go say goodbye to Molly."

"She's taking a nap with Logan," Wyatt volunteered. "I finally got her to stop crying. I'll let her know you sent your love."

Ian held the door for Lottie and opened the passenger side of the truck to help her in. "Hell of a day," he said finally as they approached Midge's farmhouse. "Want to keep driving and head into town? We could grab a bite and a drink."

"Would you mind terribly? I'm dying for a good cup of tea right now."

Ian could hear the tremor in Lottie's voice and drove straight past Midge's and onto the main road that would take them into the small town nearly an hour away.

"Lottie, I've got to know," Ian started when they'd driven nearly halfway to town in complete silence. "Where the hell did you learn to shoot like that?"

Lottie grinned. "My father. He has a passion for shooting clays. I'll confess that Wyatt's rifle is a far cry from the over/under shotgun I'm used to, but the concept is still the same. Lead the target, all of that."

"That was a hell of a shot. You could have missed," Ian started, but Lottie cut him off.

"I told you, I don't miss," Lottie said, gazing out of the window.

"How was it you even had the rifle to start with?"

"James fell into the pond and was freezing. I ran to fetch him a towel. When I left the house to head back to Molly, I saw the cat crouched in the grass. I called to Molly, who started screaming. I knew where Wyatt put his rifle—it wasn't a secret. It was loaded, so I shot him."

Ian pulled the truck into a parking space across from the coffeehouse on Main Street and slid out from behind the wheel. Lottie took a deep breath, trying not to think about how close Logan had come to being attacked by that wild animal. She reached for the door handle, but Ian was already around to her side of the truck, opening the door and helping her out.

The two strode into the coffee shop. The rich smell of roasted coffee mingled with the sweet aroma of the syrups used to flavor the lattes and frozen drinks. Today, Lottie smelled a strong hazelnut perfume in the air.

"Two hot teas, please," Ian said, ordering. "One Earl Grey black, one Ceylon, strong with milk and lemon." He pulled some cash from his wallet and handed it to the young man behind the counter.

"You remembered how I take my tea?" Lottie said, a bit surprised.

"I hope I got it right. I couldn't remember about the honey."

"Yes, I like honey, but I like to add it myself. Thank you."

The two took their brown paper cups and selected a pair of overstuffed chairs by the window, facing the street. Ian couldn't help but notice Lottie's hands shaking.

"What you did for my family today, Lottie, was—" Ian broke off, unsure of how to say what it meant to him. "I can never thank you enough. Are you OK?"

Lottie nodded. "The adrenaline will wear off in a while. I just have to stop thinking about what could have happened if—"

"Yes. Don't think about it," Ian said. "Why don't you tell me about that song you were singing to the boys in the bathtub? Where did you learn that?"

"Mother used to sing silly songs like that to my sister and me when we were scared or stressed. I'm surprised I remembered the words." Lottie snickered at herself and took a sip of her tea.

"You're good with kids. You'll make a great mother yourself one day." Ian tried his tea. It needed honey. He glanced up and saw a wash of sadness claim her face. "Did I say something wrong?"

Lottie sighed, and Ian saw deepening shadows of sorrow creep around her eyes. "I did say something wrong."

"No, you couldn't have known," Lottie said. Ian waited, silently spooning honey into his tea while he waited for Lottie to tell her story. He was beginning to doubt she would when she suddenly started speaking in a quiet voice.

"When I was fifteen, I was thrown from my horse and injured quite badly," she started. "I was told I nearly died. My injuries required surgery, and unfortunately, it also made me incapable of having my own children." Lottie sat back in her chair and let out a long breath. Ian's heart clenched in his chest. "It didn't bother me then. I never thought about wanting children when I was so young." Lottie forced a weak smile, but Ian could tell she was heartbroken that she'd never cuddle or sing her lullabies to her own babies. "But I suppose I should be thankful I can have dozens of children in my lifetime. My first three were boys." Lottie offered Ian a weak smile.

He was overwhelmed again with that obsessive need to comfort her in some way. He wanted to pull her onto his lap like he had the night he'd found Brandon and Elsbeth in the barn. Instinctively, he reached out and took her hand, stroking it with the pad of his thumb. "I'm so sorry, Lottie. I never meant to upset you."

Lottie gave her head a little shake. "It's all right. I make my peace with it day by day."

"You know the man that can't live without you won't care about that, don't you?"

Lottie softly extracted her hand from his, slid her finger around the lid of her paper cup, and gave a slight nod.

"It'll be dark soon," Ian said. She was thankful for the change in subject. "I know a really nice spot along the river where you can watch the sunset. Want to go?"

Lottie nodded, and the two set out on foot and rounded the corner. She recognized the bed and breakfast and tea room where she'd been a week ago but was careful not to mention it. Their walk took them along a cobbled path that ran along the river. As he'd promised, the sunset from that vantage point was breathtaking. The sky was so huge and empty and streaked with pinks and oranges in such vibrant hues that it stole Lottie's breath. Dark purples and navy blues crept around the edges where night enveloped the day, and one or two bright white twinkling stars were already making their way into the darkening sky.

Lottie looked up and watched the sky fade to an inky black. She felt Ian's arm snake around her waist and pull her closer. It wasn't a good idea to confide in him. It wasn't a good idea to feel so safe with him. She wasn't safe anywhere. But she couldn't stop her heart from falling. She laid her head on his shoulder and closed her eyes. She'd let herself feel all of this right now. She let herself feel his warmth, his comfort, his friendship, and the hope of something more. Even if it was just for a little while. Even if it was just for this one moment.

As the sun slipped from the sky, Ian felt the coolness of the air close around them. But Lottie's body was warm pressed against his. When she laid her head on his shoulder, he couldn't suppress his smile. He was slowly solving the mystery of her. And the more he learned, the more he grew to care for this woman, who was both fierce and fragile. He let out a breath and held her closer in his arms. Moving to stand behind her, he enveloped her in his embrace. He kissed the top of her head and let himself feel the peace he'd so long sought after. Even if it was just for this one moment.

CHAPTER NINE

Ian woke early. The sun was still held hostage by a shroud of early morning darkness. It seemed the night wanted to hold back a new day a little longer. His leg ached. His body stretched, and he felt the tightening and relaxing of muscles. He glanced toward the door of his bedroom. He sighed and closed his eyes. She was six feet away. And she might as well be on the other side of the moon.

He was already hard. Once again, his dreams had been haunted by visions of her. The golden cloak of her hair clothing their naked bodies while he made love to her over and over again. No matter how badly he wanted it, he could never find release in his dreams. He always woke just before it came, aching.

This morning had been no different. He reached a hand under the covers and tried to soothe himself—willing the flesh to soften and the visions of her to

Second to None

disappear. But his mind only taunted him all the more. He imagined it was her hand caressing him. Her body wet and sliding over him up and down. Up and down. Up and down.

He groaned silently. His eyes closed, and he just let the images come. Harder and faster. Her breasts, the smooth, creamy skin of her thighs, the gentle slope of her neck where he could bury his head and moan while he thrust deep into her, her long legs wrapped around his hips. He bit his lip. The skin under his fingers felt as if it would split. He moved his hand away. He didn't want this. He wanted her. He wanted her chocolate brown eyes half-closed and lusty, fluttering while she came on top of him. He took several slow breaths.

Wyatt had given her the day off. And he'd promised himself he was going to find a way to spend it with her. But Lord, he couldn't very well go tapping on her bedroom door with this flag pole poking out of his pants. Damn it. He let his hand slide down again, this time letting the visions and daydreams bring him into blissful spasms. He rolled to his side, muffling the quiet sounds of a pleasured moan into the pillow, and finally felt the satisfaction of a release. It would appease him—for now. But he knew. He still wanted her.

Midge had already made coffee. Ian automatically picked up the carafe downstairs in the kitchen and moved to pour the black elixir into his favorite mug. He stopped just before it spilled into the cup. He would rather have tea. He filled the kettle with water, plopped a tea bag into the mug, and searched for the honey. His body was betraying him, one organ at a time. It had started with his heart. Then his dick, and now his stomach.

The sun finally managed to shove the darkness of the night away. A new day launched quickly with beams of bright yellow light. Ian drank his tea on the front porch. While he contemplated the day ahead, the red cardinal and his mate returned to the feeder. Ian watched as they performed a courtship dance. He smiled and thought of Lottie.

"Tell me how you do it, man," Ian said to the bird. "I tried feeding her. What else?" The two birds flew away to their hiding place among the bare branches of the oak tree. He was no help, Ian thought. He went to the barn, tended to the horses, and then fed Midge's chickens. Morning chores done, he decided he didn't want to wait another minute to be with Lottie. If she wasn't up yet, he'd find a way to wake her.

Reaching the top of the stairs, Ian heard the sound of sheets rustling behind Lottie's door. He tapped and turned the knob, pushing it open a few inches. She was still in bed, her hair tousled and her eyes still a bit heavy with sleep. She was breathtaking.

"Are you up yet?" he whispered.

"Barely," Lottie said, sitting up. The thin black strap of her nightgown fell off of one shoulder and revealed the top of one breast. Ian's mouth instantly began to water. He couldn't stop thinking about wanting to kiss her again, and now, he wanted to taste her too. She pulled the cover over herself.

"I wanted to see if—" Ian began, only to be interrupted by the unfamiliar chime of a phone. Lottie's face went ashen at the sound. She scrambled from the bed, giving Ian a chance to see that her short, silky nightgown was the only thing she had on in bed. Damn, that little peek at her bare ass would torture his thoughts later. Lottie dug through a drawer and pulled out a small flip phone. She snapped it open and then turned to look at Ian.

"I'm sorry, I must take this." She moved toward the door and pushed it but didn't close it completely.

Out of the corner of his eye, he saw her hike up her black floral nightie and sit back down on the bed. This time, he was rewarded with a better glimpse of her bare behind. He could see only one side of her body and was pleased it was the side the strap had fallen down on, and the peachy nipple of one breast was just visible. She raked her hands through her hair as she listened to whatever it was the caller said.

Ian licked his lips. Wanting this woman was going to kill him. He shifted his hips, trying to adjust the part of his body that responded to her most. He should leave her in peace. She had a phone call after all, and it was clearly not something she wanted him to hear. Just as he was about to turn back to his room, he froze. A shocking realization settled over him. Lottie was talking on a flip phone. But he'd noticed she had a smartphone the other day. Was this a burner phone? Why on earth would Lottie have a burner phone? Ian could think of only one kind of person who would need one. And that person was usually his target on combat missions.

Ian pressed his ear to the small slit of an opening in the door and listened. He was ready to hear her speak words that would give an acceptable reason for the burner. He couldn't believe she would be involved in anything suspicious. He was a good judge of character. It had come as a result of years in the special forces when he'd had only seconds to ascertain whether an informant was telling the truth or trying to sell them a crop of lies.

He'd spent time with Lottie. She didn't seem the type. But his mind needed assurance all the same.

"I thought you were only to use this phone in case of emergency," Lottie said gruffly. "Is there an emergency?"

There was a pause while the other person spoke.

"Today? I . . . I'm not certain. I can ask to borrow a car. It's too risky to have Ian drive me again."

Another long pause.

"No. Not at the same place. The bookstore on Roosevelt. There's a section in the back where we can meet privately. Have your driver collect you at the rear entrance."

More silence.

"Fine, I'll be there in two hours."

Ian heard her snap the phone shut and murmur something that sounded like a curse. He sprinted across the hall to his room and flopped on the bed just as Lottie pushed his door open. She was still only wearing the short nightgown. Gown? It was more like a shirt. It barely covered her ass.

"Was there something you needed, Ian?" she asked innocently.

"I was going to ask if you wanted to waste your day off with me," he said. Seeing her in her tiny black satin nightgown, his body once again bloomed in betrayal. After what he'd just heard, his mind was opposed to her. His groin, apparently, was in favor. Heartily in favor. He was going to take to calling his dick Benedict Arnold.

"Oh, I'd like that. I have an appointment this morning. But after? I can meet you somewhere?"

"Just call me when you're back," Ian said. He hoped this conversation would be over soon. He was fairly sure if she didn't leave and close the door, Benedict Arnold was going to begin to recruit his hands and feet to drag her into his bed.

"Certainly. I'll ring you."

"You have my number in your phone, right?" Ian asked.

"Of course," Lottie answered. She waved a smartphone in front of him.

Ian's jaw clenched. Partly because he'd been right about the burner phone. And partly because lifting her arm nearly gave him a view of that sweet morsel that laid between her legs. This woman was killing him. And he needed to find out who she really was before his heart was lost to her for good.

Ian waited for Midge's SUV to crunch out of the driveway with Lottie behind the wheel before he turned the knob of her bedroom door and helped himself inside. She was a tidy creature, his Lottie. Not a thing out of place.

He'd just thought of her as his. He couldn't. His mind and heart were engaged in an all-out battle now. He tried to reason. There were too many unanswered puzzles where Lottie was concerned. His heart, however, didn't seem to care.

He hoped he could find some answers here. He started with the drawer she'd pulled the burner from. Dear God. It was her panty drawer. Silk and lace, and damn, Ian breathed out a tight stream of air. He pulled a pair of slate blue lace panties from the drawer. So much for a diminishing hard-on. One point for Benedict Arnold and the traitors.

The phone wasn't there. He checked the rest of the drawers and the closet and finally found the phone in the bottom of her wastebasket by the small desk. It had been broken, and the SIM chip and battery were removed. One point for Team Brain and reasoning.

Inside the desk, he found her passport and photographed each page with the camera on his phone. In the bottom drawer, he found a collection of letters addressed only to an "M." No full name and no address.

Each was sealed. Why had she not sent them? And who was "M"?

Ian pocketed one letter and continued his search, which revealed nothing. That in and of itself was suspicious. Where were photos of her family and friends? There was no favorite sweatshirt from the college she'd attended. No memento or keepsake that reminded her of home. Nothing. Just her clothes and the letters. Another point for Team Brain.

Ian strode across the hall to his room and closed the door. He carefully opened the sealed white envelope, noticing the quality of the linen stationery.

M—

America is nothing like what we imagined. The men here are enormous, but they have a kind demeanor that makes me feel welcomed. I am afraid I made rather a poor start with the man they call I—. He's quite a specimen of a man, I must say, and just looking at him makes me sometimes forget what I wish to say. His dark blue eyes seem to peer into my very soul, and it muddles my thinking. I find myself saying the most inappropriate things that I must later repent for. He must think me a clod, especially considering

I had quite possibly the worst first day on the job in history. He seems to reveal every weakness I feared I'd find in myself during this undertaking. I am trying to overcome them. The biggest obstacle is how lonely I feel here and how much I miss you and———. My thoughts and my love are with you every day. I can only pray that it will be safe for me to return to you again someday. All my love,

L—

His eyes re-read the lines where her elegant, slanted handwriting had described him. *He's quite a specimen of a man, I must say, and just looking at him makes me sometimes forget what I wish to say. His dark blue eyes seem to peer into my very soul, and it muddles my thinking.* Another point for the Traitors. This was getting him nowhere.

Ian stuffed the letter back into the envelope and glued it closed again. He was coming up with more questions than answers with Lottie. It was time he called in for some support. He slipped his phone from the bedside table and scrolled through his contacts until he saw John's number and dialed.

"Ian!" John's voice answered cheerfully. "How's it going?"

"Hey there, Preacher," Ian replied, smiling at hearing his best friend's voice again. "I can't complain. How's dad life treating you?"

"Oh, Allyson has colic, so that's been a nightmare. But we're surviving. How's Molly and the new nephew? What was his name, Lucas?"

"Logan. They're good. Molly's home and getting better."

"Good to hear. So did you can the nanny then?"

"No, actually, that's why I'm calling. I need you to run a check on her."

"Why? Has something happened?"

"No, it's just . . ." Ian paused. There was no one thing that he could point to, but there was something about this woman that just didn't add up. "I don't know. There's something she's hiding, I think."

"OK, what do you have?"

"Not much. A passport, a license plate number to a car I'm sure is going to be a rental, a few pictures of an unknown male contact she made here, and a number to a burner phone."

"Not much, huh? The girl's been working for your sister for what, two, three weeks, and you've run full recon on her. What do you want from me?"

"Whatever you can find."

"And what is it you think I'll find?" John asked.

"I'm not sure. But I have a feeling that you'll know it when you see it."

John grunted on the other end of the phone. "All right. I'll try a few of the usual channels and see what we can come up with. If I find anything, I'll let you know."

"Thanks, Preacher," Ian said, truly grateful.

Using a shortcut and a lead foot, Ian managed to arrive at the bookstore just as Lottie was pulling into a parking space three stores down. She walked purposefully toward the bookshop and made her way quietly toward the back of the store. He noticed she was careful not to draw attention to herself from other shoppers or the employees.

Ian pushed the door open and walked into the store. The scent of glue, paper, and ink assaulted him as soon as he stepped inside. The tinkle of a small brass bell on the door announced his entrance to an older gentleman behind the counter.

"Good day to you, sir," he said politely. He pushed his wireless glasses up onto his bulbous nose. Tufts of white hair shot out from above his ears and over his small blue eyes but from nowhere else. "Can I help you find something?"

Ian quickly scanned a colorful poster of the store's layout next to the register. He could see the rear entrance and a section of books nearby that would make for a perfect secluded meeting place. Damn, she was good.

"I know where I'm headed, thanks." Ian made his way toward the back of the store. He could hear whispered voices from behind the bookcase. One was unmistakably Lottie's.

Ian removed a handful of books from the shelves that divided the aisles. It gave him a small gap through which he could not only hear Lottie but see her as well. He could not, he was frustrated to discover, see the person she was meeting. From his voice, Ian could tell he was older and spoke with a similar accent to Lottie's. His voice rumbled like the engines of a low-flying plane. Ian wondered if he was the same man Lottie had met with at the bed and breakfast before. But without seeing him, he couldn't be sure.

"Why are you here checking up on me?" Lottie said, a bit of disgust in her tone.

"I'm just making sure that everything is going well with the job." The man whispered his reply.

"It is. You know that. I've already told you. You can go back and leave this to me."

"And the cowboy? The one you've been spending time with."

"Ian. He asks a lot of questions, but I only tell him what I have to. He doesn't suspect anything. You should stop worrying."

"There's a lot riding on this, Charlotte," the man said, his tone a bit harder than before. "We're all sacrificing a lot. We can't afford to take all these chances for nothing."

"I know. I know," Lottie replied. "I remember why we're doing this and for whom. I haven't forgotten. I think about it every day. You needn't remind me."

"How much longer do you think before the job is done?" the man asked.

"Another week, two at the most. I'll contact you as I promised. But I'll have to get a new burner. You compromised the other one."

"You destroyed it?"

"Of course. I remember the protocols we agreed to," Lottie huffed.

"Certainly. It's just that I worry. It's not as if you've trained for this sort of life, Charlotte."

"I can do this. Now, please. Stop worrying and get on your plane."

There were muffled sounds and low whispers Ian couldn't make out. But he'd heard enough. She was definitely into something up to her neck. What exactly that something was, he intended to find out next.

The loud click of the rear entrance door closing let Ian know Lottie's appointment had left. He felt his fists clench. He'd left the army, the brothers he fought alongside for more than a decade, to come and find some peace. He wanted life, not death. He wanted love, not war. In the year that passed since he'd come to live with the Hamptons, he'd never come close to feeling any of that—except when he was with her. And now, she was ... well, she was not what he thought. His disappointment morphed into anger before he realized.

Ian felt his feet moving toward her before his brain figured out what exactly he was going to say, his body apparently still at odds with itself.

He rounded the bookcase that divided the aisles and saw her. Her long legs were clad in black jeans, a long cream sweater covering her body, and a printed scarf loosely knotted at her neck. Her hair was working its way out of a burgundy felt fedora that matched the flowers of her scarf. She was beautiful. She was always beautiful. Despite his frustration from the conversation he'd just overheard, he found he couldn't suppress a smile at seeing her. His body's betrayal knew no bounds, it seemed.

Lottie's eyes shot open wide with surprise. "Ian!" she said. "I'm surprised to see you."

"Hello, Lottie." Ian stalked closer. "I thought you had an appointment."

Lottie looked over her shoulder. Yes, love, he's gone, and I'm here, Ian thought.

"I did. But I finished early, and I'd thought I'd come by here." Ian noticed her eyes darting around and her fingers nervously playing with the fringe on her scarf. "There was a book I've wanted to pick up for a couple of weeks." Her speech was hurried, her tone sharp. Ian recognized every tell-tale sign that she was lying through her teeth. Another point for Team Brain.

"A book?" Ian said. He narrowed his gaze on her, scrutinizing her face. He could see he was making her nervous. He took a few steps closer. Lottie nodded frantically. "From this section of the store?" He eased closer still until he was close enough to reach out and touch her cheek.

Without taking her eyes from his, Lottie reached over and plucked a book randomly from the shelf. She brandished the cover to Ian, forcing him to lean back an inch to avoid being smacked on the nose.

"Yes, this one," she said with feigned confidence.

Ian's eyes glanced over it. He raised one eyebrow. "This one? Are you sure?" Ian asked, his voice a husky whisper.

"Yes." Lottie's throat worked to swallow. She stammered out a few more lies.

"I thought it might be . . . use . . . useful." Lottie never glanced down at the book she held in her moistening grip. "Informative."

Ian reached out and gently took the book from her. He leaned so close that he could smell the soap she'd used in the shower that morning and the light floral perfume she wore.

Ian looked at the book in his hand. In an instant, he lunged forward and claimed her mouth with his. He gave Lottie no time to respond before he was forcing greedy kisses against her mouth, urgently teasing her lips open. He hungrily devoured her with deep, sucking kisses. He sucked her mouth with his tongue, rough and needy. Lottie let out a hum of pleasure.

Ian curled one hand to the back of her neck, clutching a fistful of hair, and pulled. She gasped, opening her mouth to him more fully. He deepened the kiss, sucking her bottom lip into his mouth, and gave it a hard nip. He had no idea who this woman really was. But he had no problem showing her right here, right now, who he was. He was the man that wanted to own her body and soul.

Ian pulled away, leaving Lottie swaying on her feet. Her eyes closed for a brief moment until her lashes lifted to meet his gaze.

Ian handed her the book and then dropped another soft kiss against her lips. Then two. Lottie looked down for the first time at the book in her hand: *The Good Girl's Guide to Oral Sex—How to Make Your Man Beg* by B.J. Smith.

"You keep letting me kiss you like that, and I'm sure we'll find that book very . . . informative," Ian breathed against her ear. He brushed a strand of hair from her cheek before leaving the bookstore.

Game. Set. Match. Winner: Benny and the traitors.

CHAPTER TEN

"Sounds like you've got yourself some sort of spy or hitman," John said. He had listened with rapt attention while Ian recounted the details about Lottie's meeting at the bookstore. He left out the portion of the encounter when he'd kissed her. "Especially when you consider what you told me about her being good with a rifle."

"Something isn't adding up with this woman, Preacher," Ian said. "She's either an incredibly good actress, or she's this really sweet woman in a hell of a lot of trouble."

"Are you falling for this woman, Ian?" John asked, his tone serious.

Ian let out a long breath. "I don't know what the hell is going on. I can't keep my hands off of her." Ian let out another exasperated sigh. "Lord, she's even got me drinking tea in the mornings now instead of coffee."

Ian could almost hear John's knowing grin on the other end of the phone. "But how does she make you feel?"

"You mean other than horny as a teen on prom night?" Ian said with a smile. "I don't know, man, I can't describe it. I feel . . ." Ian paused while his friend listened silently. John knew all too well how quickly the right woman could get under your skin. And even though Ian seemed to be having a hard time realizing it, he was thankful his friend was finally getting a chance at what he'd been wanting.

"I feel at peace," he said finally.

"I get it," John said simply. "I'll get one of my intel guys on it right away. I'm sure we can find some answers for you."

"Thanks, man," Ian said gratefully. "I don't want to fall in love with this girl just to realize it'll never work out."

"Man," John said, sympathy leaching through his voice. "I'm afraid it's probably a little too late for that."

Lottie spooned the last lemon square out of the baking dish and dropped the empty pan into a sink of sudsy water.

"That's the last of it," she announced to Molly, who was laying Logan in his bassinet by the kitchen's hearth room fire. Winter had finally decided to come and stay over the last few days in Oklahoma. A bitter wind from the west was threatening ice and snow in the coming days. Nearly all of the work on the ranch, outside of caring for the livestock, ceased. That left time for Molly to finally host an overdue girls' lunch while Wyatt and his brothers entertained their children for the afternoon.

Molly glanced out of the window to see two large white SUVs and a tan pickup pull up next to her house.

"They're here!" she said, clapping her hands. Susan, the full-figured redhead Lottie had met on her first day at the ranch, was the first to come through the kitchen door. She placed a long glass casserole dish on the kitchen island and immediately reached to bring Molly in for a warm hug. Lottie was surprised that following that, Susan grabbed her around the shoulders for a tight squeeze.

"It's wonderful to see you again, Charlotte," she said, a bright smile warming her face.

Behind Susan was a shorter, petite blond woman with an enormous, rounded belly. She had large, deep-set blue eyes and a full mouth that opened in a smile that covered nearly half of her face. She placed a large bowl on the counter next to Susan's casserole and extended a hand to Lottie.

"I'm Ginny Hampton," she said, smiling through a wide mouth rimmed with plump lips. "Mattie's wife."

Lottie gave her hand a gentle squeeze. "I'm pleased to know you."

"Which makes me Lacy," came a greeting from a tall, thin brunette. Lacy's hair was thick and long and fell in large rolling curls down her back. Her eyes were darkly shadowed, and her lips bore a shocking red lipstick against the ultra-white of her toothy smile. She was quite possibly the most glamorous woman Lottie had ever seen. Although the other Hampton wives were equally pretty, Lacy possessed a sophisticated polish that the others didn't.

Lottie took the pitcher she carried in one hand. Lacy's other hand was grasping a small infant carrier with a sleeping baby tucked inside.

"Oh gracious, look how big Clare's gotten," Molly said. She lifted the carrier from her sister-in-law and unwrapped the blankets and safety straps. "I'll put her in Logan's pack and play," she said, swaying the stirring baby to a small portable crib set up in the living room.

"I'm going to have to start weaning her. She's gotten four teeth in and bites the crap out of me," Lacy said.

She dropped a large diaper bag next to Logan's bassinet. "You're so lucky you couldn't breastfeed this one, Molly."

"Oh, Lace, I miss it," Molly replied. "Although it is nice to have Wyatt get up in the middle of the night for a change."

Ginny scooped up the sleeping little boy and cradled him in her arms. "I can't wait until Annabelle gets here," she said, cooing over the baby and leaning down to drop a kiss on his forehead. "I love newborns."

"How much longer before you're due?" Lottie asked. She had assembled the dishes the women brought on the table she and Molly had laid for their lunch.

"Just a couple of weeks. But I always go early," she said, laying Logan back down in his bassinet. "Could be any day now, I suppose. Is lunch ready? I'm starved."

"Ah, I miss those days of being able to eat whatever I want," Susan said. She poured a pink beverage into each of the glasses on the table. Lottie did a quick count of places at the table and then looked toward Molly with a questioning gaze. She had not expected to be included with Molly's sisters. She merely expected to help prepare the meal and serve.

"Let's all sit." Molly gestured to a chair beside her. "Lottie, you sit here beside me, won't you?"

Lottie nodded shyly and took her seat. Susan said a short blessing over their meal, making particular mention for patience and safety for their husbands who were alone with the children.

"Lottie?" Susan said, passing a bowl of fresh salad greens toward her. "I like that name. It suits you better. As do the jeans and boots. I couldn't help but notice. Those are one of Elsbeth Brody's creations, aren't they?"

Lottie nodded, spooning salad onto her plate. "Ian purchased them for me as a gift. I think he thought it would make me feel more at home here than my town loafers."

Susan shot her gaze toward Molly and raised an eyebrow.

"That was kind of him," Ginny said. She served herself salad. She too, Lottie noticed, raised an eyebrow toward Susan. Lottie took a chicken and rice casserole of some sort from Susan and spooned a small helping onto her plate.

Why was everything cooked here swimming in some sort of yellowish gravy? Lottie longed for her home and seared meat, grilled vegetables, and fresh pastries from the chefs in her father's kitchen. She opted to merely nod in agreement with Ginny rather than comment.

"Ian is thoughtful when he wants to be," Molly interjected. She tore a piece of bread and popped it into her mouth.

"Oh, for the love," Lacy said, dropping her napkin into her lap. "Can we please stop all this bullshitting and just ask her?"

"Lacy!" Susan snapped.

"I don't want to waste time getting to the point. I'd rather spend it hearing all the juicy bits." Lacy turned her head to look at Lottie. Molly was vigorously shaking her head, but Lacy continued. "Are you sleeping with Ian, or what?"

Lottie instantly turned a bright shade of pink, to which the four other females around the table howled and giggled, the sound like the clucking of angry hens.

"Well, if she's not, she wants to be," Lacy said curtly. "All right, girl, spill it."

Lottie was at a loss. "I don't understand. You believe Ian and I to have some sort of romantic relationship."

"Oh, hun," Ginny cut in, swallowing a bit of chicken. "This is a close family and a small town. Grace Talbot said she saw you and Ian kissing at the bookshop yesterday."

"And by her description to Midge on the phone last night, it was quite a kiss," Susan chimed in. "You know they're in the same Bible study at church, right? Everyone knows everyone around here."

"And Mears Price, he owns the bookstore, said you bought a book about oral sex. Is that true?" Lacy quieted. Lottie's head flapped back and forth among the chattering women.

"You girls, stop," Molly said. She got up from the table and retrieved another bottle of salad dressing from the refrigerator. "I'm sorry, Lottie. There's not much excitement around here. The littlest bit of gossip gets kinda thrown out of proportion. Don't let my sisters embarrass you."

"I want to know if the book is any good," Susan commented. It earned an uproarious bout of laughter from all of the women, even Lottie, whose pinkish flush had gone totally crimson. She'd been pressured into buying the blasted book when Ian caught her at the bookstore. But she was intrigued and did actually skim a few chapters.

"That book," Lottie said, shaking her head, ashamed she'd once again let Ian McGuire rattle her nerves. "I confess, was a complete misunderstanding. But . . ." She sighed and pushed a bite of salad into her mouth.

"Oh no you don't," Lacy demanded. "You read it. What did it say?"

"Why do you want to know?" Ginny teased. "Is Tim getting a little needy?"

"I have had four children in seven years. I need to find something else to do to entertain that man. Clare was our last one. And this time, I mean it," Lacy cut in. "Where's the wine?"

Molly grinned. "Cabinet above the stove."

"Should you be having wine while you're nursing?" Ginny scolded lightly.

"Weaning," Lacy corrected. "And yes. One glass won't hurt. I won't nurse again until she goes to bed tonight."

"Well, just bring four glasses for y'all. I can't," Ginny said, rubbing her rounded stomach.

"All right now, sister," Susan said, pouring a full glass of white wine into Lottie's empty cup. "Time for some truth serum. We want to hear all about this book you bought and about Ian."

"There's nothing to tell," Lottie said. She took a sip of her wine. Heaven help her, she was going to need liquid fortification to make it through this lunch.

"She's right," Molly cut in. "My brother is a serial monogamist. I couldn't name three women I know for sure he's been with. And one of them he even proposed to."

"Mmm, yes. Miranda," Lottie said absently.

"He told you about Miranda?" Molly said, a bit surprised.

"Yes. Should he not have?" Lottie wondered, a bit worried she betrayed confidence.

"Just surprised, that's all. He doesn't talk about her much. I don't even know what became of her after they broke up."

"Oh, she married some friend of his from the football team. I can't remember his name. They have a couple of children. He said she's happy."

"Really?" Lacy said. She leaned forward and took a large gulp of her nearly full wine glass.

"What else has he told you?" Ginny asked, wanting to change the subject from an old girlfriend.

"He said he thought I was beautiful," Lottie blushed. There was validation about what Susan had said. The wine was truth serum. Her tongue felt looser than she would have liked. Perhaps it was the wine. Perhaps it was just the feeling of sisterhood she'd been so long without and had so greatly missed that made her feel more like herself again. She felt she was among friends. She felt brave. Almost brave enough to risk becoming attached to these wonderful women who embraced her as a sister without even truly knowing who she really was.

"Oh, well, at least we know his vision wasn't damaged in the army," Molly said.

"And I bet the kiss was beautiful too, wasn't it?" Lacy probed.

"Which one?" Lottie asked aloud. The four women erupted into hoots and laughter as Lottie realized she'd revealed more than she'd bargained for.

"He's kissed you more than once?" Molly asked, feeling a bit uncomfortable about pressing into her brother's personal life like this. Lottie nodded.

"Was it one of those toe-curling kisses that makes you want to lay back, spread your legs, and let him just ravish you?" Susan asked. She spread her arms wide and let her head fall back while the other women laughed.

"*The Duke's Domain*?" Lottie asked. Susan's face shot up.

"Yes," Susan said. The entire table went silent.

"You read Violet Dunn?" Ginny asked in a whisper.

"Lord, Ginny, it's not like it's illegal to read smut," Lacy cut in, taking another long swig of her wine.

Lottie grinned. "My sister is a bibliophile," she said simply. As if that would explain her love for the explicit romance novelist's books.

"She's a what?" Lacy said. "Is that like she's addicted to book sex or something?"

Lottie giggled. "Not at all. She collects books. When she was eighteen, she bid on this online auction for a trunk filled with unknown books from this antique bookshop. She was certain there was an original Gutenberg Bible in it or something. Anyway, it ended up being filled with Violet Dunn novels. First editions. We devoured every single one. But had to lie to our parents lest they know what we were reading."

"I've heard Violet Dunn is just a pen name," Ginny said. "And that 'she' is really a 'he.'" Ginny raised her brows.

"Don't be silly," Molly said. "The way she describes what it's like to be kissed—no man thinks about kissing like that."

"And speaking of kissing," Lacy cut in, pouring a second glass of wine for everyone who was drinking. "What was it like kissing our Ian? That man is sin in Levi's."

"Lacy!" Ginny scolded.

"What?" Lacy took another swallow of wine. "I'm married, I'm not blind. The man is hotter than a four-dollar pistol."

Lottie grinned and gave the question serious consideration. "Well, if you must know," she began.

"We must know," Lacy answered.

"He's a cross between George in *The Count Counts* and Bix in *The Marauding Marquess*."

The five women burst into such a fit of laughter, the two babies began to wail, which only spurred on another fit of laughter.

CHAPTER ELEVEN

When Wyatt, Ian, and the two little boys arrived home nearly four hours later, all five women were seated in the living room, enjoying their third bottle of wine. Ginny was stretched out on the long sofa, her ballooned stomach poking skyward. Lacy was sitting cross-legged on the floor with baby Clare, who'd found interest in chewing on one of James' favorite superhero action figures. Molly sat in a rocking recliner behind Lacy, and Lottie and Susan were sharing a smaller sofa and happily passing a sleeping Logan back and forth. Lottie felt at home with these women. They were a true tribe of sisterhood living through the uncertainties of marriage, motherhood, and womanhood together. *A family*, Lottie thought to herself. Her stomach had become sore from laughing with them all afternoon.

Lottie beamed, seeing Ian walk in with a sleeping James in his arms. She instantly handed Logan to Susan and rose to help him usher the child to his bed. Even if she was comfortable with these women, she was still the nanny. When she stood, she felt herself sway slightly but righted herself quickly.

"I got this," Ian said in a soft whisper. "Are you staying long? I can take you back to Midge's house if you're done here."

"She's free to go," Molly said, draining the last of her wine and standing to give Wyatt and Robert each a kiss on the cheek. "We can clear this all away, right ladies?"

Each of the women gave a quick sound of agreement and moved toward the kitchen. They had half of the lunch dishes done by the time Ian came back downstairs.

"He's out," Ian said. "He may not wake up for dinner."

"Great. Two babies up all night," Molly said with a titter, her inebriated condition easily identified in her slurred words.

Ian arched an eyebrow at seeing his sister drunk in the middle of the afternoon. Wyatt took him aside and shook his head.

"You haven't lived through a girls' lunch yet. Piece of free advice. Just take her home. Feed and water her well, and put her to bed," Wyatt suggested conspiratorially. "They just get together and drink all afternoon."

"Yes, and don't be taking her to bed like Quin Quittle." Molly laughed. Her laughter prompted water to slosh around the sink. The other women joined her in enjoying their private joke with snorts of laughter.

"Our girl here needs more of a Bix Minter," Lacy said, snapping Clare into her car seat and initiating another round of laughter.

"You're not driving, are you, Lacy?" Wyatt asked.

"No," Ginny replied. "I had to skip the wine today, so I'm taking them home. I'll have the fellas come and get their cars later."

"What does that mean?" Ian said in a low voice to Wyatt. "What's a Quinn Quittle?"

"I have no idea," Wyatt said, shaking his head. "Just feed and water her and put her to bed. She'll be sorry tomorrow. They always are."

Ian had to help Lottie into the truck. She'd swayed a bit unsteadily on her feet twice while walking the short distance around the side of the house to where he was forced to park.

"Did you enjoy your afternoon?" she slurred to Ian.

"Not as much as you did," Ian confessed. He steered the truck onto the gravel drive leading to Midge's farmhouse.

"What did Lacy mean you needed a Bix Minter?" Ian asked as the truck bounced toward Midge's.

"He's just a character in a book," Lottie said.

"Oh, another book?" Ian teased.

"Ha, ha," Lottie mocked. "I'll have you know that Bix is my most favorite hero. He's a bold, take-charge man who loves women with power and substance," Lottie rambled.

"And you like men like Bix? The take-charge kind of guys?" His mind drifted back to the kiss in the bookstore. He'd wanted to kick himself for being a bit too aggressive with her. He'd thought he'd scared her off. But then she'd hummed into his mouth, and he could tell she enjoyed it. He could take charge of her. He could definitely take charge.

"Oh yes," Lottie agreed.

"And not like Quinn Quintuplet?" Ian mocked. He was having a bit of fun with a tipsy Lottie, and he was enjoying himself. If he got her talking, maybe she'd tell him what he was desperate to find out.

"Quinn Quipple. I mean, Quinn Quittle," Lottie corrected. "He's too soft. Always so delicate with women. Going slowly and being sweet. I suppose there's a time and a place for that. But sometimes a girl just wants a man, you know?"

"Oh, uh-huh," Ian agreed. There was no way he was going to interrupt her now. This line of conversation had suddenly become very interesting and entertaining. "Was Roger a Quinn or a Bix?"

"Oh, a Quinn for certain. Actually, he was a Franz. Franz was slow because he wanted the women to think he was interested in their pleasure, but he really wasn't. He was just hoping he could make it last longer than five minutes." Lottie giggled at her own joke. Ian thought she had given up trying not to slur her words. The harder she tried, the more slurred they became. She gave a hard hiccup and giggled at herself again. "Roger could never." Lottie laughed and hiccupped again.

"Never what?" Ian asked. The amusement on his face unmasked. This was too good.

"You know," she slurred. She blushed slightly and gave another hiccup. "He was always done before I could, actually." She waved her hand in a rolling motion, not saying what she was thinking.

"Ah," Ian said, catching her meaning clearly now. "Not able to get you to the mountaintop, huh?"

"No," Lottie said, a tone of disappointment and disgust in her voice.

Ian pulled the truck into the drive at Midge's and slid out to help Lottie down. The wind was picking up and felt like a frozen knife slicing the bare skin of his cheeks and neck. Lottie snuggled next to Ian's body as he helped her inside.

"Well, hello, you two," Midge said. "Did you have a nice time with the ladies today, Lottie?"

Lottie gave an enthusiastic nod, smiled dopily, and said, "It was felightdul. I mean, delightful."

Midge laughed. "Oh, they initiated her good, didn't they? I made some pasta." She spoke more to Ian than to Lottie. "It's on the stove. I'm off to the church for a committee meeting about the Snowflake Ball. There's aspirin in the cabinet in the bathroom." Still laughing, she headed outside while Lottie waved cheerily to her.

"C'mon, lush, let's get you some dinner."

Ian served Lottie a generous portion of al dente pasta and a delicious bolognese sauce. To his surprise, she ate every morsel. He'd only ever seen her pick at half portions before. "You like the spaghetti? Midge is a good cook."

"Mmm. It's delicious. I'm not used to all of the foods fried and with that gravy on it. I've liked your meal best. But this," Lottie twirled a forkful of pasta, "this is wonderful. More like home." Lottie swallowed her bite, drained her water glass, and continued.

"This whole day has been like home. Your sister and those wonderful women. And you." She gave Ian's chest a pat and then rubbed his chest under his flannel shirt. Ian's body hummed at the intimate contact. "You are home for me too. Where I'm safe. For now, anyway."

"You're always safe with me, Lottie. Do you feel like you're not safe?"

Lottie shook her head and then laid her finger over her lips. "Shh. It's a secret. We must keep Maisie safe, you know."

"Who's Maisie again?" Ian asked, laying his fork down and paying closer attention to everything Lottie was saying. It was mostly just rambling and gibberish, but perhaps under all of that, there was some vein of truth.

Lottie shook her head. "That I cannot say. My sister is off limits," she said, waving her hand back and forth. She cupped her hand over her mouth and let out a hiccup of a laugh.

"Uh-oh. I think I need to go to bed." Ian saw her eyes go a little crossed as she stood and moved toward the stairs.

"Good idea." Ian helped her up the steps. In her bedroom, Ian helped her take off her boots. He unwrapped her scarf and laid it on the chair in front of the small desk where he noticed another letter addressed simply to *M—*. The initial obviously for her sister, Maisie. He should have thought of that.

When he turned back around, Lottie had slipped her sweater off over her head and was slowly peeling her jeans down from her hips. Ian could not look away as she slowly revealed inch after creamy inch of long bare leg. She was wearing black silk and lace panties, not unlike the blue ones he'd discovered in her drawer a few days ago. Her bra matched and pushed her small breasts up and together so they were nearly touching one another.

"Ian," Lottie said, her voice low. "Would you close the door, please?"

Ian went toward the door and closed it. He should have walked through it and closed it behind him. But he knew that was not what Lottie meant. And it wasn't what he wanted. He turned to find her sitting on the edge of the bed, her long legs crossed at the knee. She crooked a finger and drew it in and out, motioning for him to come closer. He obeyed without question.

When he reached the edge of the bed, she stood up and leaned forward to kiss him. Ian's self-control was waning. He wanted this woman. He'd wanted her for weeks. And here she was, standing in her underwear, kissing him. His body responded instantly. Lottie must have felt the hardness growing because she pressed her hips closer to his, pushing a soft moan from his throat.

"Damn, Lottie," Ian groaned and kissed her back. He let his hand move around to her shoulder blades, pressing her body close to his. He pressed his tongue into her mouth, licking and sucking with bold pressure that bordered on pain. Lottie gasped and went limp, allowing him to control her body as he desired. Ian slid his hand down her back, gripping her bottom and giving it a sharp slap. Lottie let a soft scream escape her lips, then urged forward, pressing against him again.

He scraped the two-day bristle of his cheek over her jaw and licked down her neck to her collarbone. He nipped across her chest and then dipped his head down to pull a lace-covered nipple between his teeth. He pinched her tightening bud between his teeth and felt her body arch, pressing her breast closer. Ian pulled the lace down, revealing the peachy pebbled flesh, and let the flat of his tongue stroke over it. His hand slid up her side and uncovered the other breast. Lottie let her eyes close and her head roll back. She allowed him to suck one breast and twist the nipple of her other between his fingers.

"Ian," she said, gasping.

Ian released her breast and bit his way up her neck to her earlobe, capturing it in his mouth and sucking it. "Yes, love. What do you want?" he whispered in her ear. His fingers were still tweaking and teasing her nipple.

"I want to go to the mountain," she said.

Ian let his fingers drop and gave her a soft kiss. But he pulled away. He was willing to do a lot of things. He'd do anything Lottie asked. But he couldn't make love to her in this condition. It wasn't right. No matter how badly Benedict Arnold was begging him to. Lottie looked up at him with pleading eyes.

"Are you sure about that?" Ian asked. "You've had a lot to drink, Lottie."

"Please," she begged.

Ian's hands slowly slid up Lottie's back and reached for the bra clasp, only to find a seamless piece of lace stretched across her back. He wound his thumb between her breasts and easily unclasped the bra, letting it fall from her shoulders. It drifted down her arms and onto the floor. Lottie stood in silence as Ian's gaze feasted over her naked breasts. It would take all his self-control not to give in, but he wasn't going to make love to her. Not today. He'd take her to the mountain and leave. Nothing more.

"Lord, you're beautiful," he breathed. He nearly had to remind himself to do so.

"Lay back on the bed," he ordered and gave her body a gentle push until her knees were touching the edge of the bed behind her. Lottie sat down and then scooted herself up. Ian slid his hands over her ankles, then her calves, and up her thighs to her hips. He hooked his thumbs into the lace of her panties and slid them down to her ankles, where he cast them next to her bra on the floor.

"You're still dressed," Lottie said. She wrinkled her nose in protest.

"You're the only one going to the mountain tonight," he whispered. "We need to have a serious talk before I sleep with you. And you're in no condition for talk, love. Serious or otherwise."

"What are you going to do with me, then?" Lottie asked.

"I won't deny I want you. I'm going to enjoy you for a while," he said. "Because you asked me."

Ian covered Lottie's body with his, the long steel rod of his erection pressing into her hip. "My only question is, who do you want taking you to the mountain, love? Quinn or Bix?"

Lottie closed her eyes and bit her lower lip. "Bix," she moaned.

A smile played at his lips. He'd been hoping she'd say that. He let himself take a long look at Lottie's naked body. He dipped his head and took the nipple of one breast into his mouth and began to suck hard on it. Lottie's body writhed under him, grinding against his erection.

"You can't move so much," Ian groaned softly. If she kept up these gyrations, he'd be getting to the mountaintop before she'd even started.

Ian bit and nipped down her body, pushing sparks of pleasure across her skin and into her core. She arched with each taste he took. When he reached her stomach, he knelt.

"Open for me, Lottie," he said in a commanding voice. Lottie obeyed. Ian dipped his head and placed a soft kiss on the tiny brown tuft of wool between her legs. Her stomach visibly fluttered at the light touch. Ian smiled. He loved how responsive she was.

He began to softly stroke the slickness between her legs and pushed away the folds until he found the tiny nub of sensitive flesh he knew Lottie was panting for him to touch. He gave it a long soft stroke. Lottie moaned and let her legs fall farther apart.

"Please, Ian. Please," she breathed.

Ian dipped his head and licked along her seam. Lottie arched her back and let out a little scream of pleasure. Ian wasted no time. If it was a take-charge man she wanted, then he was going to take his fill. And happily. His tongue began to work greedily against her flesh, pressing her open and lathing and nipping at her sensitive bud until Lottie gasped and moaned. She pressed his head down closer to her core, begging for more. Ian obeyed. He pressed a finger inside her and began to lick and suck in tiny surges that had Lottie ready to shatter. A second finger joined the first, and he began to stroke inside her in a quick, steady rhythm in time with his kisses. He could feel her muscles tightening around him.

"You're nearly there, love," he coaxed before resuming his torturous kisses, stroking and licking her ever faster until Lottie shattered. Her body convulsed in waves of pleasure. She rode through her climax as he continued to kiss and stroke at his relentless pace, forcing her body rapidly into another ascension. In minutes, she felt a second orgasm grip her body.

"Enough," she breathed. "No more. It's too much." She was barely able to speak the words.

Ian released her gently, letting her ride her spasms of pleasure slowly down as he held her tight against his chest. He let her lay against him until her panting breath became more steady and then slower until she was asleep. He eased himself from under her, glancing down at the bright pink marks he'd peppered over her ivory flesh.

"Too much Bix, Lottie. I'm so sorry," he said, rebuking himself. He slid a comforter over her naked body and then closed the door behind him.

He would have a hell of a time trying to sleep tonight with a very displeased Benedict Arnold pulsing between his legs. He'd contemplated relieving it himself again when his phone buzzed in his pocket. Closing the door of his room behind him, he tapped the screen.

"John," he said.

"Hey, Ian." John's voice sounded grave. "Listen, I have the information you wanted, but I can't disclose it over an open channel. I'm flying to Nevada tomorrow. I've planned a long layover in Dallas around 11:00. Can you meet me?"

"Absolutely," Ian said. "A personal visit, huh? This can't be good."

"Ian," John's voice was deadly serious and low. "You have no idea."

CHAPTER TWELVE

Lottie's head throbbed. Why had she had so much wine yesterday? She sat up slowly, feeling her stomach recoil at even the slight motion. Her eyes refused to open. She held her head in her hands, trying to reassure her eyes they would not pop out of her head if they opened. They finally surrendered. First a tiny slit, then wider. When they fully opened, and Lottie was able to focus, she noticed she was naked. Tiny pink marks were sprinkled over her breasts and stomach. The tender flesh between her legs stung with ten thousand scratches from Ian's beard. He'd raked it along the sensitive flesh between her legs for several long, blissful minutes last night. The memory of what she had done came flooding back.

She sighed. So, in addition to the injury of a hangover, she now had the insult of having to face Ian after acting like a complete slapper the night before. What had she been thinking? She sighed again. She'd known exactly what she'd been thinking. She'd wanted him. And she knew he'd wanted her too. She'd felt every long, hard inch of just how badly he had wanted her. And yet, he'd not had sex with her. He'd merely pleasured her and left her asleep in her bed. She licked her lips. Her mouth had a revolting taste in it.

Finding her way downstairs had taken more energy than Lottie wanted to admit. When she made it to the kitchen, she found Wyatt sitting at the bar. He was sipping coffee from an oversized mug. The clock on the microwave announced in bright, blaring green numbers that it was just after seven.

"Good morning," he said, a knowing smile spreading across his face.

"It is morning indeed," Lottie said with a gravelly voice. She walked slowly to the electric kettle and flipped the button to make hot water for tea. She needed a strong cup of tea now more than she'd needed one in her entire life.

"Whether it is good or not depends on how much wine one consumed the night previous." She clutched at her temple. She fell into a barstool across from Wyatt.

He laughed out loud. Lottie's face scrunched. It sounded like he was laughing daggers into her ears.

"Well, if it makes you feel any better, you look a hell of a lot better than Molly." He laughed again, and employer or not, Lottie shushed him.

Wyatt pulled a plate off of the stove and handed it over to Lottie. He plucked up the kettle, poured the hot water into a mug, and then plopped a tea bag into it. He grabbed a bottle of honey and took it all over to where she sat at the bar and slid it in front of her.

"Burnt toast with butter and strong hot tea. The charcoal in the toast will help with your stomach, and the tea will help with the headache," he said. Lottie was grateful his voice was much softer now. He slid two white tablets across the bar to her. "As will these."

"Thank you." Lottie downed the aspirin. She started to nibble on the toast. To her great relief, the taste of it didn't seem to annoy her stomach as much as she had expected it would.

"What brings you here this morning?" She finally ventured to ask.

"I came to talk to you," he said. His voice held a bit of indistinguishable sadness. "I'm taking Molly to the doctor today. We expect him to give her a clean bill of health. Her pressure's been good the past few days, and the medications seem to be working."

"Would you like for me to sit with the boys while you're away?" Lottie asked. She nibbled more toast. It did seem to make her stomach feel a bit better.

"That won't be necessary. Midge is coming with us. She's going to take them to the park near the hospital while we're at the appointment. Then we're all going to go for burgers at one of the boys' favorite places in the city."

"Oh." Lottie's dulled senses were just now beginning to fully comprehend what Wyatt really had come here to say. Molly was better. The family no longer needed her to help care for the children. It was time for her to go. Her heart sank.

"Molly is back to health," he said, giving her a questioning stare. "And yet, you don't exactly look like you're happy to hear this news."

Lottie forced her face to brighten. She sat up straighter in a single quick motion. Her head rioted against the movement with a stab of pain. "No. Of course. It's wonderful news. I'm delighted for all of you."

"So." Wyatt let a heavy pause impregnate the air. "That would mean that we'll not be needing you to come by and help out with the boys anymore. I've taken the liberty of printing out a copy of the reference I sent to your agency. I made sure to tell them how terrific you were." He pulled a thin white envelope from the back pocket of his jeans and slid it across the counter to her.

She reached for it, noticing her fingers were shaking slightly. Her heart, however, wobbled like an undercooked custard. "That was very kind of you. Thank you for your good remarks."

"I have no doubt you'll be matched to another family very soon. And they'll be fortunate to have you help them—just as we were fortunate to have you bless ours."

Lottie nodded slightly, acknowledging his compliment. "You're very kind, Dr. Hampton."

"I have no doubt they'll want you to start right away, but I was hoping you could put them off until Monday. We'd really love for you to stay the rest of the week and join the celebration at the Snowflake Ball in town this weekend. Molly thought it would be a nice way to send you off with something fun."

Lottie nodded, not even realizing that she agreed to staying the rest of the week. It would be a long, painful goodbye to linger a few more days.

"You know, you could stay longer than that if you wanted to," Wyatt suggested.

"What do you mean?" Lottie's head shot up. It was her heart's eagerness to hear more. Her head knew it was nothing more than wishful thinking. She had to be on her way. There was no way around it.

"You are wonderful with kids, Lottie. Hell, if you can manage my two heathens, I dare say there are no kids you can't charm into good behavior."

Lottie offered him a weak smile. She loved Robert and James. They were high-energy children with inquisitive minds and a clever, quick wit that had enchanted Lottie nearly from the first moment she'd met them. True, they'd presented her with a bit more of a challenge than she'd been prepared for, but it didn't take long to learn the secret to their hearts.

"That's a wonderful notion, Dr. Hampton, but—"

"Since I'm no longer your employer, I do wish we could drop all this doctor business once and for all, and you just call me Wyatt. And consider it. I imagine you've made some friends and developed a couple of close—" He paused and cleared his throat. "Relationships. While you've been here, you've made a lot of people very happy. One person in particular."

Lottie blushed. She couldn't think about that. She couldn't think about him. She shifted in the barstool, crossing her legs, and felt the beard burn on her thighs. It was just that *not* thinking of him was impossible. He was all she seemed to want to think about.

"I appreciate that, but this job was a temporary situation, and now it's over. It's time for me to move on."

"Why?"

Lottie stared at Wyatt. His simple question was reasonable. The answer wasn't as simple.

"The circumstances that force me to leave can't be changed. Even if it seems easily done. It isn't."

Lottie stood up and slid the stool back under the counter.

"Lottie," Wyatt stood and met her gaze. His eyes were steely and hard. "I'm going to step out of line and say something that is neither my place nor my business. But I need to say it. He's in love with you."

Lottie's mouth fell open a scant inch, and a long breath escaped in a puff of emotion that pushed tears to her eyes.

"You didn't think it was a secret, did you?" he continued. "You two try so hard not to look like you're in love with one another. It's the only thing anyone can think when they see you together. The glances you give, those secret little touches you think no one notices. We noticed, Lottie. Don't get me wrong—we're not mad about it. It's about time Ian had someone who loves him, someone he loves. Lord knows he deserves it. And he's going to ask you to stay. Hell, I'd bet my house he's going to beg you to stay."

A single tear slipped down Lottie's cheek. She quickly brushed it away and cleared her throat, desperate to try to regain her composure again. She could not hear this. Wyatt's words were cutting through her heart like a razor.

"I just explained that I can't stay," Lottie managed to croak out. Her voice clogged with the tears she forbid to fall.

"Did you know when I decided to become a vet?" Wyatt asked. The sudden change of topic forced Lottie to do a double-take and concentrate harder on his words. "I was fourteen. I accidentally caught a rabbit in a trap designed for coyotes. It had broken her leg. Kip tried to convince me to put her in a stew pot, but I wanted to make it up to her. I wanted to mend her leg and see her back to her family again. My father helped me tend to her. She stayed in this one corner of her cage. She trembled and shook nonstop for days. It took a while for her to realize that I wanted to help her. You look just like she did in those first few days, Lottie. You look positively scared to death."

Lottie felt utterly exposed. Was she so transparent? She'd tried so hard to guard her heart. To mask her fear, her emotions. To keep her secrets secret. The fact that she was so easy to see through was frightening and disturbing. She couldn't do this. He would find her for sure. She said nothing in response to Wyatt's observations, however. She wouldn't confirm them. She was the duck again. Paddling furiously under the water and remaining stoic in view of the world.

"So, I get that maybe I'm not the person you want to tell. I'm OK with that. But, Lottie, you need someone to bear the burden with you. It won't make the weight any lighter or the journey any shorter, but just knowing that someone somewhere understands is enough to give you the strength to face whatever or whoever it is that you're running from."

Lottie fisted her hands to hide their violent shaking. He knew she was running. He knew she was running from someone. She worked to mask the fear from showing on her face. She turned to look behind her, worried Ian would walk in at any moment and force her to divulge more than she could.

"Your concerns are appreciated," the duck in her replied. "And it is a wonderful notion." She turned to leave and got two steps before she heard Wyatt's voice again.

"He's not here," he said simply. When she turned back around to glance at him, she noticed he'd stuffed his hands into his pockets. "He left early. He said he had to go to Dallas today. But he asked me to tell you he'd be back around dinner time."

Lottie shrugged, hoping the small movement would convince Wyatt that she didn't care where Ian was or when he would return. It was a total lie, of course. She cared about it more than she wanted. The duck, however, kept her emotionless gaze.

"Lottie, just think about what I said. This thing between you two is something special. It's the kind of thing that doesn't come along every day. Give it a chance. Give him a chance."

"Please give Molly and the boys my best. I'd like to come by to say goodbye before I leave on Sunday," she said coolly.

Wyatt nodded sadly in response. She turned, spine straight, shoulders back, and swam up the stairs. When she was secluded behind the security of her closed bedroom door, she let herself fall onto the bed and sob.

The USO at the Dallas/Fort Worth airport seemed as familiar to Ian as his own room at Midge's farmhouse.

There were many times he'd slept on the cots upstairs or stretched out on one of the oversized recliners in front of the big screen TV to catch a bit of sleep in between planes. And the volunteers who worked behind the snack bar were always cheerful and encouraging when a combat-weary soldier needed it most. Ian recognized John's hulking figure as soon as he entered and flashed his military ID to the volunteer at the front entrance. He also recognized the older gentleman in a camouflage duty uniform standing next to him. Short white stubble topped his head. A fierce expression seemed permanently affixed around his eyes. And deep, hard lines were carved around his mouth from more years in combat than Ian had served in the army altogether. It was his former commander, Major General Tom Bradford.

"Preacher," Ian said. He gave John a light hug and slapped him hard on the back. He extended his hand to General Bradford next. "Sir," he said as a greeting.

"Hey, Ian, how's civilian life treating you?" General Bradford asked. He motioned the trio to step into a small room normally reserved for soldiers to call home via computer video chat. Today, it would be a briefing room of sorts.

"Preacher said you're a cowboy now. Wrangling cows instead of bad guys, eh?" Bradford gave a chuckle at his own joke and closed the door behind him.

Ian's heart sank into his stomach. If Bradford was here with John, the situation with Lottie was probably much worse than he could have imagined. And he was capable of imagining a lot.

"I didn't think I was special enough to merit an in-person visit," Ian said. He took a seat in a black leather side chair. Bradford propped against the desk next to the computer, and John took a second chair opposite Ian.

"Ian, Bradford is here because this situation with your nanny is part of an ongoing national security op the General is overseeing. Actually, it's been running for quite some time." Ian swallowed and tried to prepare himself for what he was about to hear.

"I've been cleared to read you in on this as need-to-know. I'll be sharing more details than I probably should, but your clearance is still good and in effect, if you understand me, soldier?"

Ian nodded. "What's going on? Is Lottie in some sort of trouble?"

John cast Bradford a hard stare and then turned his gaze back to Ian. "Lottie, is it?"

Ian nodded.

"I'm sorry, Ian. You're not going to like this. You're not going to like this at all." John leaned back in the chair.

It was Bradford who first broke the long silence that followed. "Last year, John led his team on a hunt for Middle Eastern terrorist, Mosledek Kaymar."

"I remember," Ian said. "You found more of a dying vegetable than a man, if I recall."

Bradford raised an eyebrow in John's direction. "I'll ignore how it is that *you* came to know that piece of classified information and confirm that is in fact what we found. Kaymar's body had been on life support for nearly two years. The intel gathered to even run that op suggested Kaymar was behind the attack on your team in Afghanistan. The spooks at Langley said it was some sort of retaliation for his son being killed in a poppy field burning a few years before. A poppy field burning you, John, Tex, and the other members of that team were heading up. What we now know, however, is that the Kaymar we should have been looking for, is in fact, his son, Aymil Kaymar."

"But you just said he died in the poppy field burning. He's not dead?" Ian sounded a bit surprised.

"No," John added. "And Aymil, it seems, is even more intent on taking his revenge out on U.S. soldiers. From what we've been able to gather over the past year, he's worse than his father ever was."

"Damn." Ian raked his fingers through his hair. "What does this have to do with Lottie?"

"Chatter seems to indicate that he's upped his game from simply blowing up US targets to trying to create havoc with the US economy instead. Our Russian contacts confirmed that Kaymar is up to something else. It seems it involves a deal he's trying to negotiate with Vladimir Petrov," John explained.

"Vlad apparently wants help with his arms deals and human trafficking business in the Middle East. Kaymar wants guns and the backing of the Russian mafia in Afghanistan. A union of the two organizations would arm a whole logistical network that could move people and weapons around the globe. It would keep us looking for their next target like some sort of global shell game."

"That's a lethal combination," Ian said. He scooted to the edge of his seat. He remembered hearing about Petrov before. The man was a cutthroat and a true menace. The idea that Lottie had any connection to either of these two men seemed unimaginable. "If those two join forces, they'll wreak havoc in the Middle East and across Eastern Europe."

"Yes."

"What's the buy-in? Kaymar's gotta put something big on the table to entice a thug like Petrov," Ian suggested.

John and Bradford exchanged hard glances. Ian's heart felt like it stopped. This was where Lottie came in, he thought. Shit.

"Kaymar wants to join families. He's promised a wife—his daughter—to one of Vlad's sons, a Dimitri Petrov. Bloodthirsty bastard. Papa has him running his own brand of nasty deprivation. He wants to literally unite their families to build some sort of criminal syndicate," Bradford added.

"Syndicate?" Ian flopped back in his chair again. "It would be a damn empire of death. Who's the girl?" Ian nearly choked on the words. He'd asked. But he didn't want to know. He didn't want the nightmare that was forming in his brain to be the truth. It couldn't be. Not his Lottie.

"His only daughter, at least the only one we were able to find out about, is the illegitimate child of a mistress he had about twenty-five years ago. The mistress' name was Marjorie Burnett. She fled with the child about a year after she was born and fell off the map. That is, until her obituary turned up about a year ago. Kaymar started looking for his long-lost daughter again." John took in a deep breath. Ian's stomach turned to acid.

"Jesus Christ, don't say it!" Ian demanded. He stood out of his chair so abruptly that it toppled over. His mind instantly thought of Lottie's dark chocolate brown eyes, the dark lashes, the almond shape of them against her slender European aristocratic nose. He knew the truth of what John was about to say. His heart seized.

"His daughter is a Charlotte Louise St. John, aka Charlotte Poole," John said, regret tinging his voice.

Ian's stomach churned in his throat as John continued. Christ, there was more?

"She's more than just that. Apparently, she's a countess of some European island nation off the coast of Scotland. It's called," John paused and checked his phone, "Isle of Marishol. I think that's how you say it. Her father is a George William St. John, Earl of Somesuchplace. It doesn't really matter." John paused to give his friend time to process the information.

Ian didn't even try to hide the look of anger and frustration on his face. "Is this some kind of sick joke?" Ian spat out. "Is this your idea of 'screw with the guy who left his team'? Because if it is, I swear, I'll kill you both."

"I wish it were," Bradford said, a hint of sadness in his voice. "Believe me, son. I wish it were. But it seems after learning about what you know of this girl, Kaymar may have already gotten to her."

"I don't understand," Ian said. His brain was working frantically to piece together their story with what Lottie had told him. With what he had seen and heard. Her secret meetings with some unknown man. The burner phone. Evading his questions. That shot she made with the rifle. He didn't want it to be true, but the pieces were falling together to develop a picture he didn't want to be real.

"You think Kaymar sent her to kill me," Ian said finally.

"We think that's a very real possibility. He sent an assassin to kill John last year. Her connection to a known international terrorist organization coupled with the coincidence of her ending up at your ranch. It's too much for me. You were a part of the team that burned that poppy field that nearly killed her father and a survivor of the bombing in Afghanistan. That makes you a pretty good target if you ask me."

Ian thought back to the way Lottie talked about her father and mother. The man she described sounded more like the earl than Kaymar. This couldn't be true.

"You think she's loyal to Kaymar? No way!" Ian's voice was growing louder. "She's not been playing me this whole time. I would have seen that!"

"We see what we want to see through the veil of our emotions, McGuire," Bradford said, uncrossing and then recrossing his arms.

"Bullshit!" Ian barked. "I know when someone is lying. And when someone is truly afraid. And this girl is terrified of something, of someone. There's got to be more to the story." Ian stabbed the air with his finger, punctuating his words.

"I'm afraid there is," John added. "She has a sister."

"Yeah, I know she's mentioned her. Maisie."

"Margaret Lillibeth St. John," Bradford corrected. "And we have it on good authority she's engaged to marry the next king of this Marishol, an Oliver Peerson. Turns out his head of security is Mitchell Elliott—a former member of our own Heathen Brotherhood.

"The island is sovereign, but it's a part of the British Empire. And that's a terrorist connection a bit too close to one of the United States' strongest allies. We've already been in touch with MI6 in London."

"So you're planning what?" A dark shadow crossed Ian's face, and his stomach clenched. "Jesus, you're going to take her out?" Bile rose in his throat.

"I don't think it will come to that. I'd like to bring her in. We need to talk to her. I'm sure we can sort all this out." Bradford stood and placed a steady hand on Ian's shoulder.

Ian's stare shot daggers of fury toward his old commander. Bradford's tone didn't give Ian even a little confidence that what he said was the truth. He'd heard Bradford use this tone before. He knew all too well what he'd meant when he said, "talk to her." She'd be interrogated and possibly tortured if she refused to comply. He thought back to all the tiny pink marks across her skin from their encounter last night. How easily she could be marked. Ian felt sick.

John stood. "General, perhaps if Ian could talk with her first and verify the intel we've already collected . . ." John began. "I trust his instincts, sir. If he says our intel is flawed and presumptive, then I want him to feel this out. There are still a lot of unknowns right now."

Bradford drew in a long breath. He considered John's request. "All right. See what you can find out. And keep your guard up until we get to the bottom of this," Bradford conceded. "We'll touch base with you in twenty-four hours."

Ian stormed from the room, his face a mask of fury. He didn't need twenty-four hours. He planned to get to the bottom of this tonight.

"Think his feelings for her will hinder his ability to get the truth?" Bradford questioned.

"Actually, sir, I think it'll be the exact opposite of that. I think the fact he's fallen in love with her is the best motivation. He'll uncover what she's really about. Trust me. Ian's waited a long time for this, sir. He's not about to let her go without a fight."

CHAPTER THIRTEEN

Lottie pulled the zipper of her coat to her chin and continued to walk. She started ambling nearly an hour earlier along the gravel path leading to Wyatt and Molly's house. She felt as if she'd been walking forever, and nothing seemed to be resolved in her mind. She was determined to continue to think, to walk, and to pray until the demons that plagued her were vanquished.

The sky had turned a light gray with a thick blanket of low clouds that sought to snuff out the sun. Lottie could smell the snow. Her mother had always told her that there was no way that she could smell coming snow. But Lottie always could. It had a sweet, smoky smell to her. An odd sort of magical smell. She glanced up. They didn't exactly look like snow clouds, and the weather forecasters hadn't predicted snow. Yet, her nose would not mislead her. The snow smell was most definitely there. She walked on, leaving Wyatt and Molly's house just behind her and continued south.

Lottie and her father had made a plan. And she had to stick with it. Maisie's future was at stake, as was her beloved homeland. If she was discovered . . . Lottie shivered at the thought. And yet, much of what Wyatt had said that morning played through her mind over and over again. He was right. She did love Ian. And she wanted to be honest with him. She wanted to tell him everything. The truth was, she needed to tell someone. She needed at least one person to know.

"Lottie!" She heard her name in the wind. It sounded so far away. It sounded like Ian's voice. She turned in the direction it came to see Ian slamming the door to his truck. He stuffed his hands into his jacket pockets and walked quickly to catch up with her. "I've been looking all over for you."

Lottie smiled. She'd been anxious and worried. She debated and searched for answers. And with just the sight of him, she felt better. Just knowing he was there made her feel brave and safe and . . . she realized she did trust him. She could.

His eyes smiled at her. And just that one glance made it better. She was still scared. Her circumstances hadn't changed. But Wyatt had been right. Sharing the burden made her capable of carrying what she'd been given. Just seeing his face, just hearing his voice, knowing he'd been looking for her—she knew. She knew at that exact moment. She was going to tell Ian everything.

"You're a long way from home, love. Are you OK?"

Lottie nodded. "I just needed to clear my head and think."

"Can I walk a while with you? I want to talk to you."

"Yes. I'd like that. There are some things I need to tell you too, Ian." She swallowed and prayed she had the strength to do it when the opportunity presented itself.

He was glad he'd found her. And even more thankful she was alone. Although why she'd walked so far from Midge's, he couldn't figure. He was still struggling to process what John and General Bradford had shared. He was determined to get the truth from her. And for that, he'd need her alone.

Ian fell into step beside Lottie. She looked cold. He wanted to put his arm around her. But until he knew the truth, he couldn't. Not until he knew whether Bradford and John's suspicions were right.

"I want to talk to you about last night," he started.

"Oh," Lottie tucked her hands into her coat pockets. "That's a splendid idea. We'll launch straight into the awkward conversation. Then we can move to humiliating and conclude with impossible."

"Lottie." Ian turned his head and looked into her eyes. Her eyes were swollen and red. She'd been crying. He couldn't think of a single assassin in all his years who ever had. He was right to trust his gut about her. And he was going to prove it, not only to himself but to John and the US government too.

"There's no need for you to feel awkward, baby. Last night, I wanted you. You know that, right?"

Lottie smiled. "Yes."

"And I enjoyed you very much. The reason I brought it up was that I wanted to apologize."

Lottie's breath appeared in a white puff of smoke in front of her mouth. She was walking quickly to keep her body warm. "What for?"

"For marking you. I didn't mean to be so . . ." Ian didn't know what he wanted to say. He hadn't thought he'd been rough with her, but he left her with so many bright pink marks on her skin.

"Oh, please don't," Lottie said softly. "Last night was wonderful. My skin has always marked easily. You needn't feel bad. You didn't hurt me."

Ian let out a breath. "Good, I was a little concerned when I left you."

Lottie smiled to reassure him. They continued to walk in silence for several long minutes before Ian spoke again. He'd been considering exactly how to begin to ask her the questions that had been burning in his brain for hours since he and Bradford had spoken.

"I was hoping to get a chance to talk with you about something else too."

"About what?"

"Your family."

"My family?" Lottie looked confused.

"Yeah. Tell me about your father," Ian started.

"I've told you about him," Lottie said with a lighthearted laugh.

"What's his name?" Ian asked simply. He wanted his voice to sound innocent, non-threatening. He hoped it did, anyway. He just wanted to hear the truth. To learn her secrets. To know it was safe to love her. Because he already knew he did.

"George," Lottie replied simply.

Second to None

"George Poole?" Ian asked.

"Yes, of course," Lottie answered. She was beginning to show signs of closing herself off to him. And that wasn't a good sign as to how the rest of this conversation would go.

She cast her gaze away when she answered. She spoke too softly. Ian drew in a deep breath. He had to keep going. He had to know. He only had twenty-four hours.

"Tell me about him."

"I already told you. He likes to shoot clays. He and my mother were very much in love. He is a wonderful father."

"I would like to meet him," he said. As soon as the words left Ian's mouth, the first snowflakes started to fall.

"I knew it smelled like snow," Lottie said, her voice lifting to a happier tone now.

"What did you just say?"

"I could smell the snow. I know, you think I'm a bit mad. But I assure you, I can smell it."

"I can too," Ian said. "My team used to think I was nuts. But my nose was never wrong. I started smelling it the day you got here."

Ian recalled that day. He'd misjudged Lottie from the moment she'd stepped off the plane. He'd thought her a cold-hearted snob of a woman ill-suited to care for his nephews. But she turned out to be a woman scared of something or someone that threatened to take away everything she loved. He'd changed his mind the moment she'd apologized to him that first day. She hadn't been beneath humbling herself or doing the right thing. And it occurred to him that he'd never apologized for misjudging her.

Lottie gave him a playful wink. "I just knew there was something about you."

Ian reached over and took her hand in his. Her fingers felt like ice. The snow began to fall faster now. He picked up their pace.

"I think we should turn back," Lottie said, worry and trepidation edging her words. "The snow is really coming down. We're a long way from Midge's. Maybe we could make it as far as Wyatt and Molly's if we hurry. Although, I'm not certain they have returned from their trip to the city yet."

Ian turned and stared hard at her. Fat snowflakes fell around her face in a swirl, seeming to cling to one another as they dropped closer to the ground. They clung to her hair and her thick dark lashes in white mounds. She looked angelic.

"I don't want to go backward with you, Lottie. Let's just keep moving forward together. OK?" His words had a double meaning. He didn't want to go back to the house. He wanted to take her to the fishing camp. He didn't want to let her slink back into her shell of secrets. He wanted her to come out into the light with him. Because that's where he was now. He was in the light. Her light. And he wasn't going to just give that up.

Lottie gave his hand a squeeze, and they began walking again.

The snow swirled around them as the wind picked up. "I'm so cold," Lottie finally said. Ian felt her hands trembling in his. He practically dragged her along with him.

"There's a little fishing shack just up ahead," he said, pointing. "Near the lake. We can stop there and shelter until this blows over."

Lottie looked up to where he was pointing. She squinted through the mist of swirling snow. "Are you certain? I can't see anything."

"Trust me."

They continued to walk until the snow made a thick blanket over their boots. Ian could already feel the wetness of it seeping through, soaking his socks. Lottie's feet would be freezing. He had to get her to the fishing camp as soon as he could.

The blizzard enveloped them in minutes. Ian finally got them to the one-room cabin of the fishing camp just as the temperatures seemed to plummet. The inside of the cabin was dark and cold. But it was dry and out of the wind.

The snow began to swirl thick and fast through the window of the cabin. The ground would soon be completely covered. Lottie shivered, and her teeth clacked together. Ian too felt numbness starting to edge at his fingers, face, and toes.

"I'll get a fire started." Ian moved to the large stove in the center of the cabin. In moments, a warm blaze was glowing. Ian rubbed Lottie's arms and hands as they warmed themselves beside it.

The cabin was nothing like the shack Wyatt had described to him. When they had come to drop off Brandon's supplies, he'd found it was more like a one-room house. There was a small bedroom with a large king-sized bed and a tiny bathroom with a sink, toilet, and shower. The main area of the cabin had a small kitchen area with a sink, two cooking eyes, and a microwave. There was a central stove for heat with a table and two chairs to one side. On the other side, a sofa hugged a wall that separated the main living area from the bedroom. It was simple and rustic. And Ian thought it probably served its purpose quite well.

Lottie looked around, but her gaze was drawn back to the storm outside the window. It had come up so quickly, laying a couple of inches down in the half-hour it took them to walk to the fishing camp. It was coming down in thick sheets. Stiff winds blew swirls of it as it fell. Fresh white powder was then blown back onto the cold earth. It almost gave the illusion that the snow was actually falling up.

Lottie's ears and hands flamed to a bright cherry red. She rubbed her arms, continuing to coax warmth back into her body.

Ian found a bottle of bourbon and poured a finger's width into two glasses. He laid them on the table in front of the stove. "It looks like we may be here a while. Come sit down."

Lottie sat and sipped the bourbon. Ian took a healthy swallow of his and cleared his throat. Good bourbon had no burn, just warmth. And that was just what this had delivered.

"I'm glad we're alone here," he started. "There's something I need to tell you, and I didn't want the distractions of so many people around."

Lottie played at the rim of her cup. She twirled the glass as long ribbons of honey-colored liquid pulled along the sides of it.

Ian remained silent while she kept her gaze fixated on the glass. When she finally looked up into his face, he started.

"I'm in love with you." The words were short, easy to pronounce, and had been heard countless times in his own head. But saying them out loud for some reason took more effort than Ian thought he could muster. He watched Lottie's eyes grow wide. "And I want us to be together."

Firelight danced on the shimmering pools that suddenly appeared at the rim of her lashes. She blinked, forcing them back, but said nothing.

"Lottie?" Ian said. His voice was low and soft. "Why can't we be together? What is it, love? I need you to tell me."

Lottie shook her head vigorously. Her lips twisted into tight lines, and the dam of tears burst, allowing a steady stream to streak down her face.

Ian stood, extracted a matte black .45 caliber pistol from his back, and laid it on the table. The grip faced Lottie. She could reach it easily. Her eyes grew wide in shock, and she stared up at him.

"Are you mad?" She gasped. She pushed away from the table.

"Are you here to kill me, Lottie? Is that what this whole thing has been about? If you have a job to do, do it. I want the last thing you hear from me to be the truth. And the truth is that I love you." The words somehow felt easier to say. But Lottie's face was a twisted mask of fear and disappointment that kept the acid churning in his gut.

"What on earth are you talking about?"

"Who is your father, Lottie?" Ian asked again. His voice was firm but not unkind.

"I told you. Why do you keep asking me? I already told you!" Lottie's tears came faster, and she swiped at her cheeks in a fevered effort to staunch the flow.

"You said he was George Poole. What does he do?" Ian's jaw flexed. Why was she continuing to lie to him?

"Why do you care?" Lottie stared at the gun on the table. Then looked back up at Ian.

"I want to know how a man affords to find time to shoot, take his children traveling all over Europe, has the money to afford cashmere sweaters and handmade Italian leather loafers for his daughter. A daughter, I may add, who has to work as a nanny to pay her bills."

"What business is it of yours?"

"Who is he, Lottie?"

"Stop!" Lottie screamed. She shoved the table, pressing it into Ian's stomach with a hard *thunk*. Her glass tipped, and bourbon spilled across the table.

"Lottie, look at me." Ian's fist pounded on the table, sending droplets of drink splashing. "All I want is for you to tell me the truth."

"I . . . I can't," Lottie finally choked out. She shook her head and knotted her fingers in her lap.

Ian stood from the table and paced two steps away and then two steps back. Sweat was beading along his spine. He slipped off his jacket and threw it against the sofa along the long wall. The zipper hit the wall with a loud snap, forcing Lottie to jump in her chair. She was terrified. Of what? Of him? Or of what Kaymar had sent her there to do?

Ian raked his fingers through his hair. It was still damp from the snow. "Who is Aymil Kaymar, Lottie?"

At the sound of his name, Lottie's eyes widened to the size of tea saucers. She inhaled sharply, and Ian saw her entire body begin to tremble violently.

"He's your father, isn't he?"

Lottie sobbed. Her shoulders shook. Tears streamed down her face. Her voice was strained, and she coughed her words between sobs. "That monster is *not* my father!"

Ian studied her face. Her eyes held fear; that much was certain. But there was more. There was . . . there was fury there too. There was a rage behind her glare that Ian had never seen in her before.

"He is, isn't he?"

Lottie shook her head. "My father is a good man."

"What is his name, Lottie?"

"George . . . George St. John." Lottie slumped forward as if the truth had been pulled forth from her physically.

Ian let out a long breath. Finally. Some truth. Small bits would make the larger parts of her story easier to tell. He glanced at his watch. Time was slipping away from him too quickly.

"Who is he, baby? Tell me." Ian tried to keep the desperation from his voice, but he still sounded as if he were pleading. And he supposed he was. But he didn't even care anymore.

"My father is the nineteenth Duke of Carmichael on the Isle of Marishol, a sovereign nation under the protection of Her Majesty's Realm."

Ian's shoulders went slack. It was true. Bradford and John were telling the truth. Heat pressed at his cheeks. Was she sent here to kill him, then? Was she really Kaymar's unwilling assassin?

"Who is Aymil Kaymar?"

Lottie remained silent. It felt as if hours ticked by before she finally spoke. Her voice was quiet. "Kaymar is a madman. A deviant of humanity that doesn't deserve the right to draw a breath." Her hands shook. But this time, Ian could see it was with anger, not fear. If Aymil Kaymar had been in the room with them, he had no doubt she would have killed him with her bare hands. Was he blackmailing her then?

"My mother was kidnapped from her home when she was only fifteen. Kaymar bought her. He abused my mother in every way a man can abuse a woman." Ian saw the pallor of her face turn from a cherry red of rage to a sickening green of disgust. "When she became pregnant as a result of his . . . abuses, she was sent to live with his family in Syria. A cousin there helped her escape him."

Ian swallowed. This wasn't the story he'd been expecting. "Is he forcing you to be here, Lottie?"

She shook her head. Ian walked around the table and stood over her. Her body was slumped forward, her eyes staring emptily into the knots of her fingers twisted in her lap. His hand went to her head, and he stroked her hair softly. He spoke again, his voice a whisper.

"Did he send you here to kill me?"

She looked up into his face with an expression of outrage and confusion. "What? No! It's you he's sent to kill me. Or to take me back to him. Isn't it?"

Ian's brow crinkled in bewilderment. "Why does Kaymar want you dead?"

Lottie shook her head. "I don't know. I didn't even know who he was until after my mother died."

Ian continued to wear his puzzled expression.

"Kaymar apparently saw her obituary in the *London Times*. He found her parents—my grandparents—such as they are, and nearly beat them to death, searching for me. That's when my father told me the truth about my mother. And I left. If Kaymar was looking for me, I couldn't allow him to use me against my family."

"Why? What's so important about your family? How could he use you?"

"My sister."

"Maisie?"

Lottie nodded and sniffled. "She's arranged to be married to Oliver Peerson. He's a very close family friend, practically a brother to me, and the heir to the throne of Marishol. He's also a cousin to Queen Elizabeth. It's a remote connection, but it's there. And Kaymar could use me to get Oliver to do things. Horrible things. I can't allow that. I won't!" Lottie's face was indignant.

Ian could see her racing pulse throb against the protruding vein in her temple. "That's why I had to leave. Why I had to become Charlotte Poole."

Ian groaned inwardly. "That's why you were so scared the night I found Brandon in the barn? You thought Kaymar's men had found you?" Lottie nodded the confession.

"Why didn't you tell me?"

"Oh, yes. That would have been a spectacular idea." Lottie's voice lifted to a shrill, sarcastic snark. "Let me go crawling to you in the middle of the night to confess that a known killer is stalking me just a short walk from your sister and her family. I would have been sacked like that." Lottie snapped her fingers. "And that would have been the end of Charlotte Poole. What was going to happen to me then? There was no way the agency would have me and no other after everyone found out I'm the bastard of a monster."

Ian stared at her sympathetically. She was right.

"No, I have to keep everyone safe." Lottie glanced at the door and then back at the pistol lying in a puddle of bourbon on the table. "How did you know?" she asked suddenly.

"My meeting in Dallas today. I have friends who . . . who know things. I needed to know what you were hiding."

"What even made you think I was hiding anything?"

Ian crossed his arms over his chest. "You sneak off to meet with strange men. You had a burner phone. No personal things in your room. You wear clothes and talk like a princess, but you make less than twenty thousand a year."

Lottie's mouth fell open. "You were spying on me? You went through my room?" Outrage fueled the pink back into her cheeks.

"I'm not going to apologize for what I did. You were very close to my family. And I was—" Lottie cut him off.

"You were what? You were suspicious of me because my family had money and I met a friend in town? You had no right! You've ruined everything, Ian. Now everyone is in danger."

Ian considered her words. She was right . . . again. Now that John and Bradford had a connection, it wouldn't be long before Kaymar knew to start searching the US for a nanny named Charlotte Poole. Chatter worked both ways. He'd learned that early on in his army special forces career. Most CIA assets played both sides against one another. War was their stock and trade.

"Lottie, I'm sorry. I want to help. The men I met with today can—"

In a flash, Lottie snatched the pistol from the table and pointed it at Ian. He took two steps back and raised his hands up in an act of surrender. Shit. He hadn't expected this.

"You have helped enough, Mr. McGuire," she said through gritted teeth.

Ian glanced at the pistol. She flicked the safety off. He knew it was loaded. A round had already been chambered. All she had to do was squeeze the trigger. And after seeing what she did to the bobcat, he had no doubt she wouldn't miss him standing at point-blank range.

"Lottie, please put the weapon down. I can help you. I want to help you."

Her grip remained steady on the gun, tears still streaming down her cheeks.

"I wasn't lying before when I said I loved you. I do. And I want us to be together. I can help you with Kaymar, and we can—"

"Shut up!" she screamed. "There is nothing you can do. There's nothing anyone can do."

Ian lowered his arms and took a half step closer. "Lottie, do you love me?" His voice was soft and his words gentle.

Lottie's hands began to shake. Her tears came harder. "It doesn't matter."

"It matters to me."

She shook her head, and the aim of the gun dipped lower. If she fired now, the round would go into the floor.

"This wasn't part of the plan," she said, straightening her spine and raising the weapon again. "You weren't part of the plan, Ian. I wasn't supposed to like you. I was supposed to take care of three little boys and move on."

"But something happened, didn't it?"

Lottie nodded her head. The gun dipped again. "I . . . I couldn't—"

"I couldn't help it either," Ian finished for her. "Lottie, my whole life, I've been running and fighting. The last twelve years have been nothing but war and pain. You have been the light for something completely different. When I'm with you, I finally feel at peace. I finally feel hopeful. I can't let you go. I need you."

Lottie just shook her head again. "I'm so sorry, Ian. I truly, truly am. But you have to let me go."

Lottie raised the pistol again. Ian watched as she let out a long breath. "I do love you," she whispered. Her voice so soft, Ian barely heard her. Then, she squeezed the trigger, and the gun exploded with a bang.

CHAPTER FOURTEEN

Lottie pushed through the door of the cabin and into the swirls of white snow. The cold stung her nose. She pulled her scarf up over her ears and nose. Sharp shards of ice mixed with the snow cut at her eyelids. She had to keep them partially closed, but she pressed forward. She needed to get back to Midge's.

If she hurried, she could return, call for help for Ian, and get out of town before they all returned from the city. She had the emergency cash hidden. That could get her a ticket out of town. She'd decided to take the bus. She'd go north and contact her agency. They could have a place for her in a day or two. Then at least she could have a place to stay. For a little while anyway.

Lottie's booted feet sank into the snow. It fell in wet clumps over the toe of her shoe. Cold, wet, melted snow soaked through. Her feet were numb in minutes. But she kept moving. Ian needed help.

Ian. His face. His voice. It replayed in her mind over and over as she pushed against the howling wind. It whistled in her ears through her thin scarf. He loved her. His eyes were tender and sincere when he'd said it. Every time he'd said it. She had known. She'd known he loved her and that she, too, had been falling in love with him. But the idea was so impossible she didn't want to admit it. Not to herself and not to him.

Lottie stopped and stamped the snow from her boots. Her socks were soaked, and her toes numb from cold. Her fingers too had changed from the bright red to a pale blue color. She blew against them and stuffed them back into her pockets. The thin polyester lining offered no warmth against the biting cold.

She forced her eyes open. Looking around, all she could see was white. Swirls of snow stung her eyes. There was a dark shadow ahead. Were they trees? Were those the cluster of cottonwoods that bordered the pond behind Wyatt and Molly's house? Was she even headed in the right direction? She looked behind her. The cabin she'd left was gone behind a curtain of white. She had to keep going.

She needed to keep moving. She needed to get help to him. The man she loved more than she ever thought possible. The man she'd shot and left in a spreading pool of blood on the cabin floor.

Lottie pushed her feet through the snow. Her toes were frozen. Her hands, ears, and face stung from the bitter cold. Fierce wind blew snow at her from seemingly every direction. Her tears were almost instantly frozen on her face. The temperature continued to drop. She needed to find shelter. Soon.

The problem was she couldn't tell where on the ranch she was anymore. She felt as if she'd been walking for a long time, and yet there was no sign of Wyatt and Molly's house or the gravel drive that lead to Midge's. Had she gone the right way? She couldn't be sure. She turned but could no longer see the lake, the cabin, or the shadowy trees that had just moments ago dotted the horizon. There was no longer a visible horizon.

Lottie was ready to give up. If she just sat down right here, the ice and cold could take her. She would no longer be a threat to her sister, her father, or their family. Ian could mourn, if he wanted, and move on with his life. Oh Lord, Ian! She had meant to only graze him, but when she saw his body fall back and a pool of blood ooze across the rug, she wondered if, for the first time, she'd actually missed. He was alive when she left, but she knew he needed help. Soon. She had to keep going. For his sake. She had to get to Molly and Wyatt's.

Lottie began to walk again, this time turning to her left. She remembered reading in one of Maisie's survival books that right-handed people tend to drift to the right when walking through wilderness paths. This was no wilderness, but Lottie felt lost and needed to do something, anything to get help to Ian. Beneath the snow, Lottie's foot slipped on the edge of a stone. Off balance, the wind made short work of tossing her onto her side; her hands and face were instantly soaked from the wet, cold ground. Lottie sobbed. She couldn't walk anymore. She was too cold. Too desperate. She cried until darkness and cold surrounded her, and everything went from a white swirl to utter blackness.

CHAPTER FOURTEEN

Ian's limp body stretched across the cabin floor. He let out a soft moan and then rolled to his side. His head throbbed. He touched his temple to feel a pool of warm, sticky blood above his brow. He winced with pain at the slight touch.

"Damn it," he cursed himself. "She shot me!"

He slowly climbed to his feet and dug through the cabinet in the kitchen for the first aid kit and quickly cleaned and dressed his wound with a butterfly bandage. The round had merely grazed him. He knew she'd done it on purpose. If she wanted him dead, she wouldn't have missed from that distance. Not with the way she could shoot.

Ian's head was pulsing as he tried to organize his thoughts. How long had he been lying on the floor? Lottie was outside in what was most definitely a blizzard, and she had no idea where she was on the ranch.

Ian checked his watch and stuffed his arms into his coat. He slid on a pair of leather work gloves he'd kept in his pockets. He grabbed a flashlight and headed outside.

The force of the wind pushed the door against him violently. It nearly slapped him in the face. Lord, this was a storm. And Lottie was out in it alone. It was nearly impossible to see a foot in front of him. She was sure to be lost out in all of this. And armed, he thought as he glanced down, only to see his gun half covered in snow on the window ledge outside.

"Damn it, Lottie," he cursed again. Ian carefully tied a rope to his boot and secured the other to a heavy log at the bottom of the woodpile. If he got turned around, at least he could find his way back to the cabin and start again. He stepped out, the snow on the ground now already covering the top of his foot and any footprints she might have left.

"Lottie!" he cried out. His voice was seized by the fierce wind and silenced before it traveled beyond the edge of the cabin walls. Ian started in the direction they had come, hoping she'd head back to Midge's house. The snow was mixed with shards of ice that scratched at his face. He pulled his coat around his neck tighter. He called for her again and again. And again. The only sound he could hear was the roar of the blizzard wind.

He walked and screamed for her until his feet and legs were numb and his voice hoarse. He was nearly ready to turn around and start searching in another direction. The tether around his boot should nearly be about to run out.

He shielded his eyes to focus on what looked like something bright blue sticking up out of the snow. Lottie's coat was blue. His eyes watered from the freezing wind. He couldn't make it out. He took a step closer when the rope pulled against his foot. He groped around through the snow and found a small stone. His fingers were numb and stiff. The simple act of untying the rope and securing it to the stone was slow, painful work. Finally, he was able to take a few steps forward to examine the dark mound.

"Lottie!" Ian screamed, rolling her to face him. Her eyes were closed, and her body felt frozen. She opened her blistered lips to speak.

"Thank God." That was all he needed to know. She was alive. "C'mon, baby. I've got you." Ian hoisted Lottie into his arms. Using his rope as a guide, he reached the cabin again in little time. And a little time was all he had.

Lottie had stopped shivering, and her body was limp in his arms. Her breath became shallow.

Ian kicked the door of the cabin open, a burst of heat and light engulfing them. He stoked the dying flames in the stove and set to work, peeling away the wet clothes from Lottie's body. Her ivory skin looked burned from the cold—her toes and lips tinged with blue. He wrapped the comforters from the bed around her and laid her on the mattress he'd dragged from the bedroom to the floor in front of the fire. Then, shedding his own wet clothes, he laid his shivering body next to hers. Ian rubbed her skin, coaxing the heat back into her blood until exhausted, and he fell asleep with her in his arms.

Ian awoke to the sound of the wind whistling and howling outside the cabin. He examined Lottie. She was still asleep, but her breathing was better, the color was back in her lips, and her pulse was strong. Whether unconscious or not, he couldn't be sure. He stroked her cheek and her hair. It was still damp. He checked his watch. They'd slept for two hours. He felt her limbs and carefully examined her fingers, ears, and feet. She seemed to be OK, although her skin was still ice cold.

"Lottie," Ian spoke firmly. "Lottie, love. Wake up for me, OK? I just need to know you're OK."

Lottie stirred and blinked her eyes, letting them fall closed again. She parted her lips and tried to speak. Ian rubbed a fist across her sternum—a trick doctors used to annoy patients who would just as soon fall into the grip of sleep than force themselves to wake. And she needed to wake up. He needed to know he'd reached her in time. He needed her to be all right. He needed her.

"I . . ." Lottie licked her lips and stammered out, "I shot you."

Ian let a sigh of relief push from his mouth. He leaned forward and kissed her. It was a soft, slow kiss that ignited heat in his heart.

"Yes, you did," he uttered softly.

It took him nearly a half-hour to get her fully awake. She was tired and freezing, but she was going to be all right. Ian gathered her up in his arms and held her close.

"Ian," she finally asked when the tremors of cold eased. "I—"

But he wouldn't allow her to finish.

Lottie felt the haze of the cold begin to abate. Her skin burned as her blood warmed and heated her fingers and toes again. He had come for her. She shot him, and he saved her.

Lottie watched his naked body as he skimmed through the firelight to the kitchen. He lit two oil lamps. Warm yellow light cast soft shadows along the cabin walls. In the faint glow, she could see long and lean legs. His time in the saddle had produced thighs that could have passed for tree trunks, Lottie thought to herself. His backside was tight and curved upward to a back rippled in muscles and sprinkled with scars. He turned around and carried two plastic cups and a bottle back to the mattress, letting his semi-hard rod fall from side to side as he walked toward her. Lottie blinked, thinking he certainly knew how to make heat course through a woman's body.

When he'd tucked himself back under the comforters beside her, and the two had each taken a sip of their water, Ian spoke.

"I thought I'd lost you," he said softly, taking her hand in his. Her fingers were still cold, and his hand felt warm, almost hot, against her chilled skin. "I'm so sorry, Lottie."

"I told you to let me go. He's going to find me and you, and Molly and the boys—"

Ian silenced her with a gentle touch of his finger against her mouth.

"I love you. That means that I will always come after you. Always." Ian kissed her softly again. He sighed. "I need to confess something to you."

Lottie looked at him expectantly. What in the world could he possibly say to add to her grief? She was scared to imagine. But she nodded to encourage him to continue.

"I know why Kaymar is looking for you."

"What do you mean?"

"Drink some more," Ian encouraged. He waited while Lottie swallowed more water. She had the feeling she was going to need the bourbon again to deal with whatever Ian was about to tell her. He had a worried look on his face that sent waves of unease through her body.

Ian picked up the hand he was holding and kissed the back of it. The feel of his lips on her skin seemed to be a tonic to her unsteady nerves. Whatever he was about to say, it wasn't going to change how he felt about her. And that, Lottie realized, gave her great comfort.

"He means to trade you," Ian said flatly. "I don't know how else to say it."

"Trade me?" Lottie looked horrified. "For what?"

"An alliance." Ian took in a long breath. His muscles flexed and tightened as if he was stealing himself for what he knew he must say. "You're to be given in marriage to a Russian mobster's son in exchange for arms, political influence, that kind of thing."

His jaw twitched as he spat out the words. Lottie felt him squeezing her hand as he spoke, the anger of his words obvious in his body's reaction.

Lottie felt sick. "My God!" she nearly screamed. She tried to scramble to her feet. "I have to . . . I have to go. I need to . . ."

"Relax," Ian said. He wrapped one arm tightly around her, pulling her closer. His fingers began slowly stroking the skin along her upper arm. "That's not going to happen. I'm not going to let it."

"You? How can you stop this?" Lottie said. Ian was strong. He was well-muscled and acted like he could hold his own against anyone who tried to threaten him. But stopping Kaymar was something else entirely. No matter how much he thought he loved her, no matter how much he wanted to, he couldn't protect her from him. No one could. Terror forced her to tremble again.

"I wasn't always a cowboy, Lottie. I have experience with bastards like him. They're the kind of men responsible for the death of my brothers." Ian held her tighter.

"Brothers? What are you talking about, Ian?" Lottie demanded.

"I wasn't just in the army, Lottie. I was a special forces operator. A good one, too." Ian closed his eyes. Lottie watched as his face squeezed and then relaxed as if he were willing himself to forget something painful—to push it away to focus on her. Now.

"About a year and a half ago, I was on a mission in Afghanistan. My team walked into an ambush. An IED took out three members of my team. My brothers."

He shook his head, and one side of his mouth quirked upward. "You know, I haven't been able to say that without crying—until now. I didn't even get the whole story out to Molly after it happened." He gazed into Lottie's eyes. The hurt of the memory shining through the love that was there for her.

"Do you see? You make me able to face all of that darkness." He kissed her temple.

Lottie let her head rest on Ian's bare chest and touched an opaque puff of a scar above his nipple.

"Were you injured?" Lottie asked quietly. She wondered if the scars she touched were from the attack. Or were they from others? She didn't want to think about Ian hurt. But she knew he had been.

"Yes."

"Is that why you came here, to Oklahoma?"

"It is. Molly and Wyatt were kind enough to take in a broken-down soldier. And I was thankful enough to let them."

"But you're well now, aren't you?"

"Physically, yes. But living through that over and over, watching my brothers die year after year, I was so weary of death, Lottie. I wanted some peace. Kaymar was behind the bombing. And after the survivors got home, he tried to have my team leader killed, my best friend, John. In the process, John's father was murdered. The world lost a good man. And it was more death. More loss. I know you think I don't know what he's capable of. Trust me, I do. And you should know that I am capable of keeping you safe."

Lottie let a long silence stretch out between them. They sat and listened to the wind roaring and the gentle crackle of the wood burning in the stove.

"You deserve to be safe too," she said finally. "And to find that peace you're looking for."

Ian kissed her temple and leaned his head against hers. "I have."

Lottie snuggled her body closer to Ian's.

"I want you, Lottie. All of you. But I have to know who that is and know I can trust you. And you have to trust me. Without trust, there can be no true commitment. No love. No peace."

"You were right to follow me when I met my father." Lottie thought about how scared she had been when she'd learned he'd come all the way to America to check on her. He'd taken a terrible risk. But seeing him had filled her with hope. His love and comfort had given her strength. Was that the way she made Ian feel? The idea was overwhelming.

"Your father? He was the man you met at the inn and the bookstore?"

"It was my father. And you should know, he was suspicious of you too. You asked too many questions." Lottie gave a soft snort of amusement at knowing the two men she loved most were willing to do so much to keep her safe.

"How did your mother escape Kaymar?" Ian asked. His hands caressed her softly, rough callouses gently scratching her skin. "And when did she meet your father?"

"Even my father doesn't know how my mother got away. That was a secret she took with her. But she did get away. We did. I was told we boarded a ship bound for England. But it was forced to make port in Marishol for emergency repairs after it weathered a brutal storm. Mother and I got off, and we never looked back. She met my father a year later, working as a gardener. They married, and Maisie was born when I was nearly five."

"Which makes her . . . what, twenty years old now?"

"Yes, twenty-one this spring, and old enough by Marisholian law to fulfill the marriage contract my parents wrote for her to Ollie."

"The heir?"

"Yes. You can see how Kaymar could use a connection to a royal family of the realm to his advantage, I'm sure."

"Yes, I can." His fingers pressed harder on her skin as his emotions ran through his body.

"Lottie, you don't have to keep running if you don't want to. You can be safe here with me."

Lottie closed her eyes and listened to the sound of his heart beating in his chest, the soft thudding of it curling around her like a cocoon. She never wanted to leave him. But she couldn't stay. When the storm was over, and they were back home, she would have to leave.

Her circumstances were worse with Ian knowing, not better. But for now, she was just going to enjoy love while she could. There would never be another man like Ian. She wouldn't want anyone else. So she wanted to love him while she could. It would all be over too soon.

"It looks like I'm stuck with you for a while here anyway," Lottie said sweetly. She hoped he wouldn't detect her effort to skirt away from making a commitment to stay.

"Yeah, that storm came out of nowhere."

Ian's hand moved over Lottie's back and down to her hip. He smoothed his fingertips over her bare flesh.

"How long do you think we'll be here waiting it out?" She let her fingers tickle their way down to the rippled planes of his stomach and felt the muscles bunch together under her touch. Although she couldn't see it, she knew the hardness that was growing there.

"Long enough," Ian replied with a seductive grin.

CHAPTER FIFTEEN

Ian sat up and leaned back against the sofa. He tapped the mattress between his spread legs inviting Lottie to nestle herself between them. She leaned back against him, her hair brushing against his chest like silk. It felt every bit as erotic as he imagined it would.

He was going to make love to her. But he wanted to go slowly. He wanted to take his time and savor every second they had.

Lottie cocked her head to the side and looked up into Ian's dark eyes. Sparks of flame from the oil lamps and the light from the wood-burning stove flickered in them like embers over a bonfire. Heat coiled in his belly. Benedict Arnold, it seemed, was on fire. His fingers instinctively moved to caress her stomach. He drew lazy circles against her skin. It felt like velvet.

Ian leaned forward and kissed her gently. It was just a single kiss. He didn't taste her or urge her mouth open.

He just simply kissed her and let a breathy moan float from his throat.

"I love you. And I want us to be together. I need you to understand that."

Lottie stared back in silence. She simply offered him a sultry smile in answer and leaned up, kissing him again.

Ian let his hand drift upward to her breast. They weren't overly large, but he loved the feel of them in his palms. Her body instantly responded to his touch. Benedict twitched.

Her nipples tightened into hard buds at his first caress. Lottie hummed her approval and let her spine relax against Ian's belly.

"I want you to trust me, Lottie."

"Do you trust me?" she asked shyly.

"Well, you had the chance to shoot me, and you just grazed me. You did that on purpose."

"I never miss," Lottie teased.

Ian tweaked her nipple and forced a squeal from her. His body was beginning to ache with the need to have her.

"I want to make love to you. I want to show you that you are the one I can't live without, baby. You. I want forever with you. "

Lottie shook her head.

Ian massaged his large hands over her body. They caressed her hips and her outer thighs, then slid inward over the curve of them and stroked upward. His touch was dangerously close to her center. But he couldn't go further without her consent.

"I can't be with you forever, Ian. You deserve . . ." Lottie's words dissolved into a soft purr as Ian let his hand drift over the top of her thigh and urged her legs apart. "You deserve someone who can give you what you want. I can't."

"You are what I want. Nothing else," Ian said. She opened for him just a tiny inch. But he wanted more. Using both hands, he pressed her open farther. He snaked his fingers between her legs and allowed them to drift over the tiny tuft of moist springy curls between her legs. She was so warm. One long finger probed through the curls to feel the moisture that had gathered for him.

"God, you're wet for me already," he said. He couldn't keep the sultry growl from his voice. His erection jerked in eager anticipation. He knew she could feel the hard bulge pressing into her back and the tiny pearls of moisture there for her.

He let his fingers glide over her entrance, barely touching her, and then slowly pressed open the folds until he found the source of her heat. It scorched him. Lottie hummed and sucked in a breath as Ian's thumb found her center.

He stroked up and down, spreading her nectar over the narrow folds between her legs. In moments, her core was slick with the want of him. He didn't know how he would keep his vow to go slowly. His body was dying to feel inside her.

His movements quickened, and in moments, her body arched and moved in time with his hand. It was a slow, rolling motion that had her back rubbing against his fevered rod that nearly shattered his control.

While one hand pleasured her, the other squeezed and kneaded her breast, the sensation giving her reason to allow her legs to fall open completely. Her core now fully exposed for him to love and explore.

Her most sensitive nub of flesh was exposed fully to his touch. He stroked and teased, increasing the pressure and speed by slow degrees until her body was thrashing in his arms. A long finger pressed inside, and he nearly came undone at the tight heat that sheathed him.

Her inner muscles began to flex. She was on the verge of climax.

Before she reached it, however, he withdrew his hands and caressed her breasts again, taking her protests with greedy, hard kisses. Then, after she relaxed a bit, he slowly resumed his ministrations to her center, feeling it tighten as he let a finger enter her again.

"God, baby, you're so small," he said huskily. "You feel so good."

"Please, Ian," Lottie begged, breathless with her need to reach her climax.

"Not yet," Ian said. He withdrew his hands a second time. Lottie tried to push them back down between her legs, but he swatted them away. "Not yet," he insisted.

Ian stroked inside her thighs, pressing her legs as wide as they could be stretched and holding them in place with his own long limbs wrapped securely around her. Lottie wiggled and felt Ian's sticky, slick need slide up and down her spine. He groaned and set to work, once again rubbing, teasing, and caressing her core. He stroked two fingers in and out while his thumb danced over her center, feeling her rise nearly to her climax, and then withdrew his hands for the third and final time.

Lottie whimpered in his arms. Her body was slick and ready. He needed to pleasure her well. Despite how desperately he wanted to go slowly with her, he knew his body too well to be convinced that would happen.

He pulsed with need. It wouldn't take him long.

Lottie's hands moved over her own body as her fingertips just stroked the tingling flesh between her legs. "Oh no you don't," Ian scolded with a teasing voice. "That's mine."

"God, Ian, please," Lottie begged.

"I want to take my time with you," Ian said as he began to stroke her again. In minutes, his fingers were pressing in and out of her while she moaned. He felt her wet heat tighten around his body. Her breath came in quick gasps. She spoke his name, her voice edged with desire. It nearly sounded like a prayer the way she breathed it.

Ian lost the last shreds of his control. He released her and quickly slid around her, leaning forward on top of her.

"Lay back," he stammered in a hoarse breath, pressing her body back with his. He cradled his hips between her legs, allowing the tip to brush against her.

Lottie was writhing beneath him in anticipation. Ian leaned forward and rested his weight on his arms, pushing her legs open and sliding himself to her entrance. He held a moment. He took her mouth, tasting and licking her, devouring her moans and pleas. Her fingers pressed into his back, and she raked her nails down his sides. He bit back a curse.

"I can't wait anymore," he said. "I want to be inside you." His voice was ragged with need.

"Yes," Lottie gasped. She gripped his shoulders, pulling him closer, urging him inside her.

He pushed himself into her and was met with a vise-like tightness that pressed against him. He pushed harder. Damn, if he didn't know better, he'd think her body had never been breached before. Ian groaned as he tried to keep from hurting her. He wanted to thrust and bury himself into her in one hard press. He held his breath and pressed, firmly and urgently, over and over again until he finally felt the warmth of her surrounding him almost completely.

He drove himself home inside her in a final hard thrust, forcing out a little scream. Ian broke their kiss, pulled back, and looked into her face. He smoothed the hair from her eyes.

"I'm sorry," he said, breathless. Lottie's eyes carried a pained expression, but she shook her head and gripped his shoulders, pulling him back to her mouth and urging him on with an upward thrust of her hips.

Buried fully inside her again, Ian felt her narrow sheath grip around him. He groaned as he began to slide in and out of her. His thrusts became hard and fevered.

He lifted her knee and pressed it gently against her body. Leaning forward, he pressed himself deeper inside her.

Lottie began to moan. He felt her body clench around him. She cried out as she came in hard, pulsing spasms against him.

He plunged deep, over and over, with long, relentless strokes, while Lottie moaned and whimpered with pleasure. She arched against him, pressing him against her body, meeting his demands with upward thrusts of her own. With a primal growl, he closed his eyes, pressed in one final time, and felt himself pour into her.

He collapsed against her. He felt her lightly brush her fingertips over his back, his chest expanding against her breasts as he breathed. Tight, hard nipples pressed into the hair on his chest, and he felt his body wanting to respond again to her nearness. His breath was ragged, and he groaned as he let his forehead fall onto hers and dropped a light kiss on the tip of her nose.

"Damn, baby," he whispered as Lottie's body continued to squeeze and then relax around his swollen rod. "That was—you're . . ." but his words were consumed by Lottie's hot, greedy mouth.

"Indeed, it was," she finally released him.

Lottie pushed out a breath. She squeaked softly as Ian slowly pulled himself out of her body and laid beside her. He gathered her in his arms and laid a hand over her belly, stroking softly as their breath slowed back to normal. Ian leaned over her on one elbow and examined her body. Just as before, he found the tell-tale signs that he'd loved her too hard. Small bright pink marks were peppered over her skin. He touched one and cursed himself.

"I tried to be gentle," Ian said. "But you're so delicate."

"I mark easily. I'm not hurt," Lottie said.

"Are you sure I didn't hurt you?" Ian said, remembering the way she'd shrieked when he'd finally managed to press fully inside her.

"No. But you will certainly take some getting used to." Lottie giggled a bit and rolled onto her elbow so they were facing one another. Ian pulled a comforter over their cooling bodies.

"Too much Bix?" Ian asked, teasing. He leaned forward to kiss her. Lottie had exceeded his every fantasy. She was responsive and sensual. She had allowed herself to be directed by him. She trusted him and felt the moment every bit as much as he had. She'd been perfect.

"Too much Ian," she replied, reaching a hand to cradle his semi-hard erection.

"I didn't realize—" he started, but then suddenly stopped. He didn't know how to apologize for his size.

She had felt incredibly small. He'd have to be more careful in the future.

"Not that I have much experience, mind, but you have the largest trouser snake I've ever seen. Except for my father's best breeding stallion. But he doesn't count."

"Trouser snake?" Ian snickered and then laughed. "Well, then I'll be more careful he doesn't bite too hard next time." With that, he nipped at her earlobe and neck. His face spread into a sly grin. He'd satisfied her for certain, even if he hadn't even been able to love her for as long as he'd wanted. "Unless you wish to register a complaint, my lady."

"Oh heavens, you're not going to start 'my lady-ing' me now that you know I'm a countess, are you?" Lottie said. She stood on rather unsteady legs, Ian was pleased to note.

"Is there a loo?" She walked away as Ian realized too late he'd completely forgotten about the condoms. Damn.

He pointed toward the bedroom door entrance. Lottie slinked off to the bathroom and wet a cloth to wipe up the collecting puddle between her legs. She glanced at her face and chest in the small mirror above the sink and noticed the bright red tint over her skin, sprinkled with tiny marks where Ian had loved her. She smiled. She felt well loved, and she liked it.

When she came back into the larger room, Ian was pushing his legs back into his boxer briefs and sliding a shirt over his head. "I'm going to rummage for some snacks. Hungry?"

Lottie nodded. "Starving."

Ian nodded as Lottie reached for her bra and panties. "Don't bother with those," Ian called out. "Our clothes were soaked. Those are probably still wet. Besides, I'm nowhere near done with you, love."

Lottie gave him a girlish giggle, wrapped a thick hands-sewn quilt around her body, and folded herself onto one corner of the small sofa.

"I forgot something important just now, and I need to ask you to forgive me," Ian said. He opened and closed several cabinet doors. "I'm afraid I got a bit carried away. I wasn't careful."

Lottie's brow crinkled with a questioning expression. It relaxed when he brandished an unopened condom packet from a drawer and tossed it to her.

"I'm sorry." Ian looked chagrined and more than a little embarrassed.

"Pregnancy isn't an issue, remember?" She tried to keep the sadness from her voice. Not being able to have children was a large reason why she'd vowed never to fall in love. She couldn't give a man children. And a family was important. She wouldn't saddle him with the emptiness she felt growing inside her where a baby was supposed to be.

Ian walked back over to her, knelt down, and smiled. "I am sorry. I swear I'll remember next time."

"Don't," she heard herself reply. "You feel too good. I don't want anything separating us."

"You're sure?" Ian asked.

Lottie nodded.

"All right, well, let's get something to eat, so I can get back to what I really want to be doing." Ian's hand tickled Lottie's breast. She laughed and watched him return to the cabinets. He filled up a plate with an odd assortment of items from boxes she couldn't quite see behind his massive form.

She was just beginning to feel the warmth of the quilt sink into her skin when Ian appeared with a plate of cheese, meats, crackers, and cookies. He had two bottles of water tucked under one arm.

"You are surprisingly prepared for being stuck in a snowstorm with me, Mr. McGuire."

"Ah, well, this little fishing camp, as Wyatt calls it, is always stocked and ready for this sort of thing," he said.

"Apparently, it's tough to get some alone time on this ranch, and the brothers built this for, well . . . for some one-on-one time with their wives."

"Or girlfriends?" Lottie asked. She raised one eyebrow.

"Girlfriend? Is that what you want to be? My girlfriend?" Ian said, shoving a cracker and slice of cheese into his mouth. Lottie got the distinct impression he was disappointed at that. What else could she be? A lover? No. They were more than that. What they shared went beyond just physical satisfaction.

Lottie shrugged. "What am I then?"

Ian swallowed and gave her a meaningful look. He reached up and pushed a piece of her golden hair from her brow, her skin instantly pimpling with gooseflesh at his slightest touch.

"Mine."

"Please don't, Ian. I can't make any promises right now with this whole Kaymar issue casting a shadow over us." Lottie piled meat and cheese over a large water cracker and popped it into her mouth.

"OK, baby. Whatever you want," Ian said. He was patronizing her. But he was also feeding her a chocolate cookie. So Lottie let it go for the time.

The two nibbled and chatted easily about Lottie's life in Marishol. She told him all about her father and her sister. He shared stories of his time with the teams in the army. When the plate was empty, Lottie gave a shudder.

"Oh, the fire," Ian said. "I'll grab some more wood. I have to open the door, so wrap yourself up. It'll be cold."

Ian tucked the quilt tighter around her before he pulled open the door to the cabin. It was snatched from his hands as the wild wind pushed and roared its way into the cabin. A puff of snow billowed in the door as Ian leaned around the frame and grabbed an armful of cut timber to add to the stove.

When the fire was burning hot again, Ian slid Lottie from the sofa and brought her onto the mattress in front of the stove. His arms held her tight. "I'm not going to run again. I promise," Lottie said, wriggling against Ian's body.

"I nearly lost you today, Lottie," Ian said. "And I just can't . . ." he stammered over his words. "I was so scared. I can't remember the last time I was scared of anything."

"You're not scared when people shoot at you?" Lottie asked quietly.

"Not really. Most of the people I encounter can't shoot for shit. But today, I was so scared of losing you, of not being able to keep you safe," he confessed.

"I'm sorry I shot you," Lottie said. "I was just scared and—"

Ian soothed her with a soft "shh" and held her head close to his chest. "I understand."

"Ian, I have to keep moving," she said. "He can't find me."

"He won't, love," Ian swore. He pushed a strand of golden hair from Lottie's eyes and kissed her. One kiss turned into twenty as their lips pressed together softly over and over.

Lottie felt passion bloom inside her again. She coaxed his body over hers and wrapped her legs around his hips, feeling his desire for her stiff against her belly.

"I love you," he whispered, staring down at her.

"I love you too," she replied, smiling.

"Be with me, Lottie. Forever."

Lottie groaned as Ian slid slowly into her body again, now with the familiar slow, sweet glide of him stretching her and filling her with unimaginable pleasure. She lifted her head and kissed him, letting her body be her answer. Her heart would be his forever, even if she couldn't stay.

CHAPTER SIXTEEN

Ian slid his warm body from Lottie's and stoked the fire. They made love twice more before the sun rose the next morning. In the wee hours of the morning, Ian sent a text to Wyatt and then one to Molly, letting them know they were both safe and waiting out the blizzard at the fishing camp. But there was no reply. There hadn't even been anything indicating they received his message.

Ian watched the soft glow of firelight dance across the gentle curves of Lottie's face while she slept. She loved him. But he knew she didn't trust him to be capable of keeping her safe, not completely. One way or another, Ian vowed to himself, he would rid her of this fear of Kaymar. He wouldn't allow her to live continually looking over her shoulder—even if she chose to spend that life of freedom without him. His stomach clenched at the thought. He wanted to make her his. To have her beside him forever. But he couldn't make her stay.

Lottie stirred, and her eyes fluttered open. "You're awake," she said, half-sitting up and letting the comforter fall off of her bare breasts. Ian strode over to her and knelt by her side.

"Just watching over you, my lady. Go back to sleep." Ian smoothed the hair from her face, urged her to lay down, and draped the comforter back over her body.

"Lay with me." Her words were more of a request than a demand, but Ian happily complied.

Lottie's entire body ached from their night together. Each time they made love, they'd fallen asleep in each other's arms only to be awoken later with a rekindled fire to touch and savor each other again. When he asked her to go back to sleep, she was happy to obey. She was completely exhausted. He'd exercised her well. He was a vigorous lover. But he was also tender and generous. He enjoyed her body and offered himself up to her without reservation. He allowed her to escape the world with him to a place where only pleasure dwelt. It had been the most incredible night of her life.

She woke again several hours later to soft sounds of snoring coming from Ian. He was lying beside her, his fingers splayed possessively over her belly. The sun was streaking in through the windows with a bright fierceness that seemed to want to defy the darkness of yesterday's blizzard. Lottie eased from under his touch, feeling him stir but not wake. She pulled the sweatshirt he'd worn the day before over her body. She tiptoed to the door and cracked it open. The ground lay covered in at least eight inches of deep, soft snow. The sky, while blue and bursting with the glow of the early morning sun, revealed more snow clouds gathering on the horizon.

"Don't even think about shooting me and running again," Ian said. His voice was edged with a sleepy rumble that made Lottie's belly do a little somersault. She looked over and saw his eyes still closed and his hand resting on his pillow. Lottie responded with a light laugh.

"Ian, we're completely snowed in here. Midge must be frantic," she said, closing the door and coming to kneel back down beside Ian.

"Good," Ian said. He let his eyes drift open. He lifted a hand and brushed the back of it over her breast. His touch felt natural and familiar in a way it never had before. He'd touched her many times. But she always felt it had to be concealed. Now, her body wanted his touch all the time.

"I mean about being snowed in here with me. I sent Molly and Wyatt a text hours ago. The family should know by now that we're safe. Come back to bed. I want you," Ian said. He was completely unashamed of his burgeoning erection at just the sight of her.

"You're not satisfied after last night?" Lottie asked. She added another small log to their dying fire. Using the small iron rod nearby, she prodded it, shooting a rainbow of sparks into the air.

Ian shook his head.

"I doubt I could ever get enough of you." Ian slipped out of the bed and moved into the bedroom.

"God, it's freezing in here," he yelled. Lottie bit her lip. She had to admit she doubted she'd ever get enough of him either. And right now, there was something she did want. She blushed slightly, thinking just how badly she really wanted it.

Ian emerged from the bathroom, and his eyes scanned the small room for her. She stood with her back against the wall close to the stove. From his vantage point, he wouldn't be able to see her right away. When he finally caught sight of her standing completely naked, his groin hardened instantly.

He groaned and adjusted his growing erection in his boxers. "God, baby," he groaned.

"Come here to me," she commanded meekly. Ian obeyed immediately. She pressed his willing body against the wall where she'd just been standing.

"I'm going to test out a few ideas I read about in a book recently." Lottie's voice was teasing as she dropped to her knees in front of Ian, backing him against the wall. Ian groaned even before she slid his boxers down, and he stepped out of them. She knew he was expecting this. She just prayed she didn't disappoint him.

"Mmm," Lottie responded as she took Ian's growing member in her hand and slid it into her mouth. She licked slowly around in circles and then along each side as if it were a fast-melting ice cream cone.

Ian opened his mouth and let out a long, loud moan of pleasure. Lottie then put the tip into her mouth and scraped it along her teeth gently as she lathed the end with the flat of her tongue. His head pressed back against the wall, and his hand clutched at her hair.

"Fuck, baby," he cursed. More expletives were murmured as she sucked, teased, and nipped over his belly and his rock-hard body. The man was hewn from stone.

Lottie watched his reactions. His eyes closed, and his head tipped back. His mouth fell open while moans of pleasure poured out. He closed his mouth, opened his eyes, and stared down at her, content to watch. When it seemed watching was too much, he closed his eyes again and cursed some more.

"Damn it, woman!" He braced his melting body by placing the palm of one hand against the wall behind where Lottie was kneeling.

She took his generous length as fully as she could into her mouth and sucked hard, stroking with a firm grip up and down. Ian growled and hissed through his teeth.

"Oh God, Lottie . . . Christ," he groaned with a ragged breath, his fingers squeezing fistfuls of hair. "I want to …" Ian cut off his words with what sounded like a curse. Lottie glanced up and saw his head loll back, his eyes close, and the hand drop from the wall to cup around the back of her head with the other clutching her hair.

"Fuck, I want to come," Ian croaked. Every muscle in his body tightened.

"Stand up," he commanded breathlessly. He quickly dragged Lottie to her feet. In one easy movement, he pushed her against the wall. His mouth pressed against hers with hard, aggressive kisses. The two-day stubble on his face scraped against Lottie's tender lips and cheek.

His hands slid down her back and over the curve of her bottom. With splayed fingers around her thighs, he hoisted her up, wrapping her legs around his waist. In one long hard thrust, he impaled her with scalding heat. Lottie cried out as he stretched her and filled instantly.

He lifted and lowered her body over his. Lottie felt her core, already wet from hearing his moans of pleasure earlier, squeeze around him.

Ian thrust hard three quick times before he let himself spill hard, deep inside her. His mouth found hers again and continued to feast as he lifted and lowered her over himself. Lottie let her legs fall away and pushed her feet to the floor under her. She started to move away, but Ian pulled her closer.

"I think I'm just getting started," he said. He turned Lottie around and pulled her hips toward him. Ian leaned forward and pressed into her body, feeling her clench as she moaned her pleasure. He gripped her hips and pulled and pushed her body down over his rock-hard erection. She felt herself grow softer and more pliant with each thrust. She chased her orgasm as he loved her, hard and steady. She moaned and gasped, pressing her back against him to move faster and harder inside her.

To her frustration, Ian slowed his pace and snaked his hand around, touching the center of her body just above where he was pushing in and out of her. She squealed and pushed her hips back, urging him to give her more. "Ian, God. Yes!"

"Oh, yeah, that's it. Come for me, love." The sound of his voice humming against her skin tipped her over the edge. When she finally came against him, she screamed.

Ian hummed against her, relishing the sounds he forced from her body and the feel of her clenching him in wave after wave of pleasure. He pulled out of her and spun her around again.

"Now, I want to watch you," he said. He kissed her with unsatisfied hunger, leading her gently back to the sofa. He sat down and pulled her down on top of him, spearing her with his long staff. Lottie moaned, feeling him rub inside her on a place that made her squirm with pleasure. She rocked back and forth on his lap, feeling herself move closer and closer to another climax. Ian pressed her closer so that he could suckle on one of her blushed, puckered nipples as Lottie ground her hips over him.

Lottie called out, her breath gasping and ragged. "Ian, Lord!" she shouted. Ian growled as he emptied himself into her for a second time. Lottie collapsed against his chest, exhausted, while Ian swore and panted.

"I've never been turned on like that," he gasped. "Or come so hard in my life."

Lottie couldn't suppress a pleased grin. "I was worried I wouldn't do it correctly. I don't have any experience with oral sex."

"You learned that from that book? Holy shit. I offer up all my thanks to the good girls who wrote the definitive work on blow jobs. That was amazing." Ian kissed her mouth, her cheek, and finally the tip of her nose. "Thank you. It couldn't have been easy to try something like that."

The book had been useful, after all, Lottie thought. She'd been so embarrassed when she bought it. Secretly, she couldn't wait to get it home and allow it to fuel the fantasies she had of Ian. It had been both erotic and educational.

"That was chapter six. Just wait until we get to chapter nineteen."

Ian laughed. "Baby, I don't have the strength," he admitted, his desire finally softening. He kissed her tenderly. Lottie loved these sweet, soft kisses every bit as much as the greedy, hungry ones he gave her while they made love.

Lottie slid her body off of Ian's and rested beside him.

He wrapped them in a thick comforter and held her body close. Within minutes, the two felt peaceful and dozed together.

CHAPTER SEVENTEEN

Heavy snow clouds began to block the sun again just a few hours later. Ian stretched out on the sofa with an exhausted and sated Lottie draped across his body. She was hot. Yes, she was sexy as hell, but her body heat next to his under the comforter was just hot. Ian felt like he was boiling. But he didn't have the heart to move her. She was nearly boneless after they'd made love again, and he honestly didn't have the strength himself. She'd thoroughly exhausted him. It was the best feeling he'd had in a very long time. He thrust a leg out into the cool air of the cabin.

He blinked his eyes open in time to see Kip and Wyatt stride through the door. Kip's eyes scanned the room. There was a disheveled mattress on the floor in front of the stove. Damp clothes lay scattered across the floor. Plates of nibbled food and partially drunk bottles of water were strewn across the small table.

Wyatt picked up a half-drunk bottle of his favorite bourbon. He pulled the balaclava from his nose and mouth and gaped at the sight beside Kip.

"Damn, brother," he said quietly. "We're amateurs compared to this guy. Look at this place." Ian drew Lottie closer to his body, being sure she was covered, and put a finger to his lips to have the men stay quiet.

"We got your message," Wyatt whispered. "We brought snowmobiles. We need to go before the next wave of snow hits. It's not over yet."

Ian nodded. "Some privacy though, please, gentlemen," he whispered back. "We're . . . um," he looked down at Lottie's sleeping face, "not quite ready to go just yet."

"We'll wait in here," Wyatt said, grabbing one corner of the mattress and nodding to Kip to grab the other. They carted it back onto the bed and closed the door behind them.

"Lottie, love," Ian stroked her cheek. "Time to wake up. The cavalry is here to take us home."

Lottie gave him a sweet smile before nodding and throwing the quilt off of her body. The two dressed quickly and set to cleaning up their mess while Wyatt and Kip snuffed the fire in the stove and made a list of replacement supplies their fishing camp would need to have restocked after the weather broke.

"I can bring that stuff up here later," Kip volunteered. "Brandon's home, at least for a little while. Maybe he can hold down the fort while Susan and I bring them up there. Getting snowed in isn't such a bad idea." He gave Ian a wink.

"It's already starting to snow again. We better get going." Wyatt pulled his face covering back over his nose and mouth and secured a pair of goggles over his eyes. "Ian, you can ride with me. Lottie, you're with Kip."

Lottie straddled the snowmobile, feeling her already strained inner thigh muscles protest. She laced her fingers around his chest and closed her eyes. She was grateful Kip's body blocked most of the icy wind that whipped through her thin coat and sweater. Lottie crouched, keeping her head tucked low.

The growl of the motor roared in Lottie's ears. She nearly lost her seating twice as the machine pounded against the snow, jumping with every rock and tree root under the thick white blanket. Nearly an hour later, however, they were safely delivered back to Midge's farmhouse.

Susan was waiting inside the kitchen to usher Lottie upstairs and be sure she was put immediately into a hot shower and bundled in layers of flannel and fleece.

"I suppose it wasn't a wicked waste of money to buy this thing after all," Susan said to Kip after the group dined on a huge pot of soup Midge made.

"See," Kip said, puffing his chest proudly. "The ride wasn't bad either. What do you say we go and check on the fishing camp later today and see if everything there is all right?" He gave his wife a wink and a winning smile.

"Not on your life," she said. "I have enough babies at home, thank you. I don't need for you to be taking me fishing," Susan said, giving Kip a light smack on the shoulder. "And speaking of babies, I better be getting back home to them."

"Here, Wyatt, take some of this soup for Molly and the boys," Midge said, rising to pour some soup into a bowl. She covered it with a lid and handed it to Wyatt.

Lottie disappeared to her room and closed the door. Ian walked out with Kip and Wyatt.

"I can't thank you guys enough for coming out there for us," Ian said.

"Thank us?" Wyatt started with a laugh. "I figured you want to kill us. You're up there fucking the nanny, and we bust in and put an end to your whole get-snowed-in sex party." The bowl of soup was sloshing now as Wyatt's laugher deepened.

"At least he had last night," Kip cut in. "Let's hope the boy closed the deal before this morning."

Ian shook his head and kicked at a pile of snow. "Come on. It's not like that."

"So, we found you two naked under a pile of blankets on the couch, and you didn't have sex with her?" Kip teased.

"Course he did," Wyatt said, pointing to the wound on Ian's head. "Got mighty aggressive with it too, by the looks of it."

"OK. OK," Ian said, thinking back to their night together and then this morning. It had been aggressive. Sometimes. And slow at others. But every time had been great. "That's enough."

"Well, I certainly hope it was. Momma will have your ass if she thinks you two are he'n and she'n in her good upstairs guest room. And keep in mind, it's right below yours." Kip gave a hearty laugh. The two men turned on their heels to snowmobile back to their houses on opposite sides of the ranch.

Ian watched them leave and then turned to head back inside for a hot shower.

Lottie heard the water running in the upstairs bathroom, so she took the opportunity to head down to the kitchen for a cup of tea. The delicate bubble she and Ian had been living in the past twenty-four hours was dissolving around her, leaving a hard, loud reality in its wake. How was she supposed to act around him? It felt awkward to want to be with him now when everyone on the ranch would know before morning the two of them had slept together at the fishing camp. Would that be the extent of their relationship? Just sex? Ian had said he wanted forever. She couldn't give him that. Could there be contentment somewhere between just sex and forever?

Lottie spooned honey into her mug when she heard Midge's sing-song voice come through from the living room.

"This wonderful family of mine provides a lot of things," she started as she poured herself a cup of coffee from the carafe. "Pride, love, and a sense of purpose. The one thing it doesn't provide is privacy."

Lottie felt her cheeks grow hot. "I didn't mean to cause a problem. I . . ."

"It's not a problem for me at all. My boys think I don't know anything about that 'fishing camp' of theirs. But here's the truth, hun." Midge leaned forward and lowered her voice into a conspiratorial whisper. "Kip got the idea from my Robert."

Lottie's blush deepened. "Your husband?"

Midge nodded. "We had five kids in the middle of nowhere. Where were we going to go to be alone? Robert used to tell the boys he and I were going fishing. We'd sneak off to the lake, set up a tent, and—" Midge stopped then, the memory of her and her late husband a private moment she seemed to savor in her own mind.

"Well, I don't have to tell you," she smiled and patted Lottie's hand. "You know exactly what we did out there. The same thing you and Ian were doing, I imagine. Except Robert and I came home with fish." She gave Lottie a wink. "I suppose you'll be sticking around now? You should know that Ginny and Molly have been talking about you staying on to help her after her baby comes. Should be any day now."

"That's sweet, but my agency has already found another position for me," Lottie said, staring into her mug of tea.

"Oh, I just assumed you and Ian would …" Midge let her voice trail away as Ian strode into the kitchen. His face broke into a wide smile—a genuine expression of delighted contentment—when he saw Lottie sitting there. He dropped a kiss on the back of her neck to announce his presence. Lottie jumped at the contact.

"Well, it's none of my business anyway, now is it?" She picked up her coffee cup and walked toward the study. "I've got some things to do before the dance this weekend. I'll see you two later."

Ian's hand was resting softly on Lottie's back when she turned and walked out.

"Wanna grab some blankets and watch the snowfall on the porch? It's beautiful," Ian suggested. Lottie shook her head.

"Wanna build a snowman?" he said, grinning and giving her a wink. Lottie smiled faintly and shook her head again.

"We could just watch a movie, or—"

Lottie stood abruptly, stopping his words. "I'm quite tired, Ian. I think I'll go up to bed." Without waiting for his reply, she turned and walked up the steps to her bedroom and closed the door.

She was tired. To be more accurate, she was exhausted. She hadn't done much sleeping last night. And the long walk yesterday and strained muscles from being cold had left her joints nearly frozen and her muscles feeling as if they were made of lead. But that wasn't the only reason she'd run away from Ian just then. She was a coward.

She knew that having sex meant something more to Ian than just physical release. He'd confessed his feelings for her. He'd told her he wanted a future. He wanted her to stay. And just as Wyatt predicted, he'd practically begged her to promise she would. But how could she? Kaymar was after her. She felt him growing closer and closer to her now that she knew the American military even knew of his plan.

She didn't have to know Kaymar to understand he was a man who would do whatever he had to do to get his way. Even if that meant killing Ian or hurting Molly and her boys. No, being here was putting them in danger. She had to move on. She needed to become someone else. She loved them all too much to see any harm come to them. And would never be able to live with herself if she knew she had been the cause of it.

Lottie changed into her favorite pajamas and climbed into bed. She continued to reason with herself that leaving was best for everyone. Besides, even if there wasn't an international terrorist chasing after her, there was the issue of her infertility. She closed her eyes and relived the moments of watching Ian cradle Logan in his arms. She remembered him tossing James into the air and tousling Robert's hair. He would be a wonderful father. He needed his own children—his own family. She could never provide that to him. The truth of the matter was, no matter how much they may love one another, Lottie could never be the woman for Ian. He deserved so much more.

Lottie's eyes were closing, warm tears trailing over her nose and onto the pillow when she heard her bedroom door squeak open. Ian's familiar silhouette filled the doorway. He didn't speak a word. He walked to the bed, pulled back the covers, and slid in beside her. Lottie turned away from him. Ian just curled his body next to hers and pulled her close.

She knew he could hear her quiet sobs. No matter how she wanted to hide them, she couldn't. Ian was the man who helped carry her burdens. And she didn't want to need him, but she did.

"It's going to be all right, baby," he whispered. His long fingers began to stroke softly over her upraised hip and thigh.

"I can't stay here with you," she said finally, forcing her tears to stop.

"I need you to stay," he said. He continued to stroke her hip lightly.

"Being here is putting you and the children in danger. If Kaymar finds me—"

Ian stopped her with a kiss on the shoulder.

"If Kaymar is finished, you'll stay?" Ian asked. Lottie appreciated he wanted to help. But honestly, he was about to make her a promise he wouldn't be able to keep. He couldn't do anything to stop Kaymar. No one could. It would only be a matter of time before he finally caught up to her. She knew that. Deep down, she knew running from Kaymar would only be temporary.

"It's not that simple," she whispered. "Ian, you know I can't have children."

"You think I care about that?" Ian said, hurt in his tone.

"You should. I see you with Molly's boys. You'd be a wonderful father. I won't take your chances for a family of your own."

"Lottie, you never take anything from me. All you ever do is give. You give me peace, and purpose, and . . . love. That's enough. That's more than I ever dreamed. You're enough family for me."

"You say that now, but what if . . ." Lottie let her mind race with a myriad of scenarios where Ian would eventually regret his decision of loving her. She could never be a disappointment to him. She wanted him to be happy. Even if it meant it was without her.

"I'll say that forever. Because it will be true forever."

Ian's fingers danced up Lottie's hip to her shoulder. He caressed her softly, forcing tense muscles to relax. "You need to rest," he said. "Close your eyes. I'll stay here and watch over you tonight."

Lottie felt the hard, muscled length of him against her back. She felt the weight of his long arms covering her. In his embrace, she felt sheltered and safe. His voice began to whisper to her. She felt his warm breath wash over her ear and neck.

"I'm going to meet your father and ask him to marry you. We're going to have a honeymoon in the South Pacific in one of those little huts that sit over the water. I'm going to make love to you for a solid week. Then we'll go snorkeling. I want to build you a house with a little garden and a place for your sister to grow her flowers when she comes to visit, and . . ."

Lottie's body relaxed as she listened to him share all his dreams for their future. She fell asleep with his plans in her ear and a smile on her lips.

Ian's truck bumped along the north pasture just as the sun slipped out from its hiding place at the horizon. The sunrise was stunning, turning the remaining snow clouds a deep violet and striping the sky in shades of pinks and oranges. The storm had cleared, and the sky would be a clear bright blue later today.

He parked his truck beside the barn at Kip's house and unhooked the trailer he'd used to carry the fresh hay bales to the cattle in the field. Susan emerged, carrying two large boxes and wearing a bright smile.

"Good morning, Ian," she said brightly.

"Hey, Susan. Need a hand with those?" Ian offered, stepping up to relieve her of the boxes.

"Actually, I need you to take these to Lottie. Her new job in Colorado has her doing some homeschooling for a kindergartener. I had some things I didn't need, so I promised to send them with her when she leaves."

Ian's face instantly fell. Was she really leaving him? The devastating emotion washed over his face.

"Hey, you OK?" Susan said, dropping the boxes into the snow on the ground. She grabbed Ian's forearm. "You went white all of a sudden. Want me to call Kip?"

Ian's gaze met Susan's. She had an obvious look of concern in her eyes. Ian just shook his head. "No, I'm fine." He snatched up the boxes and shoved them into the back of the truck.

"Do me a favor," he called to Susan. He climbed into the truck and slammed the door closed with an echoing bang. "Tell Kip I'll go and look at that north pasture fence tomorrow. I've got something I need to do this morning."

"Oh, OK. I will," Susan said.

Ian's foot pounded on the accelerator of the truck, spinning the tires and spewing snow and mud into the air behind him.

Ian took the stairs two at a time but paused in front of Lottie's bedroom door to let out a long breath before knocking. He didn't wait for her to answer before turning the knob and going inside.

Lottie's suitcase was spread out on the floor, boxes piled in one corner. She was neatly folding clothes and laying them into neat piles on the bed.

"What the fuck are you doing?"

Lottie turned and met his gaze with fierceness in her own eyes. "What does it look like I'm doing? I'm packing." Lottie turned her back to him and moved to stack a neat pile of jeans onto the bed.

"You're leaving me?"

"I'm leaving Oklahoma, not you. The agency has another assignment for me. This is my job, remember. I can't stay here, Ian."

"When?"

"I leave on Sunday. I told you."

Ian's hand fell on Lottie's shoulder, and he spun her around. She wrenched from his grasp and went back to organizing her piles of clothes.

"I wish you'd stop this, Ian. No matter what we want. This is what it is. You're just making this harder than it needs to be."

"Turn around and look at me, damn it." Lottie didn't move. "What about last night? Did you not understand?" Ian's temper was rising. He let out a long breath and tried to keep it in check. His grip was loosening quickly.

"When I said I wanted to be with you, I didn't mean sex. I mean the two of us, and the whole death-till-you-part, in-sickness-and-in-health arrangement. I thought I made that pretty clear."

Lottie shook her head, cutting off his words. "I won't put you all in that kind of danger. As long as Kaymar is searching for me, it's better I leave and keep moving. What you want changes none of that."

"You are impossible!" Ian blurted out. He grabbed her shoulders and spun her around, forcing her to meet his gaze. Her eyes were red from crying, her lips trembling from the strain of forcing back sobs.

"Tell me the truth. Do you love me, Lottie?" He forced the edge of his anger to abate.

She nodded, a tear sliding down her cheek. "Yes, of course, I do."

"Then, what do I have to do? What is it you want so that we can be together? Because I know you want that as much as I do. And I'll do whatever it takes. I won't lose you, Lottie."

Lottie shrugged out of his grasp. She squared her shoulders. "Give me Kaymar's head on a platter. Short of that, I can't be certain our being together won't cost you your life. Or the lives of our family. I won't do that. I won't bring death to your door, Ian. You can't force me to stay."

His mouth turned into a frown, and he left wordlessly from the room. He could hear Lottie's sobs from behind the door. He reached for his phone. There was only one man who could help him fulfill Lottie's wish. He only hoped he'd be willing.

"So let me get this straight," John said. Ian had been talking so fast for several long minutes. He'd explained about Lottie, her relationship to Kaymar, and all he'd learned at the fishing camp. He'd also rattled on about a plan—the beginnings of a plan at any rate—to put an end to Aymil Kaymar for good. "You want to use the girl as bait and lure Kaymar out of hiding?"

"Not the girl, exactly," Ian said. "Just the promise of her. If you can leak her location through your contacts with the CIA, you know he'll come to get her. And we can have the boys ready. I don't care what you do with him." Ian let out a sigh. "But I won't have that bastard ruining my life with his threats."

"I don't know, Ian," John admitted. "You want all of this by tomorrow night? In time for that, what did you call it, Snowflake Ball?"

"I know it's a lot to ask. Please, John. She's leaving the day after tomorrow. This may be the best shot we've got to end this thing with Kaymar before it ends things with Lottie and me."

"I'll pitch it to Bradford. It's actually not a bad idea. Let me see what he says, and I'll get back in touch with you in a bit."

"Thanks, John," Ian said. "I need to end this. You understand?"

"I do understand, brother. She's the one. And when it's her, it's her."

"Yes," Ian answered simply.

"And you did help Andie and I get together, so I suppose creating a target package for a wanted terrorist is the least I can do." John laughed, and the two signed off the call.

At just a few minutes after midnight, Ian's phone buzzed with an incoming text from John that simply read, "We're good to go."

CHAPTER EIGHTEEN

On the other side of the world, clouds of blue smoke curled through a darkened room. The sickening sweet smell of its opioid powers perfumed the air. Aymil Kaymar reclined against a pile of pillows on the floor, a timid young girl on her knees before his lap. He closed his eyes and breathed out his approval of her tongue's caress over his bulging groin. A shadow of a man passed in front of the arched door in front of him.

"Don't lurk in the doorway, Sarsur," Kaymar carped to his most trusted acolyte. The man grimaced at the name, which meant cockroach. He despised it as much as the man who had given it to him. He lowered his eyes. Kaymar disgusted him—to be pleasured so openly. He emerged from the shadows.

"I can return when you are not . . . engaged, Rayiys," he said, referring to Kaymar as "master." The girl paused in her ministrations, appearing glad to be relieved of her odious chore. Kaymar reached up, grabbed a fistful of her raven hair, and jerked, forcing her to scream in pain.

"I did not give you permission to stop," Kaymar growled, giving her face a hard slap. The young girl clutched at her stinging cheek and returned to her duty. Sarsur blanched, slightly remembering all too well the blinding sting of Kaymar's rings when his hand raked across a cheek.

"We have found the girl," Sarsur said, trying not to look at the twisted sneer of pleasure on Kaymar's face in front of him. Inflicting pain pleased him. "But she is scheduled to move soon. We would need to act quickly."

Kaymar hissed through his teeth, pressing the girl's face farther down his erection. The girl choked and then gagged. But he just yanked her up by her hair and snarled cruelly. Then he crushed her now-bloodied face down over him again. He pushed and pulled faster and faster, using her mouth to pleasure himself. Then he suddenly hissed as he released himself into her mouth. He let out a long sigh of satisfaction and pushed the girl back so that she fell over onto her face, spitting the vile fluid from her mouth.

"Now you may go," he said with a wave of his hand and slid the waistband of his trousers to cover himself.

"Where is she?" Kaymar asked. He rose slowly to his feet and walked toward a small lattice-covered window. It was the only light that illuminated the shadowy space. Bright orange slants of light cut through the swirling smoke.

"America. There is a small cabin on a lake in Oklahoma where she has been hiding," the man replied. "Our source is reliable. We have dispatched some men immediately, but I thought perhaps this might be something you would want to handle yourself, personally," he began, only to be cut off by Kaymar's quickly uplifted palm.

"She is my daughter, my blood, and my future. You're right. She is too valuable to trust to those idiots you hire," Kaymar hissed. "I will go myself. Prepare my plane. I want to be in the air in an hour." He turned his back to the man, seeming to dismiss him, and reached for a cigarette on a nearby small table. Just as his man turned to leave, he spoke again. "And Sarsur, have that whore who just left me sent to . . . offer entertainment to my men tonight. She no longer pleases me."

A slimy smile slipped across Kaymar's face. "Finally," he said, his smile fading to a snarl.

"Yes, sir," the man replied with a slight bow and left the room.

Lottie crammed the last of her clothes into her suitcase and tugged the zipper closed. She was packed. She blew out a long puff of hair that pushed a stray strand of hair up out of her face. Her heart was heavier than her overstuffed bag. How she would be able to leave Ian, Molly, Wyatt, their wonderful boys, and Midge . . . she blinked back tears.

"You don't have to go," Ian said from her bedroom doorway. He was leaning on the door frame, his arms crossed in front of his chest. "But I get why you think you have to."

"Ian," Lottie said, clearly surprised to see him standing there. "Please, I don't want to go through any of that again."

"OK, let's don't then," Ian said, walking toward her. "Let's talk about tonight. Are you going to the dance?"

Lottie nodded, thankful to see him happier now. "Molly is lending me a dress. I was going to go over there in a little while to pick it up."

"Are you going to dance with anyone?" Ian asked in his most knee-melting baritone. He slid his body closer and grazed her arms with the lightest touch of his fingertips, eliciting a shivered response.

Lottie gave him a playful smile. "Well, there is this one cowboy I was sort of hoping I could dance with tonight."

"Oh yeah?" Ian said, leaning closer and letting his lips caress hers gently. "There will be lots of cowboys there. Which one?"

"You, you silly prat," Lottie said, giving his chest a playful slap and raising up on her toes to kiss him again. "You are going, aren't you?"

"I wouldn't miss it. Especially if it means I have an excuse to hold you in my arms all night." Ian gave her a long kiss filled with an unspoken vow to do just that.

"But I promised Midge I'd lend a hand to help the ladies auxiliary finish setting up. Can you ride with Wyatt and Molly? I can meet you there."

Lottie nodded and smiled. She was so glad he wasn't making her feel guilty about having to leave. His new generous attitude would make tonight truly a celebration. She wanted a goodbye she could cherish fondly, not heartache and tears. She was certain there would be plenty of that in store for her in the months to come.

"Great." Ian dropped one more light kiss on her lips and then turned to go. He paused at the doorway and gave her a smile and a wink. "Oh, and don't make any plans for after the dance. I'll be sleeping in here with you again tonight. Well, not that you'll be getting much rest."

Lottie felt a slight blush color her cheeks as she grinned. Ian had shared her bed the last two nights, both times helping himself to curl against her body underneath her covers. He did not try to make love to her. He just held her. They had kissed and laughed and whispered into the quiet darkness around them until they'd fallen asleep. It was quite possibly the most wonderful thing she'd enjoyed with Ian. It was easy to just be in his company. To just share and talk and rest in one another's arms. She felt loved. She felt safe. Her lips twisted into a frown. Tonight would be their last night together.

Ian closed the bedroom door behind him. The first part of his mission was complete. Lottie would be safely away from the fishing camp when Kaymar was scheduled to arrive. She would be safe with him at the dance while John and Bradford's special forces team set their trap to hook Kaymar. With any luck, Ian thought, this would be his last mission with these men. And it would not only free Lottie from her fear of being caught but free the world of a living devil.

His skin buzzed with anticipation. He always felt this way before an op. Although, this time was a bit different. This time, at the end of all of it, there would be Lottie.

"Let's run this again from the top," General Bradford barked. He crossed his arms and leaned against the hood of the SUV the army special forces team had brought out to the lake.

"Kaymar is expecting Lottie at the cabin," John said. "Our sources made sure he knew she was hiding from him here. Alone. We've already gotten word from one of our inside sources that he's chartered his plane to bring him here by 1700 tonight. When he arrives, our team will neutralize whatever security he's brought with him." John paused here, showing the locations of the snipers who would be cloaked in the tall, overgrown hayfields surrounding the fishing camp.

"Do we have any idea what we're expecting?" Bradford asked as if on cue.

It had been more than a year since John had planned an operation of this nature. He was proud he hadn't lost his touch.

"Intel says he's traveling with only his personal security—three men. Armed to the teeth and skilled soldiers. But only three."

General Bradford nodded for John to continue.

"We'll enter with flashbangs just in case he's armed, apprehend the target, and move for exfil. Simple snatch and grab. Couldn't be easier," John said proudly.

"Outstanding, Preacher. I'll be at our operational command at Altus. We'll be providing air coverage of the op. I've chased this bastard around the globe for ten years. I don't want to miss the chance to finally get this son of a bitch."

"Yes, sir," John said.

At his word, General Bradford slid himself inside a black SUV and bounced down the gravel road past Wyatt and Molly's house to the main highway.

John slipped his phone from his pocket and dialed Ian. "You're sure everyone is going to be far from here when this is all supposed to go down?"

"Absolutely," Ian said. "Lottie is going with Wyatt and Molly to the dance. I'll be there with her to be sure everyone stays around until I have the all-clear from you."

"Excellent," John said. "So, what's the deal with you and this girl? You gonna tell me you're in love with her and all that touchy-feely shit?"

Ian laughed. "Man, you already know."

"Wow," said Molly, taking a sip of wine and admiring Lottie's lithe figure in her favorite black floral dress. "That looks better on you than it ever did on me."

Lottie twirled around in front of the floor-length mirror in Molly's room, admiring the fit of the dress. She knew Ian would like the way it hugged her figure and dipped low in the front, revealing just enough cleavage to keep him interested. It made her feel sexy. It was the first time she'd worn anything that had made her feel that way since coming to America.

"It's so nice of you to lend it to me," Lottie said. She turned and faced Molly.

"Oh, you can have it," Molly said, taking another sip of her wine. "I've pushed three huge babies out of this body. I doubt I'll ever be tiny enough to wear that again." She shrugged, looking down at Logan sleeping quietly between two large pillows on her bed. "Not that it matters. The boys are worth it. And," she gave Lottie a wicked chortle, "Wyatt seems to enjoy the curves of motherhood."

"Already?" Lottie asked, taking a sip of her own glass of wine and laughing at Molly's raised eyebrows. "I thought you had to wait six weeks?"

"We do. We are," Molly corrected. "It's just fun to tease him a bit." The two women erupted into laughter

Second to None

as Lottie turned and looked once again at her figure in the mirror.

"I have the perfect earrings for this," she mused to herself. "I . . ." Lottie thought back to the last time she'd worn them. The night she and Ian had made love for the first time at the fishing camp. "Oh!" she said, realizing. "I think I left them behind at the fishing camp."

"Oh, well, go get them," Molly said, tossing her the keys to her SUV. "Take my truck, and meet us at the celebration. You know your way to the community center, right?"

Lottie smiled. "Are you certain?"

"Sure," Molly said, sipping her wine. "The perfect earrings are essential. My big brother deserves to see you in absolute perfection."

"Can I come too?" said a small voice from just outside the doorway.

"Robert, are you spying?" Molly said, her hands on her hips.

"No, ma'am," he lied. "I just wanted to know if I could ride with Miss Lottie to the fishing camp. I've never been to a fishing camp."

Lottie looked to Molly for an answer. "No," Molly said instantly. "You're going to be seen by at least a few people neat and clean. Now," she said, marching to the doorway, "go get dressed."

With that, she closed the door, and two women laughed again.

Ian paced outside the entrance of the town's community center. He couldn't believe loving a woman had reduced him to this. He wanted to laugh at himself for being so taken in by a woman's charms that he'd be nervously waiting for her outside of a dance. He suddenly felt like he was back in junior high school, waiting for Missy Springer's parents to drop her off. But tonight, his nervousness extended beyond just the anticipation of seeing Lottie. He was worried. Too much could go wrong. Where were they?

They should have been here by now. He felt his phone buzz in his pocket but ignored it. He needed to find Lottie. He needed to be sure she was safe. Tonight, when they were alone, he could unfold the whole plan and tell her Kaymar was no more. The two of them could start to make their plans for the future. Ian smiled. He couldn't wait.

Just as the thought rolled through his mind, he silenced his phone a second time, without bothering to glance down to see who was calling. His full attention was captured when he saw Wyatt's truck pull into the parking lot. He let out a sigh of relief.

After what felt like hours, Molly and her boys started piling out. Wyatt emerged, carrying a small infant carrier. Ian looked around.

"Where's Lottie?" he asked, his voice hurried and anxious, even to his own ears.

"Relax, Romeo," Molly said, giving her brother a pat on his shoulder. "She needed a pair of earrings and went to get them."

"Earrings?" Ian questioned, his heart beginning to hammer in his chest. This wasn't the plan. Lottie was supposed to come with Molly and Wyatt.

"Where did she go?" he finally managed to croak out. "Back to Midge's?"

Molly gave her brother a teasing snigger. "No. She said she left them at the fishing camp." She gave her brother a sly wink that he ignored.

Ian felt the blood drain from his face. His stomach instantly soured. This was not happening!

"She went to the fishing camp?" Ian's mouth went dry. His blood raced through his veins like fire. "You're positive?" He gripped Molly's shoulders and gave her a little shake. The panic vibrated from his fingers into her body like an electric current.

"Ian, what's wrong with you? Let go of me," Molly said and twisted from his grip. "She'll be here in a minute or two—" Molly began. But she never had a chance to finish. Ian was already sprinting toward his truck.

Speeding down the two-lane highway back toward the ranch, Ian heard his phone buzz again. He tapped the screen this time, still not glancing down to see who was calling. He prayed it was Lottie. It wasn't.

"McGuire," he answered brusquely.

"Ian," he heard a familiar voice say calmly. "We have a small problem." John's voice was even and low. "Your girl just pulled up."

"Tell me what you see," Ian demanded.

"I have a white SUV. Female, blonde, exiting the vehicle. She's alone. She's wearing a black floral dress and some fancy cowboy boots."

"I don't give a fuck what she's wearing," Ian barked. "Can you turn her around? Get her out of there, John."

John seemed to ignore his friend. "Damn it, son, she's hotter than hell."

"What? You can see her? Is Kaymar there yet?" Ian said, shoving his foot down harder against the accelerator.

"Not yet," John said. He scanned the horizon from his hide by the lake. From his vantage point, he could see nearly everything, including into the window of the living area of the small cabin.

"I'm on my way," Ian shouted into the phone. "God, don't let anything happen to her, Preacher."

"Marcus and I are on overwatch," John said. "We're on the north side of the lake in a duck blind. I can see everything from here."

"Roger that," Ian said, skidding the truck onto the gravel path that would take him to the lake and to Lottie. He glanced at the clock. He still had time to get to her and get her out of there before Kaymar and his men showed up.

"Ian," John said, his voice grim but still calm, "I have eyes on the target."

"Fuck! No!" Ian screamed. His foot pressed the accelerator into the floorboard. "Damn it. How many with him?"

"Ian," John said, his voice more forceful now, "this is a U.S. military operation with some serious international consequences. You are, under no circumstances, to come into my area of operations, are you clear? This AO is off limits."

"Jesus, this is all my fault," Ian said. He cursed himself for wanting to prove to Lottie just how well he planned to secure her future with him. He had wanted to ensure they could be together. He wanted to marry her. Now, he could lose her forever to that monster. And the worst of it was, she would know. She would know he didn't protect her, just as she had always feared. Ian swore and pressed the accelerator down harder, spewing gravel and dust behind his truck.

"We've got this, brother. No worries. Tex is on the long gun. He gets one shot at the target, and he's going to take it. I'll call with a SITREP when I have one." With those words, John disconnected the call.

Ian bounced violently down the road and prayed. What on earth was happening inside that cabin?

Lottie stood in the small living area of the fishing camp, looking for her earrings. She glanced down on the table and then got down on her hands and knees to search around the floor where Ian had dragged the mattress down in front of the little woodburning stove.

"Ah, there you are," she said, snatching them up from under the sofa and stood up straight.

"My thoughts exactly," she heard a low voice growl like a feral dog behind her. Lottie's blood turned to ice. She didn't have to turn around. She already knew who it was. But she did turn, slowly, to see a tall man with bronze skin and black, deep-set eyes staring back at her. He wore a blue suit that had obviously been tailormade to fit his small, light frame. A white silk shirt and tie peeked out from around his neck. A rough, ragged scar covered one half of his face, making it appear as if his skin had been raked over a cheese grater. He looked more like a disfigured businessman, not a terrorist. Lottie gulped.

"Who are you?" she managed to croak out. Her heart prayed her instincts were wrong about his identity.

"I think you already know who I am, pet," the man said, sliding easily into one of the chairs at the small table. His voice curled with a thick Middle Eastern accent, the tone crawling over Lottie like a hungry serpent. She shivered at the sound of it.

"How . . . how did you f- find me?" Lottie tried to moisten her lips, but her mouth had gone dry. Her body began to shake.

"I am wondering that myself," he said. He coolly examined the cuticles on one hand. Lottie could see the signs of many broken bones healed over and over again in his oversized knuckles. A large gold ring circled the pinky finger.

"Please, do sit," he said, motioning to the chair across from him.

Lottie didn't want to obey this man. But she needed to sit down before her knees melted under her and she fell down. Her stomach churned. She was going to be sick. Lottie swallowed, praying she could keep it together just for a little while. Someone would be missing her soon. She tried to breathe. And then they'd find her. Ian would miss her. He'd find her. God, she prayed he would find her before this devil made her disappear forever.

"You do know who I am, don't you?" he said calmly.

Lottie nodded.

"I'm happy to have found you at last. I was so distraught when your mother stole you from me all those years ago. You two have been very difficult to track down."

Hot tears sprang to Lottie's eyes. No! He did not get to speak about her mother. The woman he tortured and left alone with shepherds in a desert.

"She didn't steal me. She rescued me, you monster!" Lottie found new courage at the thought of her mother. Her mother's courage. The fierceness that coursed through her veins was the same that had given Marjorie the courage to break free from this animal. She never truly realized until right now how brave she must have been to flee this man.

Kaymar clicked his tongue quietly as if he were correcting her penmanship. His voice continued in a soothing calm, the sensation once again slithering over her and stinging her nerves with sharp, poisoned barbs.

"No, pet. You belong to me. You are my daughter. You are my property."

Bile rose in Lottie's throat at hearing these words and remembering what Ian had told her Kaymar planned to do with her. She remained silent.

"And you are a very fortunate daughter indeed." Kaymar's voice was easy, and anyone hearing him would never have guessed he planned to sell her into slavery for an alliance with the Russian mafia. But Lottie knew. She knew the evil that lurked behind that sleazy smile and slimy voice.

"I want to show you how deep my devotion is to you, pet. I have secured a very wealthy husband for you. He will provide for you well. You will bear sons for him. And live happily—so long as you are a good girl and do as you're told."

At these words, Kaymar rose and walked around the small table to stand in front of Lottie. She could feel her body begin to tremor more violently as he neared. He picked up a lock of her blonde hair and rubbed it through his fingers, then leaned forward, brought it to his nose, and breathed in. Lottie felt the acid rise into her throat. She worked to keep it down.

"Ahh, so sweet. And blonde. Just like your mother, if I recall."

Lottie grimaced. Another shiver ran through her body. She wondered how long she'd been gone. If anyone would have missed her yet. If Ian would be looking for her.

"I'm not your property. I am not going anywhere with you, and I'm not marrying anyone," Lottie spit what moisture she had left in her mouth onto Kaymar's neck and face.

He reacted as if he expected every move she made. He slowly extracted a silk handkerchief from his pocket, wiped his face, and then calmly twisted it into a rope with his fingers.

In one swift motion, he'd wrapped the strip of twisted cloth around Lottie's neck and hauled her up to her feet. Lottie coughed, sputtered, and clutched at the cloth, but it was too tight. She couldn't breathe. It squeezed against her neck, biting into her skin.

"See what living all these years away from me has done to you, girl?" Kaymar hissed, his voice harsh and filled with malice. Spittle from his foaming mouth sprayed Lottie's cheek. She gagged and coughed.

"You have had no one to teach you respect and obedience." Kaymar's voice warped into an angry croak that hissed and spit through clenched teeth. He twisted the handkerchief around her neck tighter until Lottie could hear the blood pounding in her ears. She couldn't breathe. Her eyes swam as the room swirled around her. It began to grow darker at the edges. Just as she was going to lose consciousness, he released her. Her body fell on her knees to the hard wooden floor.

Lottie clutched at her throat. Still choking and gasping, she worked to suck air into her lungs. Then, a bone-splitting stab of his pointed boot speared into her ribs. She cried out and sputtered the taste of blood on her tongue. He meant to kill her. She was going to die. Oh, God, where was Ian?

Ian parked his truck on the far side of the small lake and ran to the duck blind where John and Marcus, another former teammate, crouched. Both men were staring at the cabin through the scopes on their rifles.

"Lottie?" Ian panted, trying to angle his head to see in through the one small window of the cabin. At this distance, however, he could see nothing inside. Adrenaline now pressed his heartbeat into thunderous drumming against his ribs. John handed him his binoculars.

"We can see her, but not him," John said. "He keeps himself out of sight of the window or behind her."

"Behind her? He's touched her?" Ian's temper sent his blood boiling. His muscles twitched with the need to charge the cabin. He wanted to tear the man's heart out with his bare hands.

"Look, man. I'm sorry. I'm not gonna sugarcoat it. He's not being gentle with her," John said. Then, into a mic connected to his throat, he whispered.

"Roger. Hold for my command. We have friendlies inside. Repeat, friendlies inside."

"So we just sit here and wait?" Ian said, sweat beading across his brow.

"Our mission is to bag this bastard. As long as she's in no danger, we wait until we get our shot," John said coldly. "You know how this works, Ian."

Ian's heart clenched. He'd known too many men like Kaymar. Too many barbaric animals who would do the unthinkable to women like Lottie. In the time it took for their snipers to get their shot, Kaymar could do more than he would allow his mind to imagine.

"Lottie is in that room with a ruthless murderer, and you don't think she's in any danger? How much more danger can she be in?" Ian's voice was raising. Marcus turned and held up a hand.

"Hush, man. We got your girl," he said calmly. His voice was steady and at a near whisper. He turned back around and made a tiny adjustment to his rifle.

"I'm going in there." Ian stood to his feet, his frame nearly spilling out from behind the blind and giving away their position. Kaymar had four men patrolling the area, each carrying a semi-automatic rifle across their chests. John yanked him back down.

"The hell you are!" he snapped in a hoarse whisper. "You don't do this for a living anymore, remember? We're here for a mission. A mission *you* called us here to do. It sucks, but this is what we do. You get your head straight. You're no good to her like this."

Ian gave him a pleading look. "And if it were Andie or Allyson in there? Would you be telling me to calm the fuck down? Let me in there, man."

John gazed back at him for several long seconds. Ian knew he understood. He remembered how Andie had risked her own life on one of his missions and how the fear of losing her had sent John into a fevered rage. John sighed and let out a breath.

"C'mon, man, please." The idea that he couldn't protect Lottie nearly robbed the air from his lungs.

"SITREP, be advised. McGuire is approaching the target building. Again, be advised. McGuire is on target. So, nobody shoot the enraged white guy," John said to the men on the other end of the channel. "We execute on my mark, copy?"

When John heard back that everyone on the team received the message and was ready to execute his part of the mission, he nodded to Ian.

"There are four tangos around the perimeter. Marcus, Lincoln, and Tex can take out three. You'll take the one at the door. Just get Kaymar to the window. We'll take care of the rest." John handed him a silencer for his pistol and an earpiece with a mic to communicate.

Ian screwed the device onto the barrel of his weapon and crawled out from behind the blind, sure to keep his body hidden in the tall reeds that grew up around the edge of the lake. Ian crawled toward the cabin and took up a position of cover behind Molly's SUV. He looked into the small window of the cabin near the stove. Lottie was swaying on her feet. Kaymar's hands were at her throat. God in heaven. Mission objective or not, he was going to kill that man for touching her.

"I have eyes on target," he said to John. "He's fucking touching her, Preacher. Hurry the hell up."

"Roger that," John said softly.

Ian stilled his breathing.

"On my mark," John said. Ian let out a breath and took aim at the guard positioned by the door. He knew he only needed to worry about his target. The others soldiers wouldn't miss. In a few seconds, he would be inside with her. He needed to stay focused. She needed him to stay focused.

"Three, two, one. Execute, execute, execute." John's words came in no more than a whisper in fast succession. Ian squeezed his trigger, and by the time John finished saying the last word, Ian's target and the other guards simultaneously fell dead. The only sound was the thud of their bodies as they fell to the ground. Ian strode carefully to the cabin door.

"At the door," he whispered to his teammates.

"We can't see inside. Be ready for a fight, man." Ian heard Tex's southern drawl edge out over the radio.

"Roger," Ian replied. He inhaled and then kicked the door in.

Splinters of wood flew through the air as an exploding crack rang out. The surprise made Lottie scream. But Kaymar didn't seem rattled.

"Ah, the cowboy I've heard so much about," he said, his sickening calm tone returning. He picked Lottie up from her crouched position on the floor. Lifting her up by her hair, he shoved her in front of him. He produced a pistol from under his suit coat and jabbed the barrel into Lottie's ribs. Lottie winced with pain and let out a little scream.

Ian's jaw clenched hard enough to grind his teeth to powder. He had tried to keep his eyes from looking at her. He needed to stay focused on the threat. But he allowed himself to sneak just one glimpse at her face.

A raw line of bruising snaked around her throat, and the streaks of tears carved rivers through her makeup. There was a scarlet welt on one cheek and a thin trickle of blood at the corner of her mouth and above one eye. Lottie's body was shaking with fear. Ian raised his arm, pointing the barrel of his gun at Kaymar's head.

In his ear, Ian could hear John's voice calmly reminding him that the CIA was waiting to interrogate Kaymar. "We need the target alive if possible, McGuire."

"Killing you wasn't the plan," Ian started calmly. "But it's not off the table. Let her go," Ian demanded.

Kaymar laughed. "The very fact that you are standing here before me tells me you and, let me guess, your Heathen Brotherhood have already killed those worthless apes I brought with me. She is my ticket out of here, fool," he bleated. He pulled Lottie's hair tighter and forced a shriek of pain from her throat. The arm fisting Ian's weapon flexed.

Kaymar held Lottie's head too close to his own. Ian couldn't shoot him without shooting Lottie first. He took a step backward, hoping Kaymar would take just one step forward and into view of the window so Tex or Marcus could shoot him. Kaymar inched forward.

"No shot," he heard whispered into his ear. "The girl's blocking him," he heard Marcus say.

"No shot," Tex repeated. "He's gotta let go of the girl, Ace."

Kaymar pushed his pistol further into Lottie's ribs. Fresh tears began to flow from her eyes.

Ian could see her body sag, weakening under strain.

She let out a sigh of resignation.

"I imagine she's already tainted goods, but that's no matter. She will buy me what I want all the same," Kaymar said. Ian's muscles flexed. His heart beat wildly in his chest. Every cell of his being tingled with adrenaline. He could not allow this to happen. John may have a mission, but so did he. He promised to keep her safe. He would not allow this to happen.

An oily smile spread across Kaymar's face. "Tell me, cowboy, is she as sweet as a ripe peach? Her mother was so very, very sweet to taste."

Lottie struggled in his arms, her stomach roiling at the idea of his greasy hands on her mother. Kaymar wrenched Lottie's arm, twisting her face with pain.

"Don't worry, soon you'll be dead, and she'll belong to Petrov."

Ian had witnessed what people like Kaymar and Petrov did to women. A vision of Lottie suffering the same abuse that bordered on torture made the acid rise from his stomach and burn his throat. That would not happen to her. He'd die before he let her go.

"You are not leaving here with her," Ian ground out. "Rest assured I am prepared to die to ensure she doesn't go anywhere with you, you lousy piece of shit!"

Lottie's watery eyes gazed helplessly up at Ian. "I love you," she mouthed silently. Her lip trembled, and her body shook uncontrollably.

Ian took his gaze from Kaymar for an instant to acknowledge what Lottie probably believed would be her last words. In that brief instant, there was a flash. A shaft of moonlight glared off of the barrel of the gun in Kaymar's hand. He'd moved his head a fraction, turning it away from Lottie and toward Ian. At the same time, he leaned forward to extend his weapon to the only man that stood in his way. The tiny fraction of his movement was all he needed.

"*No!*" Ian shouted and squeezed his own trigger. An explosion shook the windows of the small cabin as both of the men's weapons fired simultaneously. Additional rounds from the sniper rifles outside aimed at Kaymar echoed their own report.

All at once, Kaymar's body lurched backward. Lottie pushed away from the man's grasp. She fell to the floor and screamed. Shards of glass rained down around everyone inside.

Ian took three long steps forward, and with one sweep of his arm, held her safe against his body. He angled himself so she couldn't see Kaymar's lifeless form sprawled on the floor. A pool of dark blood oozed from the hole in his forehead. More wounds on his shoulder and chest spread out in crimson stains under his pristine white shirt. Ian spit on his corpse.

Lottie's body crumpled into Ian's strong hold and fell against him. He carried her out in his arms as his fellow armed men in black clothes filed into the small cabin, automatic rifles raised.

———••●••———

Ian led Lottie outside around one side of the cabin. Setting her down carefully, her body doubled over and finally purged all of the acid that had been rising into her belly. Her aching throat protested, and she coughed and gagged, all the while leaning on Ian's strong arms—the only thing keeping her up.

When her body began to relax into a slight tremor, Marcus made his way to the couple, a large black bag by his side.

"Let me take a look," he said and began to examine Lottie's wounds.

"She'll have a hoarse voice for a few days, but she's lucky," he reported. "How about you? You want me to see to that?"

"What?" Ian asked. His heart was still pounding from the rush of adrenaline that hadn't yet abated. "I'm fine."

"Well, you've got a gunshot wound in your arm there." Marcus gestured at a dark spreading stain on his arm. "The bastard got a shot off before he fell onto the floor."

Ian hadn't felt it. His only thought was Lottie. Marcus reached up and squeezed the place where dark, sticky blood soaked his shirt.

"Hell, he just grazed you. You'll live. But I'll get you fixed up just the same." Marcus cleaned and dressed Ian's wound. He noticed a concerned look on Lottie's face, although her body had no strength to speak.

"Oh, don't worry about him," Marcus said reassuringly. "He's seen way worse than this. The bullet just took a bit of hide out of his arm. He'll be fine." Lottie offered him a slight nod and then let her head collapse on Ian's uninjured shoulder.

John collected Ian and his men in a fully blacked-out SUV and headed up toward Midge's farmhouse.

Lottie had no idea how they were going to explain this to her. Walking in, she could see nearly the entire Hampton clan clustered around the kitchen and dining room table. Ginny, Lacy, and most of the Hampton children were absent. She was practically being carried in his arms. Her arms and legs were drained of any strength, and her stomach still churned.

"Oh my God!" Midge said. She gaped at Ian's bloodied arm and Lottie's limp body being ushered inside. "Damn you, Tom, you broke my best hand."

Ian glanced over to see that "Tom" was actually General Bradford. Of course, he should have known he'd find a way to insert himself into this op.

"Tom?" he asked. He gave John a questioning look. "Is she allowed to call him that?"

"Susan, get Ian a clean shirt. Molly, take Lottie upstairs while I find out what the hell is happening on *my* ranch," Midge barked. The two Hampton women sprang into action without a word. Lottie reluctantly left Ian's arms and felt Molly now leading her upstairs to her room. She turned back and glanced down at Ian. "Go on, Lottie. I'm fine," he said with a smile.

Midge was already removing Ian's shirt and shaking her head at his wound. "Is this a gunshot wound? Who the hell is shooting at you, Ian? And who dressed this?" Midge turned her attention to General Bradford. "Is this how you're teaching soldiers to do a field dressing these days, Tom? This is a half-ass attempt if I've ever seen one."

Marcus listened with indignation. "I'm usually in a hurry," Marcus retorted. "Although, even I'll admit that is a pretty sloppy job."

"Wyatt, please bring me the first aid kit from the closet," Midge said.

"Good Lord, little Midget, you're still the same ball of fire I remember," Tom Bradford said with a grin.

"You two know each other?" Ian asked, surprised.

"Tom and my late Robert served together after Vietnam," Midge said. She gave the general a wink. Ian's eyes went wide. She called him Tom. And she winked at him. He'd doubted anyone ever called him that. Rumor had it even his wife called him general. The man was as hard as woodpecker lips. It seemed impossible someone who had a heart made of steel ammo casings and drank gunpowder in his coffee would have friends.

Bradford sat on a barstool, a cup of coffee curled into one of his bear-sized hands. Ian suspected he'd been there during the operation, explaining to Midge what he could. At least he was spared from having to explain it to her. He didn't think he'd be so lucky with Lottie.

Wyatt returned with the first aid kit, and Midge immediately set about removing the bandage and cleaning Ian's wound.

"Of course, Robert was just a sergeant and Tom a second lieutenant when it all started. Lord, you two were babies then. And when our service was over, we retired here to this ranch. While Tom kept on after the bad guys."

Ian flinched as Midge poked at the sizable hole in his arm. Midge continued talking. Ian was grateful for the distraction while she cleaned up the hole in his arm.

Marcus had been sugar-coating Ian's injury for Lottie. The gash was a bit larger than he led Lottie to believe. And it hurt like hell. It would be sore for a long time. He already knew that from personal experience.

"The ranch has been in Robert's family for a while, but they'd stopped farming it in the sixties. We picked it up and have been working on it ever since. This is going to need stitches, Ian," she said, frowning.

Wyatt opened another bag. "I'll do it, Momma," he said. "I think I'm the only person in this room who actually went to some sort of school for the practice of medicine."

Ian laughed at that. His face instantly morphed to a snarl as Wyatt began to stitch his wound. When Wyatt stuck him with the needle, he cursed.

"All right, Midge, I need the girl," Bradford said after he was satisfied Ian's wound was fine.

Midge let out a light sigh. "Her room is upstairs. First one on the right," she said. She and Susan were busy preparing platters of food that seemed to appear from nowhere for Bradford and his troops.

"Wait, I'm coming too," Ian insisted, wincing at the pain in his arm.

"I'm sorry, Ian," John said sympathetically. "But you're not a member of the teams anymore. I'm afraid it's just us. But don't worry. I won't let Bradford eat your girl."

"No chance," Ian protested. "Someone is going to be on her side in that room. I know how these things work. Besides, all of this is my fault. If she's going to hear about it, it should be from me."

"Fine," Bradford said, heading for the stairs. "It's your funeral."

John and General Bradford slipped upstairs while Wyatt hurriedly finished Ian's stitches. He wrapped the injury, and Ian slipped on the clean shirt Susan had brought down for him. Ready or not, it was time for him to face the music.

Ian gave Lottie's door a light tap and entered to see her sitting on the bed. John stood by the window, his arms crossed over his chest. Bradford sat down in the small chair in front of the desk. He'd turned it back so he was straddling it, leaning his forearms on the backrest. The dainty thing looked as if it might not bear his weight.

"So you'd never met him before?" he asked. Lottie looked up at Ian and shook her head.

"Do you recognize this man?" John said, handing Lottie his phone. She took it, examined the photo, and handed it back.

"Should I?"

"No," John answered. "He's just a person of interest in this whole thing. We were kind of hoping maybe you'd recognized him."

"General Bradford," Lottie started. She tore at a tissue clenched in her fingers. "How did Kaymar even find me? I was careful. At least, I thought I was."

Bradford gave Ian a hard stare, cleared his throat, and then spoke slowly. "We collected reliable intel that Kaymar had received word from an inside source you were here."

"An inside source? You mean someone who knows me was spying on me and told him? Was it someone from the agency? They only ever knew me as Charlotte Poole, but I suppose . . ."

"It was me," Ian said softly, nearly unable to meet her gaze. He was instantly sorry he had. The moment her deep, dark eyes met his, his heart shattered. Anger, fear, and betrayal were flung at him like icy daggers.

"What?"

"I asked General Bradford and Preacher here to let it leak where you were. The plan was to lure him here into an ambush."

"You used me . . . you used me as bait?" There was no hiding the outrage in Lottie's voice. Her cheeks bloomed to a bright rose almost instantly. "How could you? Do you have any idea what could have happened tonight?"

Bradford rose from his chair and tucked it carefully under the desk. John was quick on his heels as the two made a silent and hasty retreat from the room. Before closing the door behind him, John whispered, "The agency is going to be calling you both for a full debrief. Make sure you answer the call—if you survive the night, that is."

Ian rolled his eyes at his best friend's jab. He turned to face the music of Lottie's rage.

"You insufferable, arrogant, selfish man!" Lottie yelled. Ian had never seen Lottie lose her temper. It was a terrifying sight if he had to be honest. She looked as if she could take flight, swoop around the room, and then dine on his heart without blinking an eye over the effort.

"I was giving up my life to protect you all from that animal, and you lured him here? And here I was, thinking you'd discovered I was missing, saw him at the fishing camp, and called in the cavalry to save me. You are no hero. You are a manky arsehole."

"Lottie, please," he started. But Lottie would hear none of it.

"Shut up! Did you know that Robert asked to go with me to the fishing camp? Did you?" She didn't wait for him to reply. "What would have happened if he'd gone with me? Do you think Kaymar would have thought twice before killing that sweet little boy so he could cart me off as some sort of prize? I'll tell you—he would not!"

"You weren't even supposed to be there. If you'd have gone to the dance with Wyatt and Molly like I'd told you to, you would—"

"How dare you blame this on me! You should have told me about your idiot plan in the first place. Then maybe I would have done as I was told, you overbearing tosser."

"I'm not blaming you. There was a mission. I would never have intentionally put you or anyone in my family in harm's way. You know that."

"No, Ian. I do not. Do you have any idea what it was for me to pack my things and make plans to leave here? Do you have the slightest notion of how hard it was for me to leave my family and my home right after my mother died? I felt like I was dying inside. And I was willing to do that—to give up my life to keep you safe—to keep the people I love safe—and you . . . you just . . ."

"And I just gave you exactly what you asked for," Ian said, frustration mounting in his voice. "You think you were the only one ready to die to keep someone they loved safe, Lottie? You weren't. I would have given up my life for you tonight. Jesus, woman, do you have any idea?"

Lottie's mouth formed a tight line. Her eyes squinted, and she bore her gaze into Ian's face with a fury he'd never encountered in a woman before. "Why don't you enlighten me then, Mr. McGuire?"

"You said the only way we could be together was if Kaymar was dead. I had to make that happen. Even if you still left. Even if you said you didn't want me. I had to know you were safe. I had to know wherever you were that you'd never have another night so afraid you couldn't sleep. I didn't want you to have to miss another birthday without your family. And I didn't give two shits if it cost me my life, Lottie. Because without you, I don't have a life. Without you, I don't live. I merely exist."

Her lips parted. She looked as if she was about to speak but said nothing. She just closed her mouth again and turned away. Ian could see her shoulders begin to tremble with her sobs.

He stepped closer to her and reached to touch her shoulder but pulled his hand away before he did. He shook his head, and then he touched her. Her body flinched away from his touch.

"Lottie," Ian said, his voice laced with barely contained emotion. She was going to leave him. He knew that now. "I screwed up. I know I did. And I'm sorry. You can't know how sorry I am, baby."

Lottie turned to look at him. His fingers reached out, and he tenderly stroked the purpling skin at her cheek and then at her neck where Kaymar's brutal grip had marked his precious girl.

"Look what I did to you." Ian's voice choked with emotion. "When I close my eyes, all I can see is the fear on your face, Lottie. It haunts me. I promised to keep you safe, and look what I let him do to you."

Lottie's fingers closed over his. She guided his hand away from her neck. Ian felt the hot tear roll down his cheek as his gazed fixed on her skin, blotched, red, and swollen.

"It's over, Ian," she said finally. She leaned forward and put her arms around him. Ian wrapped her close to him. She was here. She was safe. For long moments, the two of them stood just clinging to one another. They, at long last, allowed the fear, the anger, and the relief of all that had happened to flow into one another in tears.

At two in the morning, Ian found himself lying in his bed. Alone. Trying not to think about Lottie. And trying to go to sleep. He was not successful at either. He let out a long sigh. He'd truly screwed things up with her. She'd taken a new nanny position for a family in Colorado. Ian had vowed to visit her as often as he could, which he was planning to do every weekend. Perhaps, over time, she could forgive him. Perhaps, he could one day even forgive himself.

The sound of his doorknob creaking forced his gaze from the stationary ceiling fan to the door. Lottie stepped through and closed it behind her without a sound. Ian half sat up in bed.

"What is it? What's wrong?" Ian knew there couldn't be any danger. But something had to be upsetting her to bring her to his bedside in the middle of the night.

"Nothing," she said quietly. Her voice did not hold the heaviness of sleep or even a hint of recent wakefulness. Just like him, he thought, she'd been lying awake, trying to reconcile all of this in her head too.

Ian pulled back the sheets in invitation. Lottie walked over to the bed and stared down at him. Ian could only see hints of deep gray shadows across her face. He couldn't make out her expression, and her voice gave nothing away. So when she climbed into the bed, straddled his body, and began to kiss him, Ian was taken completely by surprise.

The moment her lips touched his, his body ignited. Not with a furious hunger to take her, but with a fervor to plead forgiveness and to feel her love for him again despite his mistakes. Laying there that night, he'd feared she'd take the light with her and leave his heart once again to exist in the darkness. He had wondered for hours whether it was his fear of being without her or his love of being with her that dominated his emotions. Now, he knew. It was undoubtedly his love for her.

His body responded almost instantly to her. She sat up, leaving his mouth cold and wanting more of her tongue and her heat. She pulled her nightgown up and over her body, baring herself to him. His hands caressed her hips and stomach and stroked upward toward her breasts.

She leaned forward again, letting the hard peaks of her breasts press lightly through the coarse hair on his chest. The sensation fanned the flames of desire already burning in his blood. He wanted her. Not to claim her. Not to fulfill some baser carnal need for release. He wanted to love her. To worship her. To make her believe with no doubts that he loved her beyond description. That he would have died for her rather than live without her. But he would do nothing without her permission. Right now, she was just kissing him.

Just kissing? No, nothing about the way Lottie's soft lips slanted against his, nothing about the way her hands stroked his cheek or her tongue danced with his was "just" anything. It was magical.

"Ian," her voice came in a low, sultry whisper that pressed gooseflesh over his neck and down his back. "Make love to me."

"Yes," he said huskily. Ian's hands encouraged her over him, down on top of his hard length. He caressed her hips and back, rocking her into an easy rhythm of back and forth that allowed for the long, tender strokes he'd wanted to give her. They made love for hours. Slowly. He worshiped her body, taking his time to satisfy her fully. He whispered his love to her over and over, filling her heart with himself. He gave himself over to her completely. When they finally lay sleepy and exhausted in one another's arms, he was hers. Forever.

"Ian," Lottie said. She sounded so sleepy. She'd settled herself comfortably next to him, her head resting on his uninjured shoulder.

"Mmm?" Ian hummed, barely able to keep his eyes open.

"I love you," she whispered.

He hoped he said he'd loved her too. He was saying it in his mind so loudly he was certain it must have come out of his mouth too. But he didn't remember. He just felt himself being pulled to sleep by the most beautiful words he could have ever wished to hear. Lottie still loved him.

CHAPTER NINETEEN

It was the throbbing ache in his arm that finally pulled Ian from sleep. The sated feeling of having made love to Lottie the night before still clung to his heart. She loved him. That was all he needed to know. For the first time since he'd learned of Kaymar's plan for her, he'd finally felt optimistic about what lay ahead for them.

Last night, they shared more than their bodies. When they made love at the fishing camp, they were exploring, testing, and seeking pleasure for themselves and for one another. But when she came to him last night, he knew it was different. It had felt different. For him, it had felt as if he was making love for the first time. They held none of themselves back. He had felt what he thought were her tears splashing down his neck, only to realize the tears were his own.

When she climaxed in his arms, her body surrendered to emotion so powerfully, she did weep then. And he'd held her and soothed her into bliss once more. He opened his eyes, ready to claim her again, but the bed was empty. Lottie was gone.

He slowly managed to roll his stiff body from the bed and peek into the hall. Her bedroom door was closed. She'd no doubt wanted to avoid any amorous intentions this morning and had gone to sleep in her own bed at some point during the night.

He rubbed at his aching arm. He'd shower, get some coffee and some painkillers, and wait for her to wake. When she did, he'd planned to take her for a long ride across the ranch. There was so much they needed to say. So much he wanted to tell her.

He managed to shower and stuff his body into a pair of jeans and a sweater. His arm was killing him. Lottie's bedroom door was still closed. He went downstairs and discovered Molly blowing the steam off of a fresh cup of coffee and leaning against the kitchen counter. Ian gave her a warm smile.

"Hey there, Molls. What brings you over?"

"I'm on my way to the hospital. Ginny had her baby last night. Midge is staying with the boys. I thought you might like to come with and meet your new niece."

"That's great. Another girl?"

"Of course. Annabelle Grace."

"Abigail, Adelyn, Alicia, and now Annabelle. What's with all the A names?

Molly shrugged. "How's the arm?"

"It's fucking killing me," Ian said. He made a feeble effort to roll his shoulder and stretch the painfully tight muscles in his arm. "Maybe Lottie will want to come too. I'll go up and get her."

"She's not here," she said, taking a sip of the coffee.

"What do you mean?"

"It's Sunday, Ian. You knew she was leaving on Sunday."

"She left?" Ian couldn't hide the shocked expression on his face. "But last night, we . . ." he looked up at Molly, who was staring back with a raised eyebrow. "We sort of made up, I guess. At least, I thought we did."

"I don't want to know about your make-up sex, Ian. Gross."

He walked back through the kitchen, ran up the stairs, and pushed her bedroom door open. The room was empty. The bed had been stripped. He flung open the closet door to see only a handful of empty hangers. Ian pounded back into the kitchen.

"She came over earlier to say goodbye to the boys," she said sadly. "They're really going to miss her. I think we all will."

Ian threw himself on a barstool and let his head flop down onto the counter. She had said she'd loved him. But apparently, that wasn't enough.

"She also gave me this." Molly slid an envelope toward Ian. He immediately recognized the expensive linen stationery. His *Dear John* letter. He couldn't bear it.

"The least you can do is read it."

"Molly, I didn't mean to put her life in danger. And you have to know I'd never do anything that could hurt you or the boys or Wyatt. I just needed her to feel safe, so we could . . . so I could . . . Hell, I was a selfish wanker!"

Molly walked around the counter and wrapped her arms around her brother. She held on to him for a long while. When she pulled back, he could see the tears brimming in her eyes.

"I know, Ian. You just want to keep the world safe. You always have. You wanted her to trust you because you love her? Now, you have to trust her because she loves you."

"She doesn't understand," he said.

"Read the note, Ian."

He slid a finger under the seal on the envelope and extracted the letter.

My Dearest Ian,

Coming to your country was supposed to be a place to hide. But instead, I discovered who I really am. I expected to feel lonely, and I admit I did at first. But when it was time to leave, I felt loved. I am leaving a part of my heart there in Oklahoma with Molly, Wyatt, and her precious boys. And I leave the rest of it with you. I pray you find the peace and happiness you're searching for, Ian. For me, happiness will always be when I sit on a porch swing, see a cardinal, wear my boots, drink coffee, or use one of my $10 words. Because it is then I will think of you.
Always, Your Lottie

Ian folded the letter and stuffed it back into the envelope. "Molly," he said, emotion edging his voice. "She's really gone."

Molly sighed. "Defeated already, soldier? That's not like you."

"She doesn't want me. I've fucked up too badly this time, Molly."

"And what about last night?"

"Apparently, I confused break-up sex with make-up sex."

"Do you know what your whole situation reminds me of?" she asked, as if to no one in particular. "Violet Dunn's *An Heir for His Highness*."

"Jesus, Molls, not one of your silly romances. Please."

Ignoring his protests, Molly continued. "See, there's this king, and he hires this woman to be a surrogate for him and his wife, but then the wife gets cholera and dies, and well, of course, he falls in love with the surrogate."

Ian rolled his eyes. "You are killing me." He clutched at his temples.

Molly waved away his comment with a single swipe of her hand. "Anyway, at the end of the story, the woman, her name was Charlotte, ironically, is sipping Ceylon tea in Sri Lanka, and she looks to her handmaiden, the only person left in the world she can call a friend—"

"For the love of all things holy, Molly, stop it. I'm begging you." Ian's hands were folded as if in prayer.

"And she says," Molly laid a palm dramatically over her forehead, tossed her head back, and pulled out her thickest imitation of a southern drawl, "'You know, they never do come after you a second time, do they, Miranda?' At least, I think her name was Miranda. It may have been Melinda, or was it Wanda? It's been a while since I've read that one."

Ian stared at his sister blankly. "Jesus, your husband is a freakin' saint, you know that? Is there a point to this little book report?"

"It means, if the king had gone after her a second time, maybe he would have changed her mind. Or maybe she had a change of heart but didn't know how to tell him. If he'd just gone after her, he could have learned that she never really wanted to leave him at all. She just didn't know how to stay. He could have discovered that she was thankful beyond words for all he'd given her—all he'd sacrificed for her. Maybe she even confessed that through tears to her sister-in-law before she got in her Uber."

Ian quirked a brow and cocked his head to one side, now fully engaged in every word Molly was saying.

"Maybe if he had known she wasn't, in fact, going to another nanny assignment in Colorado. He might just feel a bit more encouraged to take a chance on the love of his life. If, say, I don't know, he knew instead she was flying to the Isle of Marishol via London on British Airways flight 1005."

Ian grabbed his sister's face and kissed her forehead. "I love you, Molls," he said and turned to the door.

"Ian, take your coat. It's freezing out there," she called and tossed him his coat.

Ian's truck raced toward the airport. According to what he managed to see on his phone when he was forced to pause at stoplights, her plane would be boarding in less than an hour. He skidded into a spot in the parking deck for international travel and ran toward the departures. And there she was.

She was standing in a queue outside to check her bags. Her blond hair was tied in its tight bun. She wore the black shift dress, heels, coat, and gray scarf exactly like the day they'd first met. The phone in his pocket buzzed. Later, he thought to himself.

"My lady," he said quietly, coming to stand behind her. She hadn't noticed him. She turned, her face mostly covered by oversized dark glasses that hid her expression.

"Ian," Lottie said with alarm. "You're here . . . you—"

But Ian covered her mouth with a kiss that fed her every ounce of love and passion his body could hold.

He pulled her closer, wrapping his arms around her and capturing her body and soul, and then released her.

"Please, Lottie. Please hear me out. I'm an asshole. I screwed up, and I'm so sorry." He took a breath. The phone in his pocket now both chiming a new message and buzzing with an incoming call. Damn phone, he thought.

"And I have no idea how we move past this. I only know I want to move forward with you." He kissed her softly again. "I want you. I want to build you a little house with a garden. And I want to take you fishing—really to catch fish and everything. And I don't care about children. If you want them, then we'll adopt, or we'll get a surrogate. Whatever you want. I just know that there is no life for me without you."

Lottie's hands started trembling. He clutched her fingers in his hands. "I don't care if we only have nineteen nieces and nephews to share our love with for the rest of our lives as long as I have you, Charlotte St. John. Not telling you was stupid. You have every right to hate me, but I know deep down, you don't. I know you love me. And if you can just be brave enough to give me a second chance, I swear I'll spend the rest of my life making it up to you, baby. I love you. I will always protect you, Lottie."

A tear slid out from beneath Lottie's sunglasses.

"Oi," a man with a mop of curly, light brown hair and a bad complexion called out from behind the check-in counter in an English accent as thick as London fog itself, "D'you have a ticket for this flight? Cause it's passengers only from this point forward, mate."

Ian ignored the man and just stared at Lottie. His phone chimed and buzzed again.

"I think you should answer that," Lottie said with a sniffle. She pulled a tissue from her shoulder bag. Ian slid his phone from his pocket. All the messages were from Molly.

Check your coat.

Ian stared at the message blankly and then padded the pockets of his coat. There was something in his inner jacket pocket. Ian reached in and pulled out his passport and a printout of a boarding pass on British Airways flight 1005.

"As it turns out, mate," Ian said brightly. "I do."

"You came for me?" Lottie asked. Behind her dark glasses, Ian couldn't make out her expression, but her voice was edged with what sounded like disbelief. How could she ever doubt he'd come for her? "This morning, I'd convinced myself you wouldn't come for me a second time. But Molly said—"

"Molly?" he interrupted.

"Yes, well, Molly and your friend, the one who is called Preacher, but is not, in fact, a minister of any kind. They made me see that even though . . ." She glanced over her shoulder, then, giving her head a shake, sputtered. "I was almost afraid to say his name just now. Isn't that stupid? Even though Kaymar is no longer a factor, I was still so scared. I left because I'm a coward. I was scared of Kaymar. But I was more afraid of losing you. And if I left, you couldn't leave me. If I took the danger for myself, I wouldn't have to face losing you or my family. I'm an idiot. Please forgive me."

"I love you," he said finally. His phone chimed with another message from Molly. He beamed as he read it.

Check the other pocket.

Ian felt around in his jacket again. This time, he pulled out a small black jewelry box. He opened it and breathed. "Oh, God, Molly, you didn't."

"What is it?"

"It's my grandmother's ring. She gave it to Molly before she died. It was the ring Wyatt was going to propose to her with, but he ended up using one Midge had given him."

Ian looked at the ring and then up at Lottie. He smiled broadly. "I think I'm supposed to give this to you," Ian said. He lowered himself onto one knee. He opened the box toward her and spoke softly.

"I want to marry you, Lottie. I want to live the rest of our lives with this peace that you make so real for me. Even in chaos, even in fear, when I'm with you, there's peace."

Lottie stared down at the bright red ruby ring, its square emerald cut surrounded by a ring of tiny clear, white diamonds and filigrees of gold swirling around it. "Ian—"

Ian stood and silenced her with a kiss.

"Don't say it's too soon. Don't say you don't know. Just say you love me, and you want to be with me."

"And while you're at it, say he's blocking the queue and step aside already," the young airline employee said rudely.

"I was going to say . . ." She looked at the rude young man with a disgusted wriggle of her nose and then back to Ian. "You have to ask my father first before I can marry you."

Ian scooped Lottie up into his arms and spun her around. "Well, then, it's a good thing I have a ticket."

They boarded the plane to applause by the passengers in line behind them—all enchanted by the spontaneous proposal and the touching scene that played out before them. Even the rude airline attendant gave him his best wishes in his thick, cottony accent as they walked into the airport. After they were settled in their seats, Ian dialed Molly.

"I'm going to miss you," she answered without preamble. "The boys will too. I told them Uncle Ian was going to get married to nanny Lottie. I promised you'd be back right after your honeymoon. Don't make me a liar, OK?"

"No," Ian said, his face split into a smile he could not lose. "We just boarded the plane. Molly, I . . . the ring and—"

"Don't worry. I used your credit card to buy the ticket. And, the ring . . . it's still in the family, so I don't mind. And I know Grandma Spencer would have loved to see Lottie have it."

"I love you, Molls," Ian said. "Thanks."

"You rescued me from darkness once. I'm honored to be able to return the favor to you. I love you too, big brother. Now, go and be a good husband."

Ian signed off and turned to his future wife. "I've gotta know something," he said, his brow knit together. "Was the heroine in *An Heir for His Highness* really named

Charlotte? It's so ironic that she'd drink Ceylon tea in Sri Lanka, don't you think?"

"You've read *An Heir for His Highness*?" Lottie arched a brow.

"No. Molly bored me half to death with the whole ending of how the king should have gone after Charlotte. How, if he had, he'd have won her over and saved the day. Instead, she's all despondent for all eternity, drinking tea with her handmaiden. You know, all that chick-lit bullshit you girls love."

Charlotte shook her head, a wide grin stretching into laughter covering her face.

"What's so funny?"

Charlotte's laugh faded to a giggle as she tried to explain through her happy tears, "The end of *An Heir for His Highness* is that the sister of the king uses all her powers of manipulation to trick her brother and the heroine into confessing their love for one another. The sister is the real heroine of the book, Ian."

Ian laughed with Lottie then. He realized that, after all these years of rescuing other people, it was, in fact, him who was the one who'd actually been rescued this time. He'd been saved by his sister, who turned out to be his hero after all, and by the one woman he couldn't live without.

EPILOGUE

There were only a few things her little sister had taught Lottie over the years. How to pick a lock had been the most useful by far. Lottie gently wiggled the hairpin into the lock on the doorknob of the blue guest room in the family's ancestral home. It had been the one her father had directed Ian to be housed in after they'd arrived in the middle of the night. The tumblers clicked into place, and Lottie slowly turned the doorknob. She squeezed through a narrow slot in the door, closed it softly, and noiselessly locked it again.

Ian's body was bathed in a warm yellow glow from a streak of sunlight that peeked through a slit in the drapes over the large window, his chest lifting and lowering slowly as his body slept. She let out a sigh. This man, this gorgeous human being, was the one man she could never live without. And after her father gave his blessing, which she was certain he would, they could be married, and she'd never have to.

Her robe slipped off of her naked body and puddled to the floor around her feet. Lottie slowly tiptoed to the empty side of the bed, peeled back the sheets, and slid her body in next to his, the heat from his skin warming the sheets.

"You better have a good reason for sneaking into my room at this hour," Ian teased, rolling his body around hers and drawing her close. He let out a sharp hiss.

"Oh, your shoulder," Lottie said, rolling to face him so he could turn onto his back again.

"Come here," Ian said, his voice thick with sleep. He pulled her body close to lay alongside his, nestling her into the crook of his good shoulder.

"You must be tired, huh?" Ian kissed her hair and breathed in the scent of it. They'd arrived in Marishol at just after 1:00 a.m. and didn't finish telling her father about all that had happened until nearly four.

"Not really," Lottie said. She laid her palm gently on his chest, rubbing soft circles through the hair that tickled her.

"Have a bad dream?" Ian asked.

"No," Lottie whispered and kissed his chest lightly.

"Did you hear a noise in the house?" Ian chided.

"No." Lottie giggled softly at that. She kissed his chest again and heard Ian suck in a ragged breath.

"Then what brings you all the way to this side of the mansion?"

"You," Lottie said softly. She rolled her body to cover his. She could feel the response to her unspoken request already hard and pulsing against the crux of her sex.

"Well, you have me," Ian said. His hands cupped her hips and then slid up to her waist, dragging her torso closer. Her breasts dangled in front of his mouth. Lottie watched as he captured one, quickly sending heat and a sharp prick of pleasured pain from the nipple that instantly tensed under his touch. Lottie wiggled her hips until the wet tip of his erection was softly pressing into her opening. Slowly, she slid onto him.

"You have to be quiet," Ian scolded when Lottie let out a loud sigh the moment she felt him fully seated inside her. "I don't want anyone finding you up here like this."

Lottie laughed lightly, the reaction forcing her inner muscles to squeeze tight around his shaft buried inside her. Ian groaned equally as loudly at the feeling.

"Shh," Lottie teased. "You have to be quiet too."

A wide smile spread over Ian's face as Lottie's body slowly rocked up and down over his. Long, drowsy strokes morphed into shorter, quicker ones. Warm beams of sunlight streamed into the room as Lottie felt her body quickening to ecstasy.

"Ian," she whisper-screamed as her body clenched tight around his, and a wave of pleasure rippled through her body. Ian continued to thrust inside her harder and faster, spiraling her body into readiness quickly once again.

"That's my girl," Ian groaned when her body flexed, her back arched, and she dug her short nails into his chest. Lottie held her breath as she drifted back to the two of them, still slowly rocking against one another. Their strokes became slow and languid once more.

"I could do this all day," Ian said. His grin turned from teasing to determined as he softly coaxed Lottie's weary body up and down his shaft.

Lottie's head fell back as she felt him harden further inside her. He teased and stroked with impossible rigidity until he found the sweetest, most delicate spot deep within her body. She bit her lip as her legs quaked. His fingers mimicked her body's natural response tightening around her hips, driving her harder against him.

Lottie could feel his release taking hold of him. She watched his eyes close, heard the soft sigh as his mouth opened, and felt the muscles under her thighs tense in preparation. Just as she felt the tingling of his heat shooting inside her and the silenced groan of his pleasure rumble around him, the door lock clicked, and Lottie watched with a horrified expression as the door creaked open and Maisie slipped inside.

Lottie ripped the sheet over her and Ian as Maisie's eyes flew open, and she turned. Her body lunged toward the door just as Ian's head twisted to see Maisie enter and then flew back to meet Lottie's wide-eyed gaze.

"Shit!" he cursed silently, Lottie only hearing the breath and watching his lips form the words.

"Maisie?" Lottie said. It was useless to pretend she wasn't there. This was going to be awkward no matter how the next few minutes unfolded.

Lottie slid her body from Ian's and quickly rolled out of the bed to grab her robe from the floor. Ian, too, jumped up and stuffed his legs quickly into his jeans. Lottie watched him shrug with his uninjured shoulder as he looked around for his shirt.

"It's all right. You can turn around now," Lottie said to Maisie's back, her hand already touching the doorknob to flee.

Lottie embraced her sister tight. The feel of her in her arms again a sweet reminder that her days of running from Kaymar were over forever. She'd never again be forced to leave her family. Never be looking over her shoulder. Happy tears pricked at the backs of her eyes in sweet relief.

When she pulled back, Maisie's eyes were red-rimmed and her nose pink from what appeared to be long hours of crying. So, she finally knew. Father had finally told her the truth of it all. About their mother's secret, Kaymar, and, of course, the contract.

With an all-too-brief conversation, Lottie assured Maisie they'd discuss it all in the library in an hour. When the door closed behind her sister with a soft tick, Lottie moved to the door and pushed the lock . . . again.

"You sure that thing is locked this time?" Ian said before they both erupted in a fit of laughter.

"Yes. And I think this time it will stay that way." Lottie stepped closer and wrapped her arms around Ian.

"I really do need to talk to your father, Lottie. And then, I want you to make all your plans. I'm hoping you're not in favor of a long engagement."

Lottie shook her head. "In Marishol, it's quite the opposite. Once a couple is engaged, the marriage can take place almost immediately. And I'd like it if we could get married here, Ian."

"I'd like that too, babe," he said, kissing her cheek softly. "We can have a big-ass party back at the ranch with Molly and all the other Hamptons when we get back."

"Are you sure you don't mind?" Lottie said, beaming back up at him.

Ian shook his head. "All I want is to be married to you before you change your mind about me."

"Never," Lottie swore softly. She lifted herself up onto her toes and placed a soft kiss against his mouth. "I was thinking, if it's all right with you, maybe we could honeymoon somewhere close by too. My father's villa in Italy, perhaps?"

"We can do that," Ian said, smiling again.

"Good. I want to stay close to Maisie for a while."

"Why? Is something wrong? She looked pretty upset."

Lottie nodded, her eyes going a bit soft with sadness. She knew what was coming. She knew her sister was going to need her now more than ever. The contract, Oliver, all of it. It was going to overwhelm and terrify her. Lottie was already bracing against the coming avalanche of it all.

"I probably should fill you in on a few more St. John family secrets. You may change your mind about me," Lottie said, breaking out of Ian's hold and walking slowly to the window. She pushed back the drapes, letting warm daylight fill the air around her.

"What's going on? You got an international terrorist stalking you or something?" Ian teased. "I can handle that."

Lottie turned and offered him a weak smile. "Let's just say I think my family may need a bit of the Heathen Brotherhood around for a little while."

AUTHOR'S NOTE

Each of the United States Army's unique service units carries its own motto—a few simple words to inspire, encourage, and remember. This book's title, *Second to None*, is the motto for the U.S. Army's 2nd Infantry Division. Its members were among those who stormed the beaches of Normandy and fought valiantly in the jungles of Korea and Vietnam. And they continue to serve today in the deserts of the Middle East in the nation's war on terror. Their motto was selected to honor all of the men and women who serve, train, deploy, and defend the freedoms of our nation. It's this depth of devotion that makes our armed forces Second to None.

THE END

CPSIA information can be obtained
at www.ICGtesting.com
Printed in the USA
LVHW091400240721
693545LV00003B/316

9 781736 654323